The Mark

By

Braxton DeGarmo

Christen Haus Publishing

COPYRIGHT

DEDICATION

This book is dedicated to all Believers who continue to stand strong against the world's ways while also spreading the Good News.

ONE

Inevitable: (adjective) 1. unable to be avoided, evaded, or escaped; certain; fated: an inevitable conclusion. 2. sure to occur, happen, or come; unalterable: The inevitable end of human life is death. (noun) 1. that which is unavoidable.

Adam Afton sat at his workstation, his mouth agape. Had the inevitable arrived?

His heart raced. His palms became sweaty. He tried to control his breathing. Had he become so cocksure of his programming talents that his hubris had blinded him to what was now so obvious? Did his audacity now threaten his wife and his children, as well as himself? He had always accepted the risks to himself, but the idea of being responsible for something happening to his family was anathema for him.

His fingers began to race across the keyboard. His UltraNet program had been borne out of a program designed first for PsyOps in Afghanistan that had evolved to become a master surveillance program on the U.S. populace. When his toddler daughter was kidnapped, he felt justified in using it to try to find her. Yet, in doing so, he discovered that its masters were using it for self-enrichment, human trafficking, blackmail, and more nefarious purposes. His conscience ate at him. He regretted his role in helping to develop it, and yet, he needed it to find Carolyn.

And when he had succeeded in finding her—taken by a childless couple who named her Grace, he pulled the plug on that program. He had destroyed it, and a subsequent effort by the global elites to resurrect it, thoroughly, but not without keeping it for himself to use for good purposes. Over just two years, he had helped reveal and prosecute dozens of corrupt politicians, businessmen, public servants, and more—mostly through means that were in the shadows of legality.

Then . . . he came to the knowledge of the saving grace of Christ, something his younger brother Aric had accepted many years earlier. As a Christian, he came out of hiding and reunited with his family. Now, bound by a promise, he kept his clandestine work well within legal boundaries and its results were to go through an intermediary, his friend Lynch Cully.

However, someone still searched for him. And unless he worked quickly, whoever that was, was about to trace him right to his doorstep.

Aric's first month as a senior in the Criminology Program at the University of Missouri-Saint Louis had been more demanding than he'd anticipated and yet, much, much calmer. The challenge came from moving from a start-up criminology program to the 11th best in the country, depending on whom you talked with. The level of expertise in his instructors was phenomenal. On the flip side, their expectations from him were also incrementally higher, and he was working his butt off to meet those expectations.

Yet, life had become so much easier. At the college in Wisconsin, he had become a lightning rod for controversy, thanks to the LGBTQ+ crowd on that small campus targeting him. It was an attack by such activists, in which he and his Christian friends were the victims, that led to his being asked by the college president not to return for his senior year. Not an expulsion. Nothing went on his record. Still, he, the victim, was the one asked not to return. He could have fought it in court but chose not to when he was accepted as a transfer student to the UMSL program. That in itself was largely unheard of, so he couldn't see passing it up.

He had also chosen not to live on campus. His family's home was less than 15 minutes away from campus. As a commuting student, he didn't have the "exposure" to the LGBTQ+ crowd that he'd had in the dorm in Wisconsin. He didn't know them. They didn't know him.

To say that he lived at home wasn't quite right though. His girlfriend, Jessica Larson, had followed him to St. Louis. A retired couple—Col Mike Southworth and his wife Mary—that Aric and Adam had gotten to know well through Lynch Cully, lived but five minutes from the UMSL campus in a large historic home in the community of Ferguson. As fellow believers, they had been more than happy to open their home to her, rent and board free. While Aric still slept at home, he found himself "living" at the Southworth's more often than not . . . much to his mother's consternation.

However, Jess was completing her Film and Media Studies major at Washington University, not UMSL. That campus was roughly ten minutes from the UMSL campus and 20 minutes from the Southworth home. The Southworth's generosity had enabled her to attend that year at Wash U, with its much higher tuition. Her acceptance into that program—considered one of the Top Ten in the country— had been a true miracle in itself. With only 20 to 25 students accepted each year, to transfer in as a senior was nearly unheard of. Actually, no one on the faculty could recall a senior transfer. And, unlike Aric who had the help of an "insider's" reference at UMSL, her acceptance was due purely on the strength of her portfolio.

He pulled into the Southworth's driveway and walked to the front door, where Jess met him.

"Have you been following the news?" she asked. "It's awful."

Aric shook his head. "After leaving you last night, my folks wanted to sit down and get an update on school. Couldn't very well say no, but afterward I was up past midnight preparing for that big practical I have on Monday. Then I overslept and rushed to get here. So, I haven't looked at it at all. What's going on?"

She ushered him into the Southworth's parlor where the older couple were sitting. "We've been discussing it."

"Hi, Aric. Coffee?" asked Mary, being her usual inimitable hostess.

He smiled. "Thanks. I can get it myself in a minute. What's going on?"

Jess sat down in the wingback, upholstered chair she had been occupying that morning and grabbed her mug of tea from the side table. "Hamas launched a surprise attack on Israel in their early morning hours. Over a thousand dead from first reports."

"Slaughtered is more like it." The Colonel looked at his wife. "Sorry, Mary. I know you don't like hearing about it, but he needs to understand the severity of it." She offered him a wan smile in acknowledgment.

Aric sat down in the matching chair next to Jess. His mind raced in several directions.

Mary stood. "I'll go get that coffee." She arose and left the room.

"The terrorists attacked a huge music festival celebrating

peace and shot anyone they could find. They attacked several settlements and shot people in their beds—men, women, and children. There are reports of babies being decapitated and of one pregnant woman being shot, ripped open, and her unborn baby being shot in the head. The atrocities done are, well, barbaric to say the least."

"The IDF and all of their reserves have been called up."

"And my friends in intelligence tell me that Shin Bet has already been given the mission to find and assassinate any and all Hamas leaders living in Lebanon, Turkey, and Qatar," said the colonel.

"Shin Bet?" asked Jess.

"That's the Israeli Security Service. Kind of like our CIA."

Aric shook his head. "Wow. And we were all talking about biblical end times just the other day. Could this be the start of Armageddon?"

The colonel nodded. "Wouldn't be surprised, Israeli leaders are already committing to annihilating Hamas and are preparing to invade Gaza to do so. That alone will stir up those supporting Hamas. And if Shin Bet succeeds, which they almost always do, killing Hamas leaders on foreign soil won't do anything but rile those nations and fan the flames."

Aric nodded in agreement. In their earlier discussion, they had concluded that Armageddon, also known as the War of Gog and Magog from the book of Ezekiel, would likely consist of a confederation of Muslim states moving against Israel. Many people expected that all of the nations of the world would come against Israel, but the regions mentioned by Ezekiel were all Islamic countries of the Middle East, the Balkans, and northeastern Africa. And if this was the beginning of the final battle, Christ's return was imminent.

TWO

Werner Koch lay in bed wondering how he had ended up there. In his early seventies, he and Liesl had been married just shy of 50 years. They had a good life together. They shared strong family memories and traditions with their four children and sixteen, soon-to-be eighteen, grandchildren. Two of their sons had taken on roles in the family business enterprises. The youngest son had become a much-sought-after and respected surgeon. Their daughter was active in the arts.

Werner had been a protégé of Heinz "Henry" Kissinger and co-founder of the World Order Council. Under the "tutelage" of his mentor, he had gone on to develop the WOC's depopulation policies, its climate policies, food policies, and more and had risen to prominence as a world leader, if not *the* de facto world leader. Presidents and prime ministers took his calls directly. The WOC's policies formed the backbone of most nations' newest laws, as well as resolutions in the United Nations.

The consolidation of global elites from all spheres of life to form that New World Order had become reality. True, they had been set back by four years with the unexpected election of a conservative populist, Bradley Graham, as the U.S. president. They made sure that didn't happen again, and now Charles Sidon was in office and following their game plan.

However, American conservatives were still a thorn in

their side in the U.S., and that "contagion" seemed to be spreading with conservative and libertarian politicians gaining popularity across the globe. In the U.S., they were succeeding in eliminating the Republican majority in their Congress. The ouster of one House Speaker had led to infighting within that party, conservatives versus the rest of them. Between resignations and ousters, he predicted that early in the new year, those pesky conservatives would be silenced, and the Democrats would regain control of Congress. Then, with the U.S. government totally under the "control" of the WOC and its allies in the UN and WHO, those populist leaders elsewhere would lose a major ally.

Of course, it didn't hurt that the intelligence agencies were "owned" by them. Between financial entanglements and honeypot entrapments, they had enough blackmail material to make sure most politicians worldwide would ensure that their agenda would be accomplished. And for those who wouldn't toe the line? Well, their political futures were short-lived.

His thoughts were interrupted by a glass of wine being extended toward him. As he took a sip of the excellent Cabernet, he again wondered how he had ended up in *this* bed. Not his bed. He felt a slight twinge of remorse at having succumbed to the flirting of his latest employee.

A brief thought flitted through his mind. Had he just succumbed to someone else's honeypot? No. He couldn't accept that. She had been too well vetted for that to be the case.

Yolina Zhdanov could be his youngest daughter. She was pert, attractive, and an Olympic-class flirt. She also had a brain like few people he had ever encountered. Of all of his IT folks, she had come closest to solving a major problem for him—finding the person responsible for destroying their surveillance programs, AlterNet and AlterNet2.

She had convinced him to set up her office in her apartment and to allow her to work remotely. After all, her hours would not be those of his regular employees. If her software caught the "scent" of their prey in the middle of the night, she couldn't afford the time to drive to "the office" to work. That scenario was more than likely considering that the person, male or female, he sought appeared to reside in the U.S., six or more hours "away" considering time zones.

Yet, coming to her "office" had become something of a trap. At first, she simply shared what she was finding and reported on her progress. Soon, she shared a glass, or two, of wine. Now, for the first time, she shared her bed.

He felt her snuggle up to his side, the warmth of her breast against him. Her long, black hair cascaded over his shoulder. He thought of Liesl in their younger days. What was he doing? Still, he hadn't felt invigorated like this in decades.

She stroked his cheek with a fingernail and leaned into him for a full-mouthed kiss. Her pert breasts pressed into him as his heart rate accelerated. He reached down and placed his hand between her thighs.

What? Something wasn't right. He pulled back and away.

"What's wrong?" she asked. "Have I done something?"

He gasped with his sudden realization. "You're . . . you're . . ."

"What?" She sat up, wrapping the sheet around her torso. "I, I thought you knew. I haven't exactly hidden that I was born male."

Werner jumped up from the bed, feeling dizzy at the sudden change. He forced the lightheadedness away. The last thing he needed was to pass out in this bedroom. The scandal would kill him and destroy Liesl.

As he hurriedly dressed to leave, he realized that scandal, blackmail, or both were not totally out of the question. That could never happen. And then anger engulfed him. Who had vetted this person? He would have that person's head on a platter.

"I'm, I'm sorry. I thought you knew. You speak so fervently about trans rights that I—"

Werner realized he was getting caught with his pants down, literally and figuratively. He did, indeed, promote such rights. They simply weren't his, well, his glass of Schnapps.

"No, I am sorry, Yolina. I did not know, and I was wrong, in many ways, to stay here. I must leave now."

He turned and headed for the bedroom door. Before leaving, he turned back. "However, please understand that if any word of this gets out, or if you request money for your silence, working railroad maintenance in Siberia will be the least of your worries. My friends at the FSB would make sure of that. From now on, call me with your reports."

On loan from Pozitiv Teknolodzhiz, the Russian firm contracted for cyber operations by the Russian Federal Security Service, she, or he—now he felt confused over which pronoun to use—had been offered as their best hacker. He wondered if they knew her full story. Even more, he wondered why they hadn't informed him. If she continued to work as she was doing, he would not bring it up with them. If not, . . . her silence would be guaranteed.

As soon as Yolina heard her front door click shut, she scrambled from the bed and ran to her bathroom. Why she had been asked by her FSB handlers to seduce this man was beyond her. Anything and everything for Mother Russia they insisted. What was it the Americans called it, a honey trap? Something like that. One handler called it insurance and a guaranteed promotion for her. Her other handler glibly told her that refusal was not an option.

And yet now, death still seemed inevitable. Until tonight, she faced that threat from only one front. Her compliance with her handlers' request had lessened but not eliminated their threat. Koch's threat, however, hung over her like the sword of Damocles, made worse by the fact that she did not control the information she had just obtained for "Mother Russia." Maybe now was the time to take her future into her own hands.

She brushed her teeth and rinsed her mouth several times until she was satisfied that the taste of him was gone. Fortunately, his hurried foreplay led to an earlier than expected outcome, before she would have had to . . . well, it hadn't come to that.

Next, she bent over, removed the cleverly designed scrotal appliance, and sat down on the toilet to urinate. It had been uncomfortable and blocked her ability to pee, so good riddance. Yet, it worked perfectly into fooling the great Herr Werner Koch into thinking she was a he identifying as a she. The idea of transgenderism still abhorred most in her country, and their president now promoted a law awaiting passage by the Federal Assembly that would outlaw such, contrary to the WOC's policies and those of the western Deep State. Werner Koch openly pushed for its acceptance and coerced some countries into accepting it, along with the LGBTQ+ agenda in general, despite their misgivings. And yet, when confronted with it, he bolted like a rabbit being pounced upon by a wolf. The hypocrisy was glaring.

Her bladder relieved, she thought about his threat at the end, as she walked toward her kitchen. A Siberian exile was nowhere in the cards. Would the FSB see to her safe relocation? Perhaps, but she doubted it. Even if they did, however, the man had many resources, several of which she had no doubt could make her disappear forever. She was not quite sure how to play her next hand. Did she continue with the work tasked to her? Should she leave for home, saying that her company had recalled her, and assuring Herr Koch that her leaving might be the least embarrassing move for both of them? There was one compromise. Since she worked remotely and now was expected to report only by phone or electronically, she could do that more safely at home in St. Petersburg or perhaps a hidden *dacha* outside Moscow, outside Herr Koch's direct reach.

Again, the thought struck her . . . maybe it was time to take her future into her own hands. Could she possibly find a place outside the reach of both?

With a glass of vodka in hand, she returned to the bedroom. On the bookcase opposite her bed, she retrieved the small camera, its cord, and the video recorder that had captured the man's entire stay and sudden flight. She removed the USB drive, placed it into the laptop at her bedside, and confirmed that not only was his total visit recorded but that the quality was excellent also. This file would be passed along to her handler within the hour.

With that assurance, she still debated her best move. Like Herr Koch, she now felt convinced that her prey truly existed. Whoever this programmer was, he, or she, had gone to great lengths not to be discovered. That alone intrigued her. Who had so much at stake that such lengths were needed? Well, she admitted to herself that she did at the moment. At the same time, she simply wanted to meet this person. No one before had eluded her so successfully.

She loved the chase, so she would stay. However, if her next encounter with Herr Koch proved too awkward, or if he threatened her again, that Muscovite *dacha*—no, maybe an obscure Caribbean island—would become option number one.

THREE

Adam sat back in his chair and sighed. He hoped he had been quick enough to thwart the latest attempt to identify and locate him. He jumped at the ringing of his phone, but relaxed upon seeing the Caller ID.

"Hey, Lynch. What can I do for you?"

He heard a chuckle on the other end.

"I don't know. *You* left *me* a message to call."

Adam rubbed his forehead with his free hand. "Oh. Yeah. Sorry, I'm really flustered right now."

"What? The always calm, unflappable, Adam Afton feels flustered?"

Adam smiled, not that Lynch could see him. "Yeah, yeah, yeah. It happens on occasion. Look, I've got some more info you might be interested in. It's right out of Conspiracy Theory 301 but looks like we might have another spoiler alert." He heard Lynch laugh again.

"So, what is it, disinformation, misinformation, election fraud, false flag operations, or the latest vaccine revelation?"

"Vaccine stuff. It's coming from the New Zealand Te Whatu Ora. Data released by a healthcare worker there."

"The Te Whatu what?"

"Te Whatu Ora. It's the socialized healthcare system there. A worker who says he was the original Oracle database administrator for the system has turned whistleblower. He's released actual line-item data from part of their database showing when individuals got vaccinated and when they died. Most deaths occurred around the six-month time frame, but the data shows way more deaths than the authorities there are acknowledging. Extrapolating his data worldwide shows that over ten million people have likely died from the vaccine."

"And he released this publicly?"

"It's not public yet. He's sent it to several others, statisticians or the like, to corroborate his data. It's likely to be released in a month."

"Whoa. I'll give you hundred-to-one odds he's arrested when it goes public. The authorities aren't going to like this."

"I'm trying to warn him, but I can't seem to get through. Which is odd. I can almost always get through to someone's email or texts."

"Curious. Send everything to me. The usual secure channel."

Adam pressed a key on his computer. "Sent."

"So, what's got you all flustered?"

Adam needed a moment to think about this. How much should he admit to? "You know I've told you that someone from the old AlterNet program keeps trying to find me. Evidently, I still haven't been able to throw them off my trail. Whoever's behind this is convinced I exist, and I think it's Werner Koch himself. His aide was on my trail, but he died from that paralyzing virus they released in LA. So, Koch has enlisted someone with much greater skills, and this person is doggedly hunting. He or she almost found me. I've left trails to false IDs in a dozen countries, like the Bergálfur Jónsson identity in Iceland that was exposed last spring. A total of seven of those identities have now been exposed, and I realized why. I have one tiny piece of code that I've used and reused in making those trails. It was so small that I didn't really think much of it, but whoever this is found it and has been using it to follow and expose my trails."

"Do you know who it is, the hacker, I mean?"

Adam shook his head out of habit as he answered. "Not specifically, but I've run into this person before. He or she also has a tell in his programming. It's someone in Russia, or at least from Russia, if they're now working for Koch."

"So, can you fix it? I'd hate to think of what might happen if they find you."

"Me, too, and yes. Already fixed, but I'll use it to create some more fake IDs and rabbit trails for this person to run down. Keep 'em busy. I was programming the parameters into UltraNet to begin that process."

He heard Lynch laugh at that comment. "Nothing like rabbit trails to keep someone busy. Good luck. Let me know how things go."

"Will do. Talk with you later."

Adam disconnected the call and returned to his programming. He made sure that his backstopping was more thorough this time, but he also decided to have a little fun with his hunter. He created four of his "alter egos" to appear as though they were working together clandestinely. Then, with one, he created the beginning of a trail to a fifth programmer, their ringleader. But this leader wouldn't be just anyone. He decided to link this person and his group to Alexei Baranov, the First Deputy Director of the FSB itself, and his offices on Lubyanka Square. Should the person hunting him follow that trail, it should create quite a stir in Moscow.

Yet, while working to throw off his virtual scent, Adam also acknowledged that he found this game and cat and mouse challenging. He hadn't "met" such a dedicated and talented cyber sleuth. He felt a desire to reverse their roles, become the hunter, and find this person, but something inside warned him not to. His brother said it was the Holy Spirit's warning to his own spirit. He was slowly learning to trust this inner sense.

A familiar voice interrupted his thoughts. "Daaddddyyyy! Are you downstairs? I need your help."

Grace was calling. After her kidnapping, he had spent years looking for her. And after finding her, he would never deny her needs again. He stopped what he was doing, hit 'save,' and stood to go upstairs. He could finish after she went to bed.

"Coming, Gracie. What do you need?"

FOUR

AG Derrick McFarland sat in his office at the Department of Justice reading through the briefs from the weekend provided by his staff earlier that morning. As the nation's head law enforcement officer, he held responsibility for not only the DOJ and its lawyers, but also the FBI, ATF, DEA, and other agencies involved in federal law enforcement and the prisons.

Publicly, he vigorously defended their work against those conservative naysayers calling his departments "weaponized." He, and the heads of his departments, were protecting democracy as they believed it should be—inclusive, equitable, and diverse. For too long, the government had "looked the other way" when people of color, those of alternate gender identities, and various lifestyles were victimized. These people needed their protection . . . as long as it was profitable for the elites, such as himself.

Privately, he would comply with the WOC's global agenda and aim every arrow he possessed at the hearts of those conservative nationalists. Yet, he recognized their claims of hypocrisy—that his side was avowing to protect democracy by eliminating political opponents, denying people the right to choose, and more. So what. He didn't care. He felt validated that they could use whatever means necessary to achieve their global goals.

As he thumbed through the paperwork, he set aside the brief about a Chicago-area six-year-old Palestinian-American boy who had been stabbed 22 times and killed by the family's 71-year-old white male landlord who was upset over the Hamas invasion of Israel four days earlier. The boy's mother remained in the hospital, alive but in serious condition. The AG would not be able to attend the boy's memorial in a week, but he would issue a statement that day expressing his condolences.

He continued to work through the stack of papers. He sifted through more than a dozen reports of upset parents at school board meetings. His staff would flag those parents to watch for future transgressions.

Next up was a 19-year-old white, college coed stabbed to death by an undocumented immigrant. He hated the terms "illegal alien," "illegal immigrant," and other more racist and bigoted names. No one was "illegal." They simply lacked the correct documents. He flagged that brief to remind the responsible staffer that he didn't want to be bothered by reports like that one. While he acknowledged that he, too, was Caucasian, he accepted that his race was part of the problem, not part of the solution.

As he prepared to dictate his letter of condolence, his phone rang.

"Sir, it's Mr. Zhèng. Shall I put his call through?" asked his secretary.

"By all means, Tisha."

He waited for the call to come. Zhèng Jian was President Sidon's Chief of Staff, responsible for managing the executive offices and White House. He controlled the president's schedule, access to the Oval Office and president, all staffing, and numerous offices within the Executive Branch, such the

National Security Council and Council of Economic Advisers. Despite the traditional Chinese name, the man was American-born and Ivy League trained. He had proven himself formidable in that role.

McFarland had become friends with Charles Sidon during the man's years in the Senate. He had been chief counsel to him when Sidon became vice president. During that time, McFarland had been nominated for the Supreme Court but denied that privilege by a Republican Senate. Charles had finally rewarded him for his service to their cause by selecting him as Attorney General.

On the other hand, the selection of Zhèng Jian as the White House Chief of Staff seemed to come out of the blue. It wasn't until a year or so after the appointment that McFarland learned that Zhèng was given the post at the suggestion of Werner Koch. Such powerful friends could definitely get you places, and McFarland held no illusions as for whom Zhèng truly worked.

He picked up the phone on the first ring. "Jian, a pleasure to hear from you. How can I help you?" He didn't intend to get right to business, but he had a busy day ahead.

"Good morning, Derrick. Two things. First, Zelenskyy is coming in for yet another trip to Washington. Ukraine's counteroffensive is not off to a good start, and he wants more money. The President is inclined to give it to him, but the Republican Congress is starting to balk at the continued requests. Plus, he doesn't seem to understand that Congress can't do any business with a temporary speaker at the helm, so his requests will have no place to go until a new Speaker of the House is elected."

McFarland nodded. The current status of the House of Representatives was chaotic to say the least. It would be interesting to see who would become the next Speaker.

McFarland wasn't sure where this was going. Protection of foreign dignitaries fell to the Secret Service, which was under the Department of Homeland Security, not the DOJ. He felt sure that Zhèng knew this and didn't want to offend the man by suggesting that he simply ask the Secret Service office at the White House to make those arrangements.

"Sorry, Zelenskyy's repeated pestering for money is getting thin over here. I'm venting. The President is concerned about the unsettled Congress. He wants a change there, like flipping the majority to the Democrats during the first of the year."

"Doesn't he want to wait and see who gets the speakership?"

"No. With the conservative caucus there, it's unlikely to be someone as moderate as the previous Speaker. He'd like to see more Republicans resign, and we understand you might have some files that could persuade some of them to do so."

Well, that was blunt and to the point.

"Umm, yes, we have files on all congressmen and senators, just as we have on every federal employee. I'm not sure there's anything in them that could be used to persuade them to leave, or else it might have already been used. Perhaps dangling the enticing carrot of a new position might work better. A university presidency. A top think-tank position."

He was being truthful about the DOJ not having blackmail-worthy materials on members of Congress. Despite what many believed and the old stories about J. Edgar Hoover's secret files, the FBI didn't maintain this kind of material to hold over politicians' heads. That was under the CIA's purview where subpoenas and FOIA lawsuits could vanish into the "national security" sinkhole. Zhèng knew this all too well. McFarland knew they'd both been victims of CIA honeypot operations, although he'd never reveal how he learned of the other man's victimization. Too much to drink in Washington's social circles could be damning.

He wouldn't mention the intelligence agency. Neither man liked being reminded of his failings. Besides, "they" could be listening.

"Well, see what you might have that could help. The second thing is the old man himself. He's getting worse, but when he's lucid, he insists on staying in the race. We need to convince him to move on."

McFarland hated whenever anyone in the administration referred to Sidon as the "old man." True, he was, but he deserved more respect for his decades of service to the country. At least, that's what McFarland liked to think. He was well aware of the man's enriching himself and his family through influence peddling across the globe and so-called business dealings with the Chinese. If Sidon hadn't been so successful in propelling the Deep State's global interests front and center, he would have landed in prison years ago.

"So, the adrenochrome isn't helping?"

The president, as well as others, had thought they found the fountain of youth in the blood-derived compound. However, after a couple of years, the users found themselves needing more and more for the same apparent benefit. Like opioids and aphrodisiacs, the promise at the beginning went unfulfilled in the end.

"No. We're having to pump him up with amphetamines every morning just to get through a short speech or meeting in the Oval Office. At night, he's wandering around the White

House naked, lost, and unable to find his way back to his bedroom. The staff has started to talk among themselves, and non-disclosure agreements or not, word of this is bound to leak out sooner or later."

McFarland sighed. He, too, had already heard rumors of Sidon's marked deterioration, but the nighttime roaming within the residence was sad to hear. And what if he should escape his handlers and end up outside? He didn't want to think about what the opposition media would do with that.

"So, what can I do? No one on the cabinet is willing to pull the 25th Amendment card and claim he's incompetent. That would risk reversing everything folks have worked for."

"You're an old friend. Talk with him. Talk with his wife and daughter. We need a fresh face in the race, but no one is going to step up as long as he insists on staying in the race."

McFarland nodded. "Okay. Let me think about how to approach this, and I'll see what I can do."

"That's all I'm asking. Thanks."

McFarland sat back in his chair. He knew Sidon well. The man would resist any and all efforts to remove him from the ticket. Perhaps they needed to stop his meds. He would go down in flames, but that would also bring serious embarrassment to his family. McFarland had two other options. Option one was to slowly leak bank records and other documents to the Congressional committee looking into impeachment. If a formal impeachment inquiry were to develop, the pressure on his old friend might persuade him to step down voluntarily rather than risk full exposure of his family's secrets.

Option two at the moment existed only as a possibility. Perhaps, he could nudge things along the path of probability to make it reality.

FIVE

Aric completed his second forensics practical in as many weeks and prepared to leave the lab. He looked about to see more than half of his fellow students still at their places working to complete the test. He felt good about his work and was surprised that he was among the first finishers. Until that point, he had felt under-prepared for the coursework. He was, after all, a senior transfer student from a fledgling criminology program at a small private college, and his fellow students had been with this top-tier program at UMSL since their freshmen year. If he did as well as he thought on this test, he'd know that he had earned his spot in the program through merit, not just Lynch's recommendation. The idea that he was there because of the latter had bothered him throughout that first six weeks of school.

As he left Lucas Hall and headed toward Millennium Student Center to meet Jess, who came to campus to join him for lunch, he stopped just yards outside. Loitering along the side of the walkway was a familiar looking head of pink hair looking away from him. He shook his head. It couldn't be. He had to be imagining it. Maybe it was just that shade of neon pink that caught his attention. It had to be someone else. Yet, that spike on top of the head seemed so distinctive.

Toni was the gay activist at his old college who had been part of a team dedicated to driving him out of "their" dorm. The guy had been a thorn in Aric's side for the entire three years there. He had been involved in tossing eggs at them during one of their community praise nights in a local, lakeside park. It was at that event that God intervened and all of the assailants' eggs broke in midair or within their hands.

Toni. You could spot him a football field away thanks to his bright pink spike of hair.

No way. Aric must be having a bad hallucination. Maybe he inhaled some fumes during the lab practical. Still, he pulled his hood tighter around his head and face. The last thing he wanted was a confrontation with Toni or a lookalike that would expose him to the gay crowd on campus. He enjoyed the quiet anonymity of being new and largely unknown on campus.

With his face mostly hidden, he hitched his backpack tighter to his body and continued on his way. As he passed the pink-headed individual, he turned his face slightly away to further avoid detection, but he kept the same pace. He didn't want to act suspicious. Twenty feet beyond the person, he began to sigh with quiet relief when he heard, "Hey, that's him. That's Aric the Christian bigot!"

Toni's voice was as distinctive as his hair, and that was the voice he heard. Aric took a deep breath and picked up his pace.

"That's him. That's his backpack. It even has our college logo on the back."

Aric chastised himself. Of course. The backpack. He hadn't considered a new one. After all, who at UMSL would have recognized it? Why discard a perfectly good and useful backpack when he had just months to go before graduation.

He heard the scampering of feet behind him. Not just one set, however. There must have been half a dozen individuals hurrying up behind him. He was almost to the student center when he felt someone tug on and pull his hood off his head. He stopped.

"Hey!" He turned and, sure enough, there was Toni. "Toni? What are you doing here? Did you miss me?" He smiled as he reached for Toni to give him a hug.

A puzzled look flashed across the guy's face as he jumped back to avoid contact with Aric. He looked as if Aric was about to infect him with bioweapon-grade cooties. Aric knew him well enough to know that an unexpected response would always throw him off balance. He laughed inside but resisted the temptation to display that amusement. He would give up his advantage if he did so.

"I . . . I . . ."

"Toni, it's good to see you. I've missed that hair waking me up in the dining hall at breakfast. It's shining brighter than I remember. What brings you to St. Louis?" His comment produced a few chuckles from Toni's comrades.

The man, using that term loosely, stood there speechless. Aric had no doubt that being greeted as a friend was the last thing Toni expected . . . or wanted.

"Hey look, good to see you, but I'm late. I need to meet someone inside, so gotta go."

He held up his thumb and index finger to his head as in saying "Call me," turned, and hurried into the building. Jess stood near the doorway at the large adjacent windows, her mouth wide open in disbelief. Aric grabbed her elbow and pulled her away from the window, moving quickly into the interior of the center and out of sight of the doors.

"Is . . . is that who I really hope it isn't? Wha . . ."

Aric nodded. "Yep. Good ol' Toni from Kenosha. I didn't wait around to find out why he's here. I don't want to know."

And yet, he did kind of want to know. The man appeared

to be waiting for him and seemed intent on exposing him, if that was the right word to use. No, identifying him or pointing him out to others was the more accurate description. Why else would he have yelled, "That's him," if it had been an accidental meeting? At that moment, Aric understood how the apostle Paul must have felt when antagonistic Jews followed him and called him out from city to city. Was Toni so vindictive that he sought out the school where Aric transferred and now wanted the local LGBTQ+ activist mob to continue their gay vendetta against him?

Sadly, Aric knew the answer to his question.

SIX

Denton Pierce, JD, was swimming with alligators. He had started the Midwest Justice and Freedom Defense Alliance over 20 years earlier as a Christ-centered firm committed to protecting the religious freedoms of all religious groups, protecting the unborn and declaring the sanctity of life, defending the constitutional rights of free speech as well as parental rights, and defending marriage and the family as God ordained both to be. From humble beginnings, he had developed a team that grew the firm to a size he had never envisioned in its earlier days. And the need for their services grew daily as the alligators of the Deep State swamp and immoral culture around them grew more and more powerful.

While most lawyers would take great personal pride in their successes, Denton gave God the glory. The firm itself had 70 attorneys, and they now had a network of over 2,500 lawyers nationwide and nearly 5,000 worldwide. MJFDA had played positive roles in over 70 Supreme Court victories, a dozen of which they could claim as their own just in the past decade. Counting state and local victories as well as lower federal cases, they had nearly a 90% success rate, with an 80% success rate in the U.S. Supreme Court. Their work had benefited cake decorators, website designers, photographers, pastors, churches—as well as synagogues and mosques, religious groups, pro-life pregnancy centers, family businesses and more. Yes, there was no way this all could have been achieved without God's help.

But now, Denton was at a personal crossroads. He loved his position as CEO and General Counsel of the firm. He found he had talent in managing and mentoring younger attorneys, and he enjoyed both roles. Yet, he missed wading into the fray, the battle of the courtroom, and the jubilation of victory. He wanted one more fight, maybe his last fight, because after 37 years in practice, he was getting tired.

His wife was always saying that life is like a roll of toilet paper. The closer you get to the end, the faster it rolls. As the age of 65 loomed larger and larger in front of him, he found that he relished time with the grandkids and his wife more and more.

One more battle. Just one big one. He'd be ready to bow out, go emeritus.

"Here's another batch."

His legal assistant, Twila Teague, had been with him for the past 15 years. She knew him better than he knew himself, almost as well as his wife, and he was the first to admit it. As such, he had confided in her his desire to participate in one more big case, the more earthshaking the better.

"Anything out of the ordinary?" he asked.

One of his roles was to review requests for their services. While he hated to turn away anyone with a real need, the firm still had its limits. Seventy-five percent of the requests he turned over to one of the vice presidents, who in turn, would usually respond with a referral to someone in their network of affiliated attorneys, mostly volunteers, across the country. International requests went through their Austrian office and its leadership.

The other 25% were requests that the firm would consider taking on directly. He would select them to be discussed at an upcoming executive committee meeting. If approved there, they would get farmed out to the appropriate team. If not, they joined the 75%.

"Maybe. I think you'll agree that most of these can be passed on to affiliates. It's the last ten you might want to take on in-house."

He looked up at her. She was correct 95% of the time. "You still sure you don't want to just do this job for me?" He grinned.

She shook her head. "Above my pay grade."

"You said 'maybe.'"

She nodded. "Yeah. Look at the last three. It's not that each case is particularly unique or egregious, but they point to a concerning trend."

Her interest in those three piqued *his* interest. He flipped over the stack of papers and retrieved the three on the bottom. He took time to not just read each request, but to ponder its implications. First, he noticed that all three were referred to them by other law firms. Not just by a lawyer who thought the case was beyond his ability or resources, but by senior partners of three large firms that he was personally familiar with. They all had the talent and resources for such a case.

However, all three mentioned their case as one potentially destined for the Supreme Court. And apparently that was the deciding factor for each referring attorney. With its track record, the MJDFA had a dozen attorneys credentialed by the highest court in the land. You could appear before SCOTUS only if you had such credentials. None of those three firms, despite their size, had ever taken a case before the Supremes.

Denton set those three requests to one side of his desk.

"Thanks, Twila. You might be right. And this just might become *my* project."

She smiled. "Just might? I see your name written all over this one." She turned and left his office.

He settled back into his chair, swiveled toward the large windows, and gazed into the distance. He would need more than those three cases, but like she said, there seemed to be a trend developing. He chuckled. *Oh, she knows me too well*, he thought.

Over two weeks had passed since the Hamas invasion of southern Israel and the slaughter of hundreds of innocent people, and the nation's leadership still promised to send their military into Gaza to eradicate the terror group. Adam scanned a dozen news sites looking for the latest updates but could only find information on the most recent aerial attacks against Hamas strongholds and rocket sites, many situated in or next to schools, hospitals, and civilian-occupied apartment buildings. To use civilians as human shields was a violation of international law and the Geneva Conventions, but the world looked the other way at those infractions and instead, criticized Israel for its bombings.

Adam remained bewildered at the world's blindness. How could anyone side with terrorists who attacked innocents in the early morning hours, raping and killing women, shooting entire families as they slept, and decapitating babies? And the call for a two-nation solution to the problem? In all of history there had never been a Palestinian nation. If one looked at the so-called Palestinians' genetics, they would discover that they were all of Egyptian heritage, even though Egypt refused them refuge in the Sinai.

Adam had to agree with his brother—and Lynch and the Colonel—that this was a spiritual battle. That was the only way he could understand such global hatred against such a small, but industrious, country.

He glanced at the time on his screen. *Welp, lunchtime is over*, he thought. *Back to work.* No sooner had he resumed work on a client's website security package, than his phone rang.

"Pelethites Cybersecurity. This is Adam."

Aric's name for his company was still perfect. Just as the Pelethites guarded King David, Adam's company guarded the websites and computer systems of believers. Still, Adam and his clients continued to stumble over the correct pronunciation: pel-ay-thee'. Adam realized that the only way he was ever going to understand and speak Hebrew was if the Lord supernaturally gifted him that language, downloading it directly into his brain.

"Hey, Adam, this is Terry Weaver at America First News. We have a problem."

"Uh-oh. Is this another denial-of-service attack? Ransomware?"

The start-up news portal posted stories reflecting the attacks on First Amendment rights, election integrity, medical rights and vaccine safety, political corruption, and the like. They had come under attack by those who didn't like what they posted, even though their journalism was truly fair and balanced, well-researched, and corroborated by facts. To their opponents, just the presentation of verifiable facts made them guilty of spreading "misinformation" and the Deep State's latest favorite, "*dis*information."

After a year in operation, their viewers numbered in the hundreds of thousands daily, making them a target for left-wing hackers. Actually, Adam had verified that the hackers were state-sponsored, and not by some Middle Eastern or communist nation. They had suffered a denial-of-service attack by one of the United States' own intelligence agencies. Adam had provided services that stopped the attack, back traced the source of the attack, and warned the attackers that they would be identified and prosecuted. Of course, that was all a bluff. Prosecution would never happen, but the fact that the hackers had been tracked and warned was enough to stop the DOS attack and future ones. So far.

"Nothing like that. We've been de-platformed. Our hosting service has told us they will no longer do business with us after Amazon Web Services notified them that they're dropping our site. They've given us no reason, but as of midnight our website will go dark. We checked with a couple of other services, and they won't take us on without AWS. I'm not sure you can help, but we figured we'd call and check."

"Hey, sorry that happened to you guys, but I've got you covered. Did you guys forget that I offer hosting services? I have main and backup fiberoptic connections to the internet and offer a scalable service just like AWS. In reality, I believe I can provide you with better service at a cheaper price. I can send you a contract right now, and if you're good with it, I can have you online by tonight or tomorrow morning, without missing a beat. It'll take a few days for the new nameservers and addresses to permeate the web, so traffic might be down until that process is over."

"Wow. Ricardo hadn't passed that info on to me. Send me the contract ASAP. I'll need to run it by our legal guys."

Adam called up the blank contract on his system, added it to an email, and hit "Send." "Sent. You should have it momentarily."

"Already in my inbox. Thanks. I hope to get back to you within the hour."

Adam interlaced his fingers on top of his head and leaned back in his chair. This was the second client in less than a week who had been removed by AWS and their hosting company. That group, a law firm whose managing partner wrote a daily blog exposing vaccine myths and providing medical facts backed by studies ignored by the MSM, had nowhere near the web traffic of America First News. Yet, his blog had a readership of over 20,000 people . . . and growing daily.

At the time, Adam had postulated that the blog's rate of growth was rattling the-powers-that-be, producing the pressure on AWS to remove his websites—both the blog website and the man's legal firm's site. The attorney was developing a lawsuit against AWS, but he would need all of his ducks in line before filing it since AWS could outspend him a million to one and delay the case forever with motion after motion. The case was a classical David vs Goliath moment, but as a Christian, the lawyer liked his odds.

What bothered Adam was that even though he was a small internet service provider this was his second such case. He wondered what some of the bigger ISPs were seeing. Plus, he specialized in a niche group that would be more likely to be the targets of a de-platforming effort. While that might be good for his business, what kind of harbinger did this bring?

He took a few minutes to set up UltraNet to search for de-platformed companies and to try to ascertain why they had been removed. He had no trouble infiltrating AWS, Microsoft, and other cloud service providers, so he expected results quickly. In the meantime, he resumed the work that had been interrupted by the AFN call.

Within the hour, as promised, an email arrived from AFN with a signed contract. He finished his current project and began to set up the website for AFN. This would take him several hours between transferring the current site from the other provider, setting up all of security parameters on his own server, testing the site, changing the nameservers, setting up an SSL certificate for secure transactions by the website, testing the company's eStore, and more.

If all went smoothly, he might be finished by dinner. If not, he felt confident he could meet his self-imposed deadline of midnight. He didn't like the possibility of it hanging over until morning.

Not too far into the process, UltraNet alerted him to having completed his query and having its results. He stopped to peruse that data. He didn't like what he saw.

SEVEN

"Я нашел тебя на этот раз," said Yolina to the empty room. *I've found you this time.* She clenched a fist and jerked it toward her in a show of victory. Her prey's tell consisted of three simple lines of code. Easily overlooked, and yet consistent. She had found it on Koch's deceased aide's computer, as well as on computers that survived the devastating "attack" on the AlterNet2 hard drives. She had found no other examples of this code used by any other programmers, known or unknown.

Her fingers flew across the keyboard. Yes. One more step closer. Then another. From one IP address to another. She had to admit this person was genius in using VPNs to route and reroute "his" work. She had decided that her prey was male. Call it female intuition, but something about his code came across as brash and bold, like that of certain male hackers at Pozitiv Teknolodzhiz. Her code, and that of her fellow female hackers, seemed, well, more refined and finessed.

вот ты где, she thought. *There you are.* What? Igor Karamazov? A fellow Russian? Or at least someone with a Russian heritage. Was this his real name, or just a play on Fyodor Dostoevsky's infamous novel, *The Brothers Karamazov*?

With a name and certain account information, she began her scrutiny of the man. Age: 42. Yes, a fellow Russian by birth but taken to the U.S. as a child by parents fleeing some kind of persecution in the homeland. She made a note to try to find what that might have been, but records from 35 years earlier were unlikely to be easily found in the records of the old U.S.S.R. since few of such records had been digitized. She would have to decide later about whether or not to involve her handlers in finding this information.

Igor appeared to have done well in school and ended up at the California Institute of Technology. She nodded in approval. That computer science program was in the Top Ten in the U.S. He certainly could have developed his skills there. With some additional digging she learned that he held multiple certifications in advanced logic and algorithms, Linux, database design and security, and more. His skill set became more impressive with each thing she discovered about him. He certainly could be her guy.

Yet, with each of the previous false identities, their stories failed when she began investigating personal facts—marriages, children, the children's schools, social media accounts, and such. Igor was married—20 years—and the marriage certificate, church, and other supporting documents still retrievable after 20 years supported him. They had one child, and she found school registration documents and grades to support the boy's existence. A new search found the wife's birth certificate, school records, and employment data.

With the previous fakes, their histories had failed by now. If this guy was another fake, her prey had vastly improved his ability to backstop his creation.

Then she found something totally unexpected—a link to another programmer. Was "he" actually "they?" Should she really be hunting a *pair* of programmers? That could explain some things. One could be wiping clean any trail left by the other, and vice versa. Maybe that's why they had had so much difficulty finding the "man" responsible for killing both AlterNet program.

Another thought hit her. What if it wasn't even just a pair or programmers? What if more people were involved?

She sighed. Any thought of getting to bed on time just went out the window. It was going to be an all-nighter.

"Sir, are you okay? You seem distracted."

Werner turned to his new assistant, blinked twice, and gave a subtle shake of his head. "Sorry, Ilse. Yes, I'm a bit distracted, but I'll be fine. Where were we?"

Ilse Adelsperger at age 40 was a no-nonsense woman with strong Germanic traits—direct, rule-bound, organized, punctual, and somewhat distant. Werner had discovered that she loved her beer and soccer and also had a fondness for American football. What she wasn't was a blue-eyed, blonde-haired Aryan beauty so favored by the Nazis of the previous century. *That* wasn't a trait he wanted confronting him at the moment. As such, she seemed perfect for the role as his new aide.

She became the third candidate for the position since Edvin Bergstedt, his previous aide, had died from the crippling enterovirus that had to date killed millions across the globe. Created to further their goal of depopulating the world—a goal Werner remained dedicated to—the virus had mutated in unexpected ways, leading to the sudden, unexpected, and severe paralysis of its victims. It was this acute nature of the virus that had caught multitudes of people, including Edvin, in positions where they could receive no help in time.

He missed Edvin. The young man had become like one of his sons. He was never supposed to catch the virus, and for the first time, Werner had had a crisis of conscience over the manmade and WOC financed epidemic. Yet, his pragmatism won out. That so-called evil genie was already out of its bottle, and nothing was stopping it, except its very nature to quickly mutate. The latest variant caused only mild to moderate weakness and not the deadly paralysis of its earlier progenitor.

So far, Ilse seemed up to the tasks. Her breadth of experience outmatched Edvin's shorter career, and she held the same insightful ability to analyze a situation or project. However, her grasp of details did not seem to match his. Perhaps that was illusory. Maybe she seemed slower to do so because she took that time to review those details in greater depth. While her two immediate predecessors lasted but weeks, he would give her the time needed for him to fully assess her abilities.

"We were reviewing policy changes for the upcoming annual meeting."

"Ah, yes."

The WOC's annual meeting in Switzerland was just over two months away. The elites and power brokers of the world would be there, and he needed to be fully engaged, at the top of his game. And yet, right now, that was not the case. In fact, for the past two weeks, he had slept poorly, lost his appetite, and found himself becoming increasingly reclusive. Ilse's concern matched that of his wife. Liesl had suggested twice in the past week that he should consult their doctor, the latest suggestion coming that very morning. How could he tell anyone what was truly wrong?

"Ilse, I need to make a couple of confidential calls." He handed her a stack of papers. "Please review and summarize these contracts for me. I'll call you when I'm available."

She took the paperwork, nodded, and quietly left his office. As the door closed behind her, Werner began to pace. His mind was in turmoil, a continuing eddy of worries and disgust with himself swirling about. So far, Yolina had kept quiet. She, or he, had made no demands of him and, in fact, had kept him abreast of her work via phone as he had requested. She appeared to have found something significant just that morning, something that would very likely keep her working throughout the night.

However, the thoughts of having been lured into a gay honeypot operation by her or someone else controlling her kept threatening to accelerate the eddy into a ship-sinking whirlpool. How had he been so foolish?

Part of his struggle had been what to do about the situation? He couldn't simply have her eliminated . . . for a variety of reasons, not least of which was his worry about someone else being in on it. There he was again, assuming the worst. Assuming it was a trap. Maybe it wasn't. Maybe it really was her, um, him, being attracted to him. Many were sexually attracted by power, and he was among the most powerful men on the globe.

Also, she held the greatest promise of finding the person responsible for AlterNet and its demise. Finding that person—they now agreed that it was most likely a man—had become a minor obsession with him, if any true obsession could be considered minor.

Of late, though, he had come to recognize that part of his struggle, perhaps the largest part, was pride. He didn't want to confide in anyone—anyone—that he had been unfaithful to Liesl. And unfaithful with a trans-woman at that. Despite his public rhetoric, his true feelings of that "movement" were those of disgust. It went against every fiber of whatever morality he held. Morality as he defined it for himself, of course. He did many things without guilt that his religious grandparents would have found abhorrent.

He realized, however, that to rid his mind of this torment, he would have to swallow his pride. He would need to pull someone into his confidence. And he had decided who that someone would be.

He retrieved a certain cell phone from within his desk and dialed the only number in its contact list. There would be no answer. Just the appearance of his number on the phone's call log would tell that person he was needed.

Yuri—the only name he would be called by—had been placed into Russia's FSB as a mole for the WOC. Well, specifically for Werner. The WOC's influence within the Soviet country was nil, despite their attempts to lure a number of Russian oligarchs into their sphere of influence. So, Werner, playing the long game, carefully placed men of influence, men he could trust, into the FSB and Kremlin. Their roles were not to try to push the Soviet leadership into the WOC, but to rise in rank and wait until their services were needed.

Within ten minutes, the phone rang.

"*Ja?*"

"Yolina Zhdanov. FSB asset or not. If yes, who are her handlers? And what is her background?"

"*Ja*, Herr Koch. Three, maybe four days. I will send information through usual channel."

"*Danke.* And payment will be sent likewise."

EIGHT

Aric began to feel optimistic that his encounter with pink-hair Toni a week earlier was truly a fluke and that nothing would come from it. He had not seen the guy since, and no one else had approached or heckled him. Of course, by not living in the dorms, his comings and goings on campus were not as easily discovered. Plus, he could, and did, vary his times arriving at and leaving campus if for no other reasons than taking opportunities to study in the library or grabbing a quick snack before or after a class.

He and Jess finished lunch at the Southworth's, and he drove her to her early afternoon class before heading back to campus for his own class. He still had an hour to kill and planned on using that time in the library before his computer forensics lab.

After parking in the north student center garage, he exited and headed toward the Thomas Jefferson Library. However, rather than take the most direct route through parking lot E and the student center, he ducked out the back of the garage and picked up the Cross Campus Trail that would skirt the south garage and recreation center before crossing the greenway to the library's entrance on the south side of the building. He told himself that it was a nice fall day. Enjoy the walk. Yet, he also admitted to himself that he was least likely to encounter other students using the trail than if he went through the student center.

He hoisted his new UMSL backpack over his also-new hoodie. He didn't try to fool himself that these two purchases were because he needed them. What he needed was to continue the peace he found in anonymity on campus. If his old Carthage gear gave him away, then he decided to pack them away.

He spent half an hour in the library, reading, before packing up to head to Express Scripts Hall. Outside, he could turn right or left, as he simply needed to walk around to the northwest corner of the library to get to the other building. He chose to be lazy and go left to avoid the stairs down and then back up to get to the hall's entrance.

"Hey, watch it!" The sidewalk was nearly empty, and yet, another student bumped into and jostled him as he rounded the northeast corner of the library. The student didn't reply or even slow down, but Aric noticed he managed to avoid others as he continued walking. Aric shook his head at the guy's lack of manners. The least he could have done was say, "Sorry."

Aric settled into his seat within the lab. The room, which seated 40, was already nearly half full. The Cybersecurity and Information Technology Innovation Lab—CITIL for acronym lovers—functioned as an interdisciplinary center and the hub of the university's state-of-the-art facilities for cybersecurity education, research, and outreach. He figured Lynch's love of computer forensics had rubbed off on him because he had found this particular class intriguing and stimulating.

"Okay, folks. Let's get started. There's a lot to cover today."

Aric stopped chatting with his neighbor and turned his attention to the instructor.

"Today, we have a special guest." He nodded his head toward a man seated in front.

The guy had a physique like Jason Mamoa but with sleek, silky hair pulled back into a ponytail like that of a romance novel cover model. Aric thought for a moment. Was it Lynch, or maybe his brother, who had described someone like that? Was this the guy?

"This is Mike Jurgesmeyer, the director of the St. Louis County Computer Forensics Center in Clayton."

Aric smiled. Yep, this was the guy.

"Mike is internationally known for his work in facial recognition, and today, he's going to talk to us about the technical aspects of facial rec, its limitations, the legalities of its use, and its admissibility issues in court. Pay attention. From past experience, I know you're about to get three hours' worth of information in just under 80 minutes here. Please welcome Mike."

The instructor turned aside and sat down as their expert stood and took to the podium, without notes. A second later, Aric's head appeared on all three plasma screens, rotated 360°, and was covered with green vector lines just like in the movies. Everyone turned to watch him and laughed as Aric squirmed in his seat. He hoped he wasn't visibly blushing, but he felt flushed. Within another second, his first name appeared under his image. Then a second student underwent the same scrutiny, followed by a third.

Mike walked over to the third student and handed him a pair of Groucho Marx glasses. "Please put these on." The young man complied, laughing as he did so, and now his image with the glasses in place appeared on the screens. Again, the vectors measured his face and came up with his name, but with an 85% rating following his name. Mike went to the second student and handed him a wig. Same instructions but the hair didn't change the program's ability to identify him. Then Mike reclaimed the wig and classes and approached Aric.

Aric knew he was blushing this time, as he expected to be asked to put on both. The others in the glass began to laugh, expecting the same. Instead, Mike surprised them all when he pulled out a wildly abstract shirt. "Here, put this on over your shirt."

Aric complied. To the class's amazement, the computer couldn't lock onto Aric's face, much less identify him.

"With this quick demonstration, I've shown you both abilities and limitations of facial rec." Their guest speaker then moved on and for the next 80 minutes, fulfilled their instructor's expectation.

As the class ended, Aric felt both overwhelmed and wanting more. He was glad he had recorded the class on his phone. As he picked up his backpack, Mike Jurgesmeyer approached him.

He extended his hand, and the man responded to shake hands. "Mr. Jurgesmeyer, thank you. That was fascinating. I'm going to have to listen to it a couple of more times to let it really soak in though."

The man smiled and pointed to the shirt. Aric realized he still wore the abstract garment.

"Oops. Sorry. I got so engrossed in the material, I forgot I still had it on." He doffed the shirt and handed it back to its owner.

"Aric, it's nice to meet you. I've heard a lot about you over the past few years."

Aric knew he shouldn't feel surprised, for some reason, and yet, he was. "Oh?"

"Yep. Lynch and I are old friends. He actually helped me establish the county computer forensics lab back in the day. And I worked closely with your brother . . . on a project that I can't really talk about."

Aric leaned closer and whispered, "The Remnant?"

Mike's head flinched back a bit in surprise. "Well, I—"

"Don't worry. My lips are sealed."

"Look, any time you want to come by the lab and check it out, let me know. Here's my card." He extended a business card to Aric.

"Thanks. I'd love that. Maybe during our fall break at Thanksgiving next month."

Mike nodded. "Should work. Not going anywhere for the holiday."

Aric pulled his backpack onto his shoulders and turned to leave. He felt a tug on the pack.

"Aric? Wait a sec."

Aric turned back to Mike.

"No. Turn back around."

He felt Mike tug on his backpack.

"Okay. Now you can turn around again."

Aric faced the man to see him extending something toward him.

"This yours?"

Aric recognized the item as an Apple AirTag. He shook his head. "No. It isn't."

A thought hit him. The collision on the sidewalk. Just as a pickpocket physically bumps into his victims to distract them from what's really happening, that guy had used the encounter to paste an AirTag onto his backpack.

"Well, looks like someone wants to track you."

Aric nodded. He went on to explain what had happened

right before class, as well as the run-in with pink-haired Toni two weeks earlier.

"I can bring this up to your department head, if you want."

Aric shook his head. "Nope. Lynch and I had a similar encounter on campus in Wisconsin. Whoever tagged my car there found himself driving to Madison that evening. I saw a groundskeeper's cart outside as I came in. I think the owner of this tag can have fun chasing it all around campus."

Mike chuckled and gave him a thumbs up.

NINE

Monday afternoon became evening and marched well into Tuesday morning before Yolina came up for air. Yes, there had been lots of coffee and the corresponding potty breaks, even a quick trip to Andy's Krablergarten at the Sendlinger-Tor-Platz underground station for a take-out of schnitzel and *pomme frites*—French fries as the Americans would call them. The food was good and inexpensive, and the restaurant was a short distance from her apartment on Lindwurmstraße. Plus, it didn't close until 11 pm. Yet, as tempting as it sounded, no beer. She needed the caloric energy of the food but not the drowsiness the beer might produce.

Her investigation into Igor Karamazov ultimately had yielded not one but two links to others. That hadn't made it any easier, however, to suss out those people. Warm trails led to blind traps that stopped her cold. Backtracking her steps sometimes helped, but often it didn't. And then she would find those three telltale lines of code and zoom in for the reveal. The whole thing sounded simple, but it took her hours.

Coder number two was a Dormán János—Hungarian, so his last name came first under Hungary's traditional Eastern naming order, like the Chinese or Japanese. He was in his mid-thirties, so he was unlikely to recall anything about his native country under communism. His parents were socialists who fled the country when the national conservative party, the Fidesz, won a supermajority in the Hungarian parliament. The family ended up in the U.S. where his parents became active in the Democrat Party, but János became a Christian conservative, the black sheep of the family.

Like Karamazov, the man had a top-notch education—systems engineering at MIT. He was married with three kids. Also, like Karamazov, the family passed inspection—marriage certificate, birth records, school enrollment records. She even went so far as to comb his state's DOT records to find two vehicles registered to them and county land records listed them as owners of their home. Emails were overtly ordinary. Phone text messages and call logs reflected a "normal" life.

Programmer number three was American by birth but also Russian by heritage—Danil Kiselyov. He was, however, a second generation American. His grandparents had immigrated to the U.S. at the fall of the czar and rise of the Bolsheviks. She discovered hints of links between the grandparents and the ousted royal family but that could never be proven. All records of the family had been systematically destroyed in Moscow and St. Petersburg.

Kiselyov also went to MIT where he and Dormán had met. As with Dormán, the records for Kiselyov supported his existence, although he was divorced and had four children. She even found records of the ex-wife's remarriage. Again, emails and phone records were unremarkable. Emails between Dormán and the older Kiselyov reflected a student and mentor relationship at the American university, so that explained their connection.

She nodded her head in quiet approval. If her quarry had

invented these two men, he was certainly thorough in his creations. She couldn't think of anything else to look for in her attempt to break the charade. No, these men must be real, and that meant that perhaps she was indeed looking for a team.

She sat back in her chair and stared at all three of her monitors, gazing from one to the next to the next and back again. The details of these three men glowed from those screens and bathed her with light. What didn't envelop her was a sense of motive. She shook her head. Something didn't add up, but she couldn't put a finger on just what was wrong. She found no direct emails between Karamazov and the other two.

She took a deep breath and sighed. She acknowledged her fatigue and was about to call it a night and get some sleep when she remembered something. It was another factor in Karamazov's emails that had led her to the other two—cryptic references to an organization for which she could find no details. She hadn't searched for it with them. She leaned forward and began to type on her keyboard. As her system began to search and analyze, the same references began to appear. She had expected such a result since that's what had led her to these men in the first place. Yet, from this data she discovered a link to yet another man.

How big was this team? Who was the leader? How did they communicate? What were their goals? Were they indeed behind the destruction of the WOC's surveillance programs, and if so, why? Were they part of the group that had developed AlterNet in the first place? That would have certainly given them the knowledge of how to destroy the program permanently. No. Their work histories didn't seem to support that, but then, work histories could be altered or faked.

She sat back again. She was too tired to tackle these questions at the moment. As she stood to head to the bedroom she recalled how, not even ten years earlier, an all-nighter like this would have been no problem for her. Now? A long sleep was in order.

TEN

Adam listened to his new voice mail recording.

"Hi, this is Adam with Pelethites Cybersecurity. Sorry we can't take your call directly but honestly, we've been overwhelmed with calls since the article on the America First News website came out. Please leave your name, number, and reason for your call, and I promise we'll get back to you as required. Thanks."

Satisfied with the message, he saved it. He had never been one who liked having to leave a voice mail with a company, so it seemed wrong to have to now rely upon it himself. He wasn't ready to hire a sales team to field the new volume of calls that had resulted from AFN's article about their debacle with AWS and their old hosting company and being saved from virtual extinction by Adam's fledgling company. Over a hundred calls had come in within the past 24 hours, and when he looked at his email inbox, double that number had arrived. More than double.

"Okay, so I've eliminated over 30 of the calls and cataloged those you should call back," said Jess. "I simply added them according to date and time of their call 'cause I have no idea how you would prioritize them."

"And I've deleted over half of the emails. The trolls have come out from under their bridges in force." Aric laughed. "Might be fun for you to run some back traces to see where these are actually coming from. Most of them don't appear to have English as their primary language."

Adam nodded. He might do as his brother suggested, just to see where the opposition came from.

"Thanks, you two. Rachel was helping, but she had to run errands, get groceries. You know, the normal stuff for daily life."

Jess gave him a serious look. "I don't really know anything about computer hardware, but if the legit messages I screened are serious inquiries, you might need another server or two."

Aric nodded in apparent agreement. "Same with some of the emails, and as I look at this list Jess made, some of these folks must be serious because they called *and* emailed."

Adam smiled. "I'm ready for them. I was working on two new servers before yesterday when this tsunami of interest rushed in. Of course, it'll depend on how big the sites are and what kind of resources they'll need. If they're low volume sites, I could put hundreds on a single server. If they're like AFN, they could take up one or more servers all by themselves."

He felt pleased that he'd followed that inner sense—that quiet leading that Aric said was the Holy Spirit—to build a separate, dedicated server building on the property he'd acquired after returning to St. Louis. It was state-of-the-art, had room for several dozen server racks, and yet, seemed nondescript and uninteresting from the outside. Nothing to attract attention.

The ten wooded acres in north St. Louis County also held their home, and neither building was visible from the road. If there was one thing he'd learned after years of hiding from some very dangerous men, it was the need for security. No one could get further than five yards onto their property before alerts would warn him of their presence. And, unless they were very cautious and forewarned, they would likely be identified using facial rec by the time they penetrated ten yards onto his land.

Jess smiled as she retrieved the list she'd compiled from Aric. "You might want to check out this guy." She pointed to the third call from the bottom on her list. "He said he wasn't a betting man, but he guessed that after that AFN article, you might be looking to hire a network administrator."

Adam looked at the name and brief info jotted down by his brother's girlfriend. Why did that name sound familiar?

"Logan Mathias. Does that name ring any bells with you? Seems I should know that name."

Jess shook her head, but Aric seemed to find it familiar, too.

"Aric?"

His brother cocked his head sideways a bit. "Not sure but wasn't there a man named Mathias who was sued and heavily fined by the State of Colorado for refusing to create and host websites for gay weddings and gender transition documentaries. Stood up for his religious beliefs and rights."

Adam snapped his fingers. "That's it. Sued twice by the state leftists, and his rights were upheld twice by the Supreme Court. Kind of disappeared after that second victory."

Aric nodded. "Rumors started about his having some kind of hiking accident in the Rockies and dying in the fall."

Jess' eyes lit up. "Hey, I remember that part. All kinds of conspiracy theories about his being taken out by the lefties who didn't like him."

"Guess that didn't really happen." Adam laughed. "If this is the same guy, I'll be a betting man and give ten-to-one odds he started those rumors himself."

"Smart move, if he did," replied Aric. "Hey, look at the time. We need to be heading back. I can't help tomorrow, but I might be able to come back in two days if I don't get a bunch more work from my classes."

Jess grabbed her coat and shook her head. "Sorry, but the rest of my week is really busy."

"No problem. I suspect the load of inquiries will drop off over the next day or two. If I call for help towards the end of the week, you'll know I'm truly overwhelmed."

Adam waved them farewell and rushed back to his desk. He began to return the phone calls, and as he called, he eliminated any emails from the same people from his inbox. By dinnertime, he had worked through half of Jess' list. From those 34 calls, he had secured 18 new accounts, along with 11 maybes. And yet, he also noted 42 new voice mails in the same time period. If this pace continued, he was definitely going to need help.

With that in mind, he recognized that one way or another he would need help. Before Aric and Jess arrived, he had already signed up 23 new accounts. Now, with 18 more, how was he going to get these installed and running within their desired deadlines? Even after that initial phase, how could he maintain those sites and their servers *and* handle phone calls *and* deal with sales and marketing *and* manage his "front office" *and* have time to eat, sleep, and be a dad and husband? What had been a comfortable one-man operation had morphed overnight into a significant business. He now needed employees, but under the circumstances—his peculiar situation—he couldn't simply put out a "Now Hiring" sign. Anyone he hired would have to be screened to the nth degree.

"Earth to Daddy. Earth to Daddy."

His mental meanderings snapped to an end. His daughter, Grace, stood next to his desk waving her hand in front of his face.

"Mom says it's time to eat."

Adam glanced at the time on his monitor. He took a deep breath and acknowledged that it was time to head upstairs. "Great. Let's go." He stood and feigned a running start. Grace bolted to the stairway, laughing.

"I'm gonna get there first," she cried.

Of course, he wasn't about to upset her but stayed close on her heels as they "raced" up the steps. In the kitchen, he helped by dishing up the food for their kids' plates and getting drinks for everyone. Yet, after saying grace over their meal, his mind returned to the problem at hand and what he would need to do after helping put the children to bed. And that task was to find out as much as he could about Logan Mathias.

ELEVEN

For the past two days, Yolina survived on caffeine from numerous sources, four hours of sleep, and one *zu mitnehmen*, to go, meal each day. The chase was on. She had no time for leisurely meals or nonproductive time in bed. Her time on her computers had paid off—she found two more members of this programming cabal.

First up was an Arno Prinsloo, of Afrikaans descent in South Africa, age 35, a graduate of Carnegie Mellon University, Magna Cum Laude in computer science with an emphasis on programming languages and systems. His doctoral degree was also at that university, ranked number one in that field. His expertise appeared to be critical to the group's success in avoiding detection. He, too, had been married with two kids. His wife had died mysteriously and suddenly at age 32 from what was reported to be a heart attack. Yolina read between the lines—she was yet another victim of the COVID vaccines. He moved back to South Africa where he was dating a divorcée, age 36, also with two kids. All four children seemed to be excelling in school and were active in various extracurricular programs.

As with the others, she could not find any weak links in the man's back story. And she certainly tried to find them. The better part of the past two days had been spent trying to pick apart the man's history and prove him to be fictional. She had concluded that his existence was factual.

The second member had been uncovered just that morning—Christopher Solovyov. Yet another Russian surname. She found that odd . . . and disturbing. A Hungarian, Afrikaner, and three Russians, at least by name. Why?

And where was the American whom Herr Koch was convinced was behind all of his trouble? True, three of the four men were American citizens, but their school and work histories conflicted with Koch's belief that the man they hunted had worked for a military contractor doing PsyOps in Afghanistan. Had she missed something? Was there a gap in one of their histories? Had one of their stories been changed to remove any reference to Afghanistan? She groaned at the thought of having to validate every employer and workplace listed in each man's file.

She set her computer to work looking at the last man's story. At this point, much of what she needed could be hacked and found by routines she had automated. To dig even deeper would take a herculean effort going one by one to vet every point. She sighed. Yet, that's what she was being paid—and paid well—to do.

And then a thought hit her. She stood and paced, shaking her head as she did so. She didn't like the implications of that thought. As a contractor to the FSB, she had the clearance to access certain files at the Kremlin. To do so, would, however, raise a red flag. Maybe several red flags. Did she want that hassle? Or worse?

Four hours of sleep was bad enough. She couldn't sustain that pace for long. Yet, she knew that if she didn't answer the questions swirling about in her head at the moment, she'd get no sleep at all.

Shaking her head at her decision to open this can of worms, she sat back down at her computer. Within a minute, she found the files containing the names of old USSR KGB sleeper agents sent to the U.S. As she worked through the dozens of names, both men and women, she learned that most had assumed American names. Those who hadn't, had been granted asylum based upon false stories of their being dissidents under threat by the Soviet regime. Those were the names that interested her the most.

And she wasn't disappointed. After only a short time, she discovered that all three names—Solovyov, Karamozov, and Kiselyov—were among those listed. Were all three men descendants of these sleeper agents, people never called to duty and who became complacent living the American way of life? She didn't like the implications of that, considering the world in its current state.

She finished reviewing the old KGB file and turned her attention back to her search. Unlike the others, Solovyov was single, entrepreneurial, and fancied himself something of a ladies' man. His financial records showed that his business acumen had been successful. His medical records revealed that his choice of ladies left a lot to be desired. Like the others, however, he had a link to each of the others in the group. Was he the ringleader? This discovery further strengthened her conclusion that they were dealing with a group,

In addition to the names she had already uncovered, there was one other name she had not encountered yet—a David Watson. Now, that name sounded American. While her system continued to ferret out information on Solovyov, she turned her programming loose on Watson, too.

She looked at the time. A bit early for dinner, by European standards, but she was hungry, and her programming would take time to collect the data she sought. She called up the website for the restaurant down the street. She had the menu memorized, so she quickly placed her order for her daily to-go meal. For the fourth Wednesday of October, the weather had been slightly above average with sunny skies and pleasant temps in the upper teens, Celsius. She decided to walk to get her food, but light rain was on its way, so she needed to be quick about it.

As she entered the restaurant, she spotted a young woman whom she met two weeks before. She waved, and the woman waved back as she crossed the to greet Yolina. They hugged.

"Yolina, I have not seen you in here for a while."

"Hi, Marta. I've been working late into the night and coming here much later than usual. How have you been?"

"Working too hard. I need a vacation. By the way, my friend Horst has been asking about you. He keeps calling you my sister." She laughed.

Yolina smiled. Their resemblance had not gone unnoticed.

As dawn arrived the next day, Adam was stunned to find 52 more voice mails in his system . . . overnight. He'd barely made a dent in returning the previous day's calls. How long would it be before he could deal with the new ones? He definitely needed help.

However, before attempting any more callbacks, he checked UltraNet. He had initiated a search for Logan Mathias after dinner the previous night. He couldn't wait to see what his software had uncovered.

After helping get both kids fed and ready for school, he waved goodbye to his family as Rachel drove off to take them to school. She promised to help with the phone upon her return. For that, he was quite grateful.

He grabbed a bowl of crunchy raisin bran cereal, a large mug of coffee, and a banana and headed for his basement office. He set down his food and glanced around. He liked working within his home, while his servers were but 50-plus yards away in their own climate-controlled building. He had designed that structure to hold some office space, but he hadn't expected to make use of it so quickly. Still, if he was going to hire help, he was destined to move his office there in the very near future.

As he called up his search results on Mathias, another alert caught his attention. He grinned as he read that more of his rabbit trails had been followed—Igor Karamazov, Dormán János, Danil Kiselyov, Arno Prinsloo, and Christopher Solovyov. If his breadcrumbs continued to work as he had designed them, the hunter would uncover David Watson next. Then would come the big surprise, if he, or she, was as astute as he suspected. And so far, whoever was hunting for him hadn't quit the search. To him, abandoning the search before completing his snipe hunt would be a significant indicator that his fictional characters had been discovered to be just that, fictional.

He double-checked that his alerts were still in place for the Watson and Alexei Baranov identities. The trail to Baranov was credible but would take some real skill to follow. He was, after all, the director of Russia's FSB and one of the most powerful men in Russia, a prominent member of the *silovik* faction of the Russian president's inner circle. Adam could imagine his hunter's state of mind upon "discovering" that the FSB was behind all of Werner Koch's AlterNet troubles.

To Adam, creating the fiction of the FSB being responsible

for the demise of AlterNet and AlterNet2 made sense. The global elites of Koch's WOC used Russia as their never-ending bogey man and punching bag. To discredit a political foe, they created stories of that foe's ties to Russia. To launder U.S. and European taxpayers' money and enrich their own coffers, they went after Russia using Ukraine as their proxy. It was all Russia's fault, even though Russia had offered to meet Ukraine at the peace table in 2022—a deal turned down by the globalists. Ukraine's president had admitted publicly at a Polish press conference that 70% of U.S. aide money never left the U.S. Indeed, the globalists made sure that money went into their own military-industrial pockets. So, to attack the WOC with the destruction of their pet project could be seen as the perfect payback.

Well, his planted info was working. Now he needed only to wait and see if his hunter would continue down the trail he had designed.

He stood and stretched. He'd been sitting too long. He grabbed his laptop and perused the data on Logan Mathias as he paced within his basement. Wow. The guy had creds out the wazoo. A bachelor's degree in computer science with an emphasis on systems and parallel computing from Stanford, followed by a master's at the same institution focusing on both artificial intelligence and network security. He took that degree to qualify for and complete a doctoral at Carnegie Melon where he worked in Algorithms, Combinatorics, and Optimization. If Adam had still been in the midst of developing UltraNet, this guy would have been a perfect fit. He might still be, if Adam were ever to bring him into his confidence about UltraNet.

Why in the world had the man been designing websites for people? His skill level was galaxies beyond something as mundane as that. But then, that's what Adam was now doing, so how could he castigate the man? It paid the bills.

As he continued to read, he saw that Mathias had been involved in far more esoteric work than that which brought him his 15 minutes of fame. His CV listed publications and articles that Adam suspected might require security clearances to fully read. He had multiple publications a year for several years and then nothing. Nada. A trail that ran cold.

Shortly after that, the website design business registered as a Colorado LLC. What had happened? Had the man simply burned out? Or had he run afoul of some employer or government entity?

With regard to a personal life, Adam found little. Twenty-eight. Single, never married. Parents were still alive in the Denver area. Maybe that explained his return to Colorado. No social media presence. Ever. But the last bit of info was of particular interest. Mathias was a staff member at Church Alive right there in west St. Louis County. What was he doing there?

The questions about this man multiplied like Tribbles in a vintage Star Trek show. He needed to talk with this guy.

TWELVE

Almost a month had passed since his unfortunate "indiscretion," and Werner was feeling less and less concerned about it. That unfortunate evening was water under the bridge at this point. Yolina had made no monetary "requests" or other threats and had been compliant with his request to keep reporting by the secure phone he had provided. It was that very phone that now called his private line.

"Yes." His answer was curt on purpose.

"Herr Koch, I have details for you, but they are too many to report over a phone call."

He mentally debated his next act. Having "her" come to the office remained a possibility, as it would be quite public during regular office hours. Yet, he had no desire to see "her" face-to-face.

His investigator had confirmed the transgender background of this Russian hacker, something that still astounded him. The great Soviet bear would never have tolerated what they saw as perversion. Modern Russia, with its Eastern Orthodox religious heritage, seemed unlikely to tolerate it either. That she had risen to her rank at Pozitiv Teknolodzhiz under the current regime attested to her computer skills. Why else would they tolerate him, er, her?

Still, he had to acknowledge that his repulsion—and that was the right word—to her was more deeply rooted than he had admitted to himself. Was his public support of transgenderism, indeed the whole array LGBTQ+ lifestyles, simply virtue signaling, as right-wingers would say? He preferred not to think of himself as a hypocrite and to think that he was open-minded to alternative lifestyles, even if they weren't his preference. But he couldn't ignore the aversion the encounter with this individual had stirred within.

"I'm too busy to meet with you. Have you found him?"

"Not him, sir, them. I anticipated your busy schedule, so I have put all of the information onto an encrypted thumb drive and sent it by courier to you. The package should arrive shortly, if not already."

"*Sehr gut.* We will check it out to verify your findings. If all is in order, your payment will be deposited into your account, as initially agreed upon." He emphasized the last three words to make it clear that no additional payment would be made.

He disconnected the cell call and pressed a button on his desk phone. "Anja, I'm expecting a package by courier. Has it arrived for me?"

"*Nein*, Herr Koch, not yet. I will check with the front reception. Shall I bring it in when it arrives?"

He nodded as he replied, "*Ja, bitte.*" He hung up.

In the meantime, he returned to the task he had started before the phone call. He shook his head as he reviewed the briefing on Charles Sidon. The U.S. President was failing rapidly. They needed to control the situation before conservative nationalists in that country could take real advantage of his deterioration.

Zhèng Jian and others within the U.S. federal and state governments had launched a full court lawfare press against the previous president, Bradley Graham. He had been a wound in their side, delaying their global efforts by a full four years. Now that the wound had been healed, they could not afford his return to the presidency. He had learned how to truly set them back by decades and had to be stopped, by whatever means.

He picked up the phone again. "Anja, please get Derrick McFarland, the U.S. Attorney General, on the phone for me."

Yolina paced from one end of her apartment to the other. She could not settle the turmoil within. She had indeed sent Koch the data on the men she had discovered as the likely team responsible for sabotaging the AlterNet programs. All but one.

The trail had been difficult to follow, but she had persevered. Now she wished she hadn't. The trail also ended . . . with one man: Alexei Baranov. Baranov was the director of the FSB and one of the most powerful men in Moscow. He controlled the contract under which the company she worked for, Pozitiv Teknolodzhiz, performed cybersecurity as well as espionage, aka hacking. Her bosses would not take kindly to outing that man as the one behind the destruction of AlterNet.

Yes, she could understand the FSB wanting the WOC's AlterNet programs to disappear. Russia had been the WOC's and U.S.' punching bag for a long time. Every time they needed someone to blame or someone to oppose in order to feed more money into their intelligence services or military-industrial complex, they used Russia. Even though China posed a bigger threat to the west, the powers-that-be picked on Russia.

However, to find Baranov as the ringleader seemed out of

place. It did not ring true. No matter how secretive he might have wanted such a project to be, he would never have spearheaded it personally. Would he? She could see him delegate such a project to the CEO of her company, but to lead it himself?

She struggled with those thoughts. She knew the man only by reputation. True, she had stood in line with her fellow hackers when Baranov did a walk-through of Pozitiv Teknolodzhiz and shook everyone's hand. In that sense, she had met the man, but such an encounter didn't count. She didn't even know if he was married or had kids, much less what his personal foibles might be. Maybe he was the type who liked getting his hands dirty on occasion. Maybe he wanted the personal satisfaction of "defeating" the WOC in some way.

She shook her head at that thought. What was the term coined by the CIA 60 years earlier? Plausible deniability? Yes, that was it. The man was in such a position where plausible deniability was a true asset. If she could find him, others could, too. For all she knew, Werner Koch had others also working on finding whoever canceled AlterNet. The man was known for getting what he wanted . . . at whatever cost.

And then a thought hit her that made her blood run cold. She ran to her workstation, grabbed her phone, and dialed a friend at Pozitiv. Well, Sergei Agafonov was a bit more than a friend.

"привет, котик. У меня для тебя сюрприз, когда ты вернешься домой."

Yolina smiled. She had been so immersed in her search that she hadn't talked with him for almost two weeks. She wondered what surprise he had for her when she got back home.

"Милый мой, я тоже скучаю по тебе." She missed him, too. She explained her dilemma to him.

"Ah, my little fish. I think your instincts are right on. Baranov would have farmed out a project like that to us. That means one of two things. Baranov alone was a false trail, or you have been chasing goose altogether."

Both thoughts had already crossed her mind. Koch knew nothing about Baranov, so it was the latter option that scared her. If Koch discovered that none of the names she had sent him were real, she would need heavier clothing for Siberia . . . if she was lucky.

"Sergei, do you have contacts in the U.S. who could help me? I need to verify that some names and addresses are real before Herr Koch does."

"I-I-I-I might." There was hesitation in his voice. "Send me the data."

She hit "Enter" on her keyboard. Names, addresses, places of work—the data necessary to prove their existence and nothing more. "Sent. Quickly, please. I don't want to end up in Siberia or a shallow grave."

"On it. I will call as soon as I have something."

She knew he wanted to talk, but he hung up first. She wanted to talk, too, but her safety had priority, and she knew he was already working on her problem.

What had she missed? She could think of nothing that would have indicated these men to be fictional. And yet, she marveled at the brain that could have created such an elaborate ruse. If indeed it was a ruse. The thought of it being such made her think that perhaps Koch was correct. It would have to be a one-man job. A team would require unheard-of coordination to have created everything so flawlessly. The slightest miscommunication of a detail here or there would have left gaps, however trivial, in the trail.

What now? Sitting at her workstation, she called up her bank accounts. She felt only minimal relief on seeing that she had the funds to escape, if necessary. But where? Where could she go to escape Werner Koch and the WOC? And if she could find a place where he couldn't reach her, she still needed to worry that the FSB would be able to find her. Unless . . .

THIRTEEN

AG McFarland already looked forward to the upcoming holidays. The pressures of the job were weighing heavily on him despite enjoying the perks of his position and the prestige of being on the world stage. What burdened him the most was kowtowing to outside powers, particularly when it came to "betraying" an old friend.

As his driver navigated the awful, Washington morning traffic to take him to the RFK Department of Justice Building, he reviewed the latest briefings on their efforts against Bradley Graham. The civil fraud trial in St. Louis moved along well. However, the effort now seemed to be backfiring on them as public sentiment grew in the ex-president's favor. The judge's rush to declare the man guilty of fraud even before hearing any evidence, along with his denial of numerous motions by the defense, was now seen as prejudicial. Plus, to be found guilty of fraud when no one was defrauded went against all common sense for the common man.

Their other efforts likewise appeared to be moving along well, but they, too, seemed to have only increased the man's popularity. The rise of alternative conservative media had not been fully appreciated. They had been much more effective at presenting the inconsistencies within these trials. In addition, they were digging into the backgrounds, finances, and relationships of the prosecution teams, judges, and others. What they might uncover could unravel every case against Graham.

McFarland's legal training also told him that Graham had a better than 50-50 chance of reversal in every case at the appeals level and an 80-20 chance of reversal at the Supreme Court level, should any of the cases reach that far. He had no doubt that most, if not all, of the cases brought against the man would be appealed to the highest court. Their biggest hope was to derail his campaign long enough to upend his chance of re-election. That this didn't appear to be happening concerned McFarland.

Graham's trial for mishandling classified files held great potential. The charges were federal felonies which could be used to prevent his election. Still, several snags existed. Graham's defense team had developed a presidential immunity argument, and while the judge had been instructed to disregard that argument, his action would no doubt be appealed all the way to the Supremes. The appeals process would take weeks, if not months, and that delay threatened their planned timetable to convict Graham before the November 2024 election.

However, there was one other bigger obstacle. McFarland stared out the window as they crossed West Potomac Park. He watched as they passed by the Jefferson Memorial off to his left followed by the National Park Headquarters to his right. A growing majority of the populace already recognized the differences in how his department treated Graham for holding old, classified documents in a secured, Secret Service-protected room at his well-guarded St. Louis home and how they treated his old friend, President Sidon, for a similar infraction but where the documents were kept scattered over several locations without any security whatsoever. He had even given documents to his ghost writer to use in his upcoming "autobiography." Plus, Graham had certain rights as president that Sidon didn't enjoy as vice president when he took the documents.

His thoughts were disturbed by the ringing of his secure car phone. The interruption was unusual. Only a handful of people had the number and fewer still would dare to call him during his morning commute to the office. He picked up the handset.

"Sir, I'm sorry to interrupt your drive, but Werner Koch is on the line for you. Should I connect you?"

Werner Koch? He had met the man once at an annual WOC gathering in Switzerland, but that simple introduction hadn't led to any form of communications between the two. The WOC's globalist intentions were typically transmitted to him via intermediaries such as Zhèng Jian. What could possibly have led the WOC's director to contact him directly?

"By all means." A moment later, he was in direct contact with the global leader. "AG McFarland here. To what do I owe this honor, Herr Koch?"

"*Guten morgen*, Mr. McFarland. Thank you for taking my call."

"My pleasure, sir." Well, not exactly, but what else could he say? It was precisely the WOC's pressure on him to betray Charles Sidon that made him look forward to a holiday break. "How may I help you?"

"It has come to my attention that President Sidon's mental health is failing. I understand that Zhèng Jian has enlisted your help to remove him from the upcoming election before he becomes a major liability."

McFarland knew he needed to choose his words carefully. "He has, Herr Koch."

"And will you be invoking your constitution's 25th Amendment?"

Yes, he needed to be very careful. "No, sir. At least, not yet."

"Oh?"

"Herr Koch, please understand. Charles is a longstanding friend of mine. His family and mine are close. I will not betray him, but I understand our predicament and the need to discourage him from running. For me to openly invoke the 25th Amendment would crush him and destroy the relationship my family has with his."

There was silence on the other end. Had he overstepped his position, crossed over some red line?

McFarland continued, "I believe I've found another way to approach this, one that won't make me the fall guy."

"Please, continue."

"As I assume you are aware, I was forced to initiate an investigation into his mishandling of classified materials, as well as other accusations of corruption. Our Republican Congress has started investigating this as well, as part of their impeachment inquiry. I hope to beat them at their own game by releasing our investigation's report first. I have been reviewing the initial draft of that report."

"And this will help us how?"

"Our special counsel has included firsthand observations of Charles' mental decline—his loss of memory, confusion, and more. He still thinks he's the vice president. The special counsel is reporting these observations directly within the report, and his conclusion, with my approval, will be that Charles is a confused old man with memory loss, who would be incapable of standing trial. He will avoid being charged criminally because no jury would ever convict such a man who cannot understand what he's done wrong."

"Ah, Mr. McFarland, that is genius and will certainly keep you off the hot seat. When will this report be released?"

"There are some additions and corrections to be made, and some things we need to get in place to handle the fallout. So, we're realistically looking at three months, early February."

"What do you envision as the fallout, as you put it?"

"Charles, of course, will vehemently deny a problem but that will help. His confusion comes out on full display when he's distraught. There are likely to be Republican voices calling for my invoking the 25th Amendment. After all, if he's incapable of standing trial, they'll argue he's also incapable of leading the country. We have White House staffers lined up who will reinforce the message of dementia by leaking information to the press. The pressure will build to a point where, if he continues to insist on running, I will have no choice but to declare him mentally incapacitated and invoke our constitutional means of removal. I hope that he will see what he's up against and bow out while ahead."

"Very good. Zhèng Jian was correct in stating we could rely on you. I assume the Vice President will be prepared, yes?"

Ah, that was a topic for a different meeting. McFarland knew her background well, and while he sought to support the diversity of people who had not had the benefits of being white in order to get ahead, he had trouble with this one. He would never admit it in public—probably not to anyone in private either, his opinion would remain his own—but he had to agree with certain conservatives that she was the ultimate diversity hire—a term he disliked but found fitting in this case.

"That, Herr Koch, is one of the things we need to still arrange. She is not ready for prime time, as some would say."

"And the upcoming election?"

"Yes, sir. There, too, we need to find a viable alternative to Charles and begin to show him, or her, favorably as a strong candidate."

"Let me know who you decide upon. We will need to approve. Have a good day, Mr. McFarland."

McFarland hung up as they passed the Washington Monument. Who indeed?

FOURTEEN

Denton sat at his large mahogany and pulled out the three case requests that Twila had given him over a week before. To that folder he added four more similar cases. Of those, two had come in directly while the other two were referrals from large firms, just like the first three. If this trend continued, a major first amendment, freedom of speech battle was about to ensue, and he would lead the charge.

After all, they had been the targets of a similar situation. Their credit card processor elected to cancel their account, which led to being unable to process donations by credit card on their website. Just the threat of a lawsuit had reversed that decision, but the bad taste it left in Denton's mind made these cases more enticing for battle.

There was a knock at his door and Twila poked her head into the office. "Here's the material I had Eric and Cara collect. It's not much, as there have yet to be any legal challenges leading to court."

Denton nodded. "I knew that much, but it will be interesting to see what the banks' recent responses have been."

She laid them on his desk. "Anything else?"

He shook his head. "Not at the moment. Thanks."

As she closed the door behind her, he grabbed the papers written by the two research aides. The two most prominent cases of debanking in the U.S. involved the National

Committee on Religious Freedom and a law firm similar to his own, Alliance Defending Freedom, in the spring of 2022. The NCRF had opened a checking account at JP Morgan Chase bank in April of 2022 only to discover that weeks later, the bank had closed it for reasons unknown. In pursuing the issue, Chase changed its story three times. At one point, they told the NCRF they could reopen the account if they revealed the names of their top donors and listed the political candidates it would support. NCRF refused and took the issue to Washington and the press. The backlash against Chase had been prompt and furious.

The other law firm learned that Fidelity Charitable was refusing to allow donors to use their donor-advised funds to support the organization. Upon asking for such a grant, the donor would be required to give up his anonymity and put his name on the grant. One donor reported that he was told he would have to give up his anonymity for donations to four different conservative groups, but not for four left-leaning organizations. The bias was clear. That situation, too, led to significant backlash against Fidelity Charitable.

The repercussions to both financial institutions had been well laid out. On paper, as they say. Their DEI—diversity, equity, and inclusivity—initiatives were discriminatory, as were their ESG—environment, social, and governance—goals. These violated the First Amendment of the U.S. Constitution, and should they continue, the banks' and investment firms' favored status by the government would be in jeopardy. These big banks received numerous government benefits leading to greater lending power, lower FDIC insurance rates, subsidies, bailouts, and a chartering system that reduced their competition. Various members of Congress had pledged to seek the removal of such perks if the banks continued to discriminate.

Denton shook his head as he read about the seven additional recent cases. He interlaced his fingers across the top of his head and leaned back in his chair as he pondered where these might lead. Sitting forward, he picked up the phone and speed-dialed a colleague whose office was down the hall.

"Hey, John, if you have a moment could you come by my office. I'd like to pick your brain."

"Sure. Your timing was perfect. On my way."

A moment later, John Hood, General Counsel and VP of Corporate Engagement, sat down in front of him.

"So, what's up?"

Denton handed him the papers. "Take a moment to scan these." Denton saw him shaking his head subtly as he read and pursed his lips a couple of times. After a few minutes, he lifted his head and looked at Denton.

"Looks like things are heating up, not going away as we'd hoped."

Denton nodded. "I agree. We hoped the DEI movement had plateaued, but I think that was only cosmetic."

"Yep, several major corporations have or are in the process of closing their DEI offices, but from what we're picking up, that was just cost cutting and the practices sponsored by those offices are just being continued in their HR divisions. You know, it's just like a politician espousing a position he knows has no chance of success simply to be able to claim he supported it. These companies are touting the closure of their DEI initiatives for the positive PR, while simply transferring those roles elsewhere."

Denton understood. As for the politicians who raised concerns, they may have been sincere, but the reality of being able to touch those big banks was another story. The big banks had the upper hand, and they knew it. As such, they grew bolder in pushing the agenda of the elite class, to the detriment of the middle and lower classes.

"So, what do you think? Is this an issue we need to take on?"

John offered a non-committal wag of his head. "Maybe. I mean, the big banks do get a bunch of government perks, but they're also still general corporations, not branches of the government, and corporations have rights to do business as they see fit. These seven cases aren't exactly big-name ministries or celebrities— "

"But we're not— "

"I know what you're going to say, we're here for the little guys, too. I know, I know. That wasn't the point I was going to make. Bigger ministries have a following that's big enough to generate some public pressure on the banks." John shifted around in his chair. "Look, we know how powerful the banks are. Remember, they manipulated Congress and the public into creating the Federal Reserve and turning our entire monetary system over to the private bankers a century ago. Congress will never pass anything that curtails their business or digs into their profits. So, we will need as much public pressure as possible to make any headway against them."

"Good point, but it's easier to nip something in the bud than to let it grow into something unmanageable and then try to knock it back down."

John nodded. "That's true, too. I'd be curious to see what kind of numbers, dollars, we're talking about with these seven cases. If we're looking at totals only in the low six figures or less, we'll know that the banks are targeting folks without the resources to fight back. Then, maybe it's time to fight for the underdogs. If we're talking millions, then, well, that's a whole new ballgame. Banks don't like to lose accounts worth millions. If they're now targeting such big accounts, then the level of censorship is shooting up to new heights, or down to new lows depending on how you look at it. Anyway, that's when it becomes more than fighting for the little guys. Then it's fighting for everyone."

Denton was glad he'd called on John for his opinion. The man had always offered sound advice and excellent insights.

"Look, we're heading into the holidays and this place always quiets down then. Maybe more cases will come in, and they'll help provide better direction. Or you can bring this up at the next executive meeting and get everyone's input."

Denton agreed. "Or both. I'll put it on next month's meeting agenda, *and* we'll see if new cases arrive. These all arrived in the past two weeks or so, and the next meeting is after Thanksgiving. Should give it time to see if this is a growing problem or not."

FIFTEEN

Aric continued feeling optimistic that his run-in with pink-hair Toni was a one-off, despite the nagging concern about the guy's comments at the time. Over two weeks had passed and no further encounters with the local LGBTQ+ crowd had occurred, except maybe the AirTag incident. That one he couldn't blame on the LGBTQ+ folks without evidence.

As he left his morning class, he checked the time. If he hurried, he could pick up Jess and take her to her afternoon class at Wash U. He'd found a perfectly secluded spot to study while he waited for her. He would park himself there, read, and prepare for his next day's classes. Once she was done with class, they had some errands to run before a planned dinner outing at Sugarfire Smoke House. Jess had never been a big-league bar-b-que fan, but then, southeast Wisconsin had no quality bar-b-que options. It was a land of great cheeses, but one where grilling was usually confused with authentic smoked goodness. Sugarfire and Pappy's in St. Louis had made a convert of her. Still, she hadn't yet warmed up to the idea of a weekend trip to Kansas City just to make the rounds of their famous smoke houses. He remained determined to win her over.

He had parked in the student center's south garage and now headed that way to get his car. He continued to take a variety of circuitous routes between car and class but began to wonder if that was still necessary. He climbed to the second floor of the garage and walked toward his car. As he rounded a corner and spotted his car, he stopped short. Clearly, he'd been wrong about taking various paths to and from his car. It hadn't helped.

The back of his car had the word "bigot" sprayed across it. One back tire had been flattened. As he moved closer, the side closest to him displayed the word "racist." He imagined that the other side and front hood would be equally decorated. He hoped whatever the vandal had used to paint on the slurs was washable, but he suspected he wouldn't be so lucky.

His heart sank. Sure, it was just a car, but the coming inconvenience and expenses were not something to look forward to. He had another big expense that required his capital.

He pulled out his phone and dialed Jess as he further examined the car. "Hey, babe."

"Are you on your way?"

"Sorry, but you're gonna have to drive to class without me." He explained the current state of his car.

"Oh no. Have you called security?"

"They're next. I needed to give you the heads up first so you can get to class. I'll keep you posted. We might need to postpone our errands and dinner plans."

"Okay. Call security and let me know."

"Will do. Bye."

His next call was to the security office. At times like this, he would have had an advantage in Kenosha where one of the campus officers was a friend of Adam's, and by default had become his friend as well. He had no such "ins" with the campus officers at UMSL. He said a quiet prayer for favor and was surprised when an older officer arrived within five minutes.

"I'm Officer Kenniston. You the guy who called about his car?"

Aric nodded. "That's me." He pointed to his vehicle. "I'm Aric Afton. I just came from class and found it like this."

The man grimaced. "Ouch. Who'd you piss off?"

"Your guess is as good as mine. I live at my parents' home and commute in. I've made it a point to keep a low profile, focus on my classes, and graduate next spring." He went on to give his story about seeing pink-hair Toni who seemed intent on finding him and exposing him to the local LGBTQI+ activists. He then explained just who pink-hair Toni was and the problems he'd encountered at the college in Kenosha. He didn't offer any info on being asked not to return for his senior year.

"Kenosha? That's Wisconsin, right?"

Aric nodded. "Yep. Southeast corner of the state."

"Yeah. I retired from the Ladue police and took this job. Best detective I've ever known was with our department, and he went to a small college in Wisconsin to start a new forensics program. I'm pretty sure it's in Kenosha."

Aric smiled. "That would be my friend Lynch Cully." Mentally, he thanked God for an answer to prayer. Not only was favor being shown, but a new contact within the campus security team was in the making.

The officer's face lit up. "Yeah. You know Lynch?"

Aric nodded. "Yep. He's the reason I went to that college, and when things got bad, he used his contacts here to get me accepted to the forensics program here for my senior year."

The officer smiled. "I have another friend in the department here. He told me they'd accepted a senior transfer student. The first and only such transfer in the department's history is how he phrased it, and they've been real pleased with you. Congrats."

Aric felt a slight blush rise to his face. "Thanks."

"Okay. So, forensics senior, how would you go about processing this?"

Aric was taken aback at first, thinking that would be the security department's job. But then he realized he had a real-life practical right in front of him. And having a vested interest in the crime was an added incentive.

"Well, we start off with photos from every conceivable angle. Then I'd get the obvious scrapings of the paint or whatever it is they used for the letters."

The officer nodded and then returned to his car where he pulled a medium-sized case from the trunk. Upon opening it, Aric noted that it appeared to be a complete forensics tool kit.

"There you go. Go for it. Show me what you got."

Aric got busy with photos and scrapings from every word. Sadly, the material appeared to be paint, not something he'd be able to remove at the car wash. He then began to inspect the area surrounding the car, marking every stray item within 15 feet of the car as well as under it. He collected three cigarette butts, a pull-tab, a discarded soda can, two pairs of plastic gloves, and more. The gloves appeared to have paint on them.

Officer Kenniston nodded. "I'd probably go wider with the search grid, but what you've done so far looks good. What else?"

"Inspect the video footage from that camera . . ." He pointed to a nearby security camera. ". . . as well as cameras from all of the entrances. From that camera, we should be able to see the vandalism in progress. That will give us a time stamp for reviewing the other cameras. They become important because the vandal, or vandals, would likely hide their faces while doing this, but might not have thought to hide from other cameras."

"And if they are astute enough to hide from all of the cameras here?"

"Well, we'd be able to backtrack them across campus, perhaps to another car. That could give us a license plate to use."

"What else?"

Aric thought for a moment. He figured the plastic gloves were used by the perps to prevent fingerprints, so dusting his car would likely be unproductive. The gloves could produce useful DNA, however. He explained his thinking to the officer.

"Sound reasoning, but you'd still want samples of every print you can find. What if they didn't don the gloves until they used the spray cans? They might have leaned against the car while looking inside and left usable prints on your door. If we're able to ID them from video or DNA, the prints would reinforce your case. If you don't collect them, you're missing that opportunity. Kind of like wearing layers of clothing when it's cold. If you get hot, you can always take off what you're wearing, but you can't put on what you don't have if you're cold."

Aric laughed. "Now you're sounding like my father."

Officer Kenniston smiled. "And my father before me."

They discussed the nuances of inspecting a crime scene as Aric dusted and searched for prints. He already had Jess's prints as well as his own and those of his family. They had been the subjects of his practicing different techniques. As his on-the-scene mentor handed him tape to collect prints as he found them, Aric smiled and pulled his laptop and a device from his own backpack. "Got something better." He used the small device to digitally scan the prints as he found them and upload them to his computer.

"I'm impressed. Our department doesn't even have those yet. Where'd you get that?"

"Mike Jurgesmeyer. Do you know him?"

The man laughed. "Of course. I should have figured that if you were a friend of Cully's, you might know Jurgesmeyer."

"That, and Mike and my brother worked on a special project together a year or so ago." He offered no further details on that "special project." "If you want, I can send these prints to Mike. He might be able to fast track them for us."

"I'll need to certify them first for chain of custody, but sure, go for it. Let's go look at video."

Aric packed up his laptop, picked up his backpack, and joined the man in his car. As they drove toward the security office, the man leaned toward him and said, "Say, you want a part-time job? You processed that scene better than half of our department. Lynch would be proud."

SIXTEEN

Adam grabbed his tray in the line at Sugarfire Smokehouse and placed his combo plate, baked beans, and potato salad onto it. Right behind him in line was Logan Mathias with a pulled pork plate consisting of the meat, house fries and coleslaw. Adam settled for a soda, while Logan waited for an apple-pie shake.

Adam paid for both meals and began looking about for a spot to eat among the communal tables. He wanted someplace a bit more private.

"Logan, you okay with eating outside?" As far as Adam was concerned, it was a perfect day for outside dining—55 degrees, full sun, and only a slight breeze. His family would prefer it to be 20 degrees warmer, but he didn't have to concede to them today. Besides, it was now November. They wouldn't have many days left for eating outside this year.

"Sure, I'm dressed for it."

As Adam exited the building for the outside tables, he noted only two others out there. *Guess more folks are like my family*, he thought. But as he sat down at a table away from the other hardy souls, he realized the sun was too low to hit them directly. Its warming rays were blocked by the building. He zipped his jacket fully up to his neck.

Logan joined him a minute later. As he sat down, he said, "A bit brisker than it looks. We'll have to eat fast if we want warm food, but good news is, my shake won't melt as quickly." He grinned. "Shall we bless the food?"

Adam nodded and let the man continue.

"Lord, we come to give You honor and to thank You for Your boundless provisions. We thank You for this food and bless it to nourish our bodies. We thank you, too, for new friendships within Your body and ask that You guide our conversation and any decisions to be made. Thank you again, Lord. In Your name we pray. Amen."

"Amen." Adam took a sip of Coke and then said, "I've learned a bit about your education and background, but there are some gaps. You had a number of publications and then nothing. Next thing I found was you in Colorado building websites. What happened?"

Logan was already several bites into his pulled pork, finished chewing, and answered. "My employer, who will remain nameless, decided my social credit score was lacking. I supported a local pregnancy center and wrote a short article about abortion's toll on our society for their newsletter. About the same time, a co-worker, with whom I had a good relationship, asked me my opinion about transgenders in girls' sports. I answered honestly. Somehow both of those issues and my stand on them got back to my bosses. When I stood up for my opinion, my position there suddenly disappeared. My life had grown increasingly hectic, so I figured some time off, staying with my parents for moral support, and prayer would help me figure out where to go next." He took a bite. After swallowing, he continued. "Guess I'm still trying to figure that out. A friend was hired by Church Alive here and through her, I was hired to rebuild their entire media presence—social media, live streaming, WiFi within the building, and so on. That's about done." He took a spoonful of shake. "So, what about you? Sounds like you were able to find out stuff about me that a typical search engine would never find, and yet, I wasn't able to discover much about you at all. That makes me curious."

Adam nodded as he chewed. He washed it down with another swig of soda. "Yeah, well, about that, if I told you, somebody'd have to kill you."

Logan laughed. "Not you, just somebody. Well, that's a different take."

"Yeah, I, well, let me just say it was a highly classified position, but, like you, certain things didn't work out. I actually had to run for my own life for a while. Went to ground, and that's when I made sure my online history, well, made sure it disappeared. What you can discover about me online is only what I've allowed to be there."

"Curiouser and curiouser." Logan continued to eat. "Umm, starting to cool off pretty fast."

"My whole family is Christian, especially my kid brother. I was the black sheep of the family. I think their prayers, especially his, finally worked because I accepted Christ just over a year ago. I came out of hiding, reunited with my estranged family, and decided to put my skills to use helping Christian organizations with their online presences, particularly those who've been deplatformed from other internet providers and AWS. I developed a whole set of security tools to help them prevent denial of service attacks and such. From there it seemed natural to begin hosting them and providing web services comparable to AWS. The name, Pelethites Cybersecurity, was my brother's idea."

Logan nodded. "Good name. Very appropriate." His food gone, he now finished off his pie shake. "I like what you're doing. I believe I could be a big help. My tasks at Church Alive will finish up in about a week, maybe two, and then I'm available full-time."

Adam sighed. "From what I've learned about you, I agree. I was hoping you'd be available sooner 'cause I'm swamped. After helping America First News, they did an article on me, and the response has been overwhelming."

Logan nodded. "I figured as much. That's how I learned about you, and I was surprised to find you here in St. Louis. It was as if God planted me here to ultimately help you."

Adam scrutinized the man. "Are you sure? I mean, the stuff I'm doing is way beneath your training and skill sets."

"Sounds like it's way beneath yours, too."

"Yeah, guess I can't argue with you there."

"Look, I'm in. I won't even quibble over salary. Well, as long as it pays the bills. I want to serve the body of Christ, and I see that that's what you're doing. It's right up my alley. Between us, we ought to be able to raise the level of web hosting, design, SEO, and security that most of these companies are getting now."

That fit right into Adam's desires for his company. They discussed salary, and Logan seemed pleased that Adam's initial offer was higher than he'd expected. But then, Adam knew what Logan's skills were worth and with the influx of business, he could afford that. Yet, could he wait two weeks?

"You said you were swamped. The church is closed on Mondays, and I'm not expected to be there either. I can come to your place then and begin to get a feel for what you have and what you might still need."

Monday. Four days away. He could have the employment contract ready by then. Adam nodded. "That would be great."

SEVENTEEN

Yolina had not slept at all. Yes, she had pulled all-nighters many a time before but that was when she was preoccupied with a project. Adrenaline had provided the stimulation she needed for those nights. However, she was sure that last night it was cortisol controlling her body. The stress hormone never dropped to let her sleep. Too many what-ifs flooded her mind throughout the night . . . and in none of the scenarios did she fare well.

As the sun topped the spire of the Town Hall Tower in the Marienplatz, she knew that trying to find sleep at that moment would be a lost cause. When would Sergei call back? Had he found anything useful to her?

One thing was sure. She needed to change locations. Koch had much better resources than she and Sergei. If he discovered that what she hoped wasn't true actually was, she would be in a world of hurt. Not getting paid was the least of her worries. And yet, she had concluded overnight that what she hoped wasn't true probably was. She had spent days hunting down fictitious identities . . . and once Werner Koch understood that, the understated anger he was known for would be energized against her.

Her last resort would be to offer to trade the video recording of them together for her safety. Of course, she no longer had sole control of its contents, having forwarded the video to her handlers. Could she be convincing? If she tried to fool him into thinking she had the only copy, once he had the flash drive, there would be nothing to keep him from exterminating her and making sure her body was never found. No, she would have to lead him into thinking that she would keep that recording as insurance.

And should he discover that she didn't have the only copy, much less that she sent it to the FSB, her fate would be likewise sealed. Yes, no matter which way she turned, trying to use the video as an explicit threat was a tactic that would return to bite her. Perhaps the simple implication of having a video, without expressly admitting it, would best keep him off-balance.

As she forced down a Monster drink through the nausea of her stress, her phone rang. She sighed in relief noting that it was *her* phone, not Koch's phone. Sergei?

She rushed into the nearby bedroom and snatched it up from the nightstand. Yes. Sergei.

"моя дорогая, тебе нужно бежать."

I need to run? Yolina's knees buckled as she collapsed onto the bed.

"You need to clear out of there. Come home. Find a place to hide. Whatever. So far, my friends have tried to identify three of the men whose names you gave me. Not one is a real person. I think you have been, what do they call it, catfished."

She shook her head in disbelief. How? She had been so thorough. Yet, she did not have the resources to back up her findings with physical investigations, so naturally any information she found would have to be corroborated in person. Surely, Koch did not expect that of her. Did he? Had she not been so assured of her findings in her report to him, she might have been able to use that argument. But that was not the case. She had practically guaranteed her findings to him, and that's what could become her downfall.

She would appear a fool to him, and he didn't take kindly to fools. As long as she was useful to him, the "extracurricular" mission she had foolishly agreed to take on and that had caused him so much embarrassment, could be seen as a cost of doing business. However, not being useful to him made her a real liability. At this point, she didn't appreciate the FSB's painting a target on her back.

"I will be in touch."

"But—"

She hung up and ran to her workstation. The first thing she did was transfer all of her funds to a Caribbean account that only she knew of on the small volcanic island of Nevis, part of the nation of Saint Kitts and Nevis. With its population of 11,000, the island's bankers doubled down on secrecy in 2008-9 when others, such as the Cayman Islands, caved to international political pressure to open their books. The account where Koch was to forward her payment would be empty. As that transfer took place, she composed a brief note:

Herr Koch,

I performed all of my work with due diligence and was as thorough as I know how to be in vetting my findings. However, I do not have the resources or ability to confirm my findings physically, and it has come to my attention that I have been catfished. I expect no payment. Please forgive my failure to uncover the person or persons you seek, and other transgressions.

Yolina.

She added the last three words in the hope of further mollifying his anger. She reread the note. Her German was mediocre, but it would get the message across. After printing that out and placing it next to the computers, she used her hacking skills to make sure her bank transfer was untraceable. Next, she erased and reset all of the computers in the apartment. They were Koch's anyway, so a factory reset would not jeopardize any personal data.

She glanced down to the street. Nothing suspicious.

She hurriedly grabbed her clothing and stuffed it all into her carry-on case. From a compartment within the lining of that case, she retrieved a passport and a credit card in that name. She glanced about the apartment. Koch's men would find nothing to point to where she had fled. Wherever that was going to be. She needed first to get out of harm's way and then figure out her next steps.

A thought crossed her mind. She opened her bag and retrieved the nanny cam she had used to record her tryst with Koch. She ran into the bedroom and positioned it on the shelf where it would be easily discovered next to the secure phone Koch had provided for her.

As she emerged from the apartment, she smiled. She had one stop to make, one person to meet, but now, the only thing his men would find was evidence suggesting that she recorded her bedroom activities. That should throw his world off-kilter, but would it simply enrage him further or make him tread lightly?

EIGHTEEN

Aric sat in the waiting room of the auto body shop waiting for the manager to call him. Ten days had passed since discovering his car vandalized in the campus parking garage. His new acquaintance, Officer Kenniston, had arranged to have the car hauled—under a tarp so as not to call attention to it—to a body shop nearby in the suburb of Maryland Heights not far from Aric's parents' home.

Although having to rely on his family and friends for transportation to classes was bad enough, his biggest hassle was the insurance claim. He'd had to jump through hoops followed by going to great lengths and then more hoops to prove that he had not provoked the vandalism. Never mind that the damage was a criminal act, the company didn't want to pay his claim if he'd somehow been involved in hateful speech or actions against those who perpetrated the act. Even more galling was when the adjuster asked his religious preferences, as if the company had any right to know. Aric stood his ground on that one, stating that religion, like politics, should have no bearing on someone committing a criminal act. In this case, it was felony property damage because of the expected cost of repair.

And that's what Aric was about to find out—the cost. The 2019 Altima had held its value pretty well, so the insurance company's first attempt to "total" the car, saying it wasn't worth the cost of repainting didn't fly. He'd acquired it from a distant elderly relative, and it had only 30,158 miles on it at the time. He could easily expect another 150,000 from it.

"Aric?"

He looked up from his cell phone and nodded. He stood. "Hi. That's me."

"Figured as much," the guy replied as he looked about the room and smiled. Aric realized the room was otherwise empty.

"I'm Jay." They shook hands. "So, who'd you piss off?"

Aric smirked. "That's exactly what Officer Kenniston asked me. No one that I know of."

The man nodded. "Yeah, Kenniston told me the story. He also said you're a student of Lynch Cully's. Cully used to refer folks to us all the time. Good guy. So, look, we're gonna give you the Cully discount, but the color and type of paint still determines a lot of the cost. Also, if you want us to fix any cosmetic issues while we're at it, that adds to the cost."

"I know. I did a bit of research on this last week. Other than a few door dings, I don't think there's much else."

"Yeah, a small dent in the right rear quarter panel, but the paint's intact there. The respray should cover it okay, but up to you about fixing the dent itself."

"Okay, let's not worry about it."

"Color?"

Aric hadn't been fond of the generic silver color. "So, the whole car has to be repainted, right?"

Jay nodded. "Yeah. We can do pretty much any color you want at this point."

Jess wanted to go with a metallic hunter green, while Aric thought a chameleon paint that changed color depending on the light angle would be cool. When she pointed out that such paint cost more, was expensive to apply and hard to repair, he suggested the Frozen Portimao Blue Metallic color he'd seen on a BMW i4. He changed his mind again upon learning that the upcharge for that color was around $4,000.

"I'd like a dark blue metallic."

"Sounds good."

Jay showed him some samples, and Aric picked the one he liked.

"Good choice. Okay, so with the Cully discount, basic sanding and prep, and the metallic blue, we're talking about $4,325, plus tax."

Aric took a deep breath. He had expected a couple of grand, but where was he going to come up with over $4K? He needed the money he'd been saving to make a bigger purchase. His thoughts calmed a bit upon realizing that he wasn't looking at over $8,000 with the Portimao Blue he liked.

"And if I just go with a flat, solid blue?"

"Actually, same cost. The metallics are so popular, the paint price has come down from when they were first introduced. They're both single-step applications. It's when you get into the three-step applications that things really get expensive."

"Got it. Let's stick to the metallic then."

"Gotcha. We've got some paperwork for you to sign, and there's a 30% down payment. Should have it done in a week."

Aric felt defeated. He hadn't expected a down payment, and he'd never used his credit card for more than textbooks. Those were expensive enough. But what choice did he have? He needed his car. Jess relied on him often, too.

After completing the transaction, he exited the shop and called his mom to pick him up. As he waited, he tried to think of ways he could make the money he needed. Those thoughts were interrupted by his phone—a number he didn't recognize.

"Hello?"

"Aric, it's Jack Kenniston. Thought you'd want to know that your forensics work on your car paid off. We found the two culprits. Remember what I said about getting the fingerprints?"

"Yep."

"Well, that's what sealed the deal. They matched. They're facing felony property damage charges, and as students, expulsion from the university as well. It's unlikely they'd get any jail time over this, but we can probably get them to pay for the damages. Have you gotten an estimate yet?"

"Just now. I'm waiting at the body shop for a ride home." He gave the security officer the final cost.

"Great. I'll pass this along to the prosecutor." He paused. "By the way, that part-time job offer still stands."

Aric smiled and said a quiet prayer of thanksgiving. Yet again, God was watching over him.

Adam checked the time. Logan said he'd be there at noon. It was 11:55. Adam didn't understand why he was nervous. Was it that Logan was to be his very first employee? Was he concerned the guy would take one look at his setup and criticize it and want to redo it? He was, after all, more of a systems wonk than Adam had ever been.

Maybe he was anxious because he'd rarely worked with a partner, with someone who might be looking over his shoulder to see what he was doing on the side. True, he'd worked with Mike Jurgesmeyer and the Colonel on The Remnant, but there he'd been part of the team working on a specific "project." UltraNet hadn't openly come into play then. Only Lynch and his brother knew the full extent of his software's capabilities.

At 11:59, his security system picked up on a car coming into their driveway. The thought *Showtime!* entered his head, but it was really going to be more *Show 'n Tell* time as he gave Logan a tour of his server center and gave him the rundown on what he was doing . . . and how far he was backed up.

He met Logan at the door.

"Welcome." They shook hands. "C'mon in. Get you something to drink?"

"No thanks. Grabbed lunch to eat on the way here. This is more secluded than I thought possible in St. Louis County."

"The more secluded, the better." His wife emerged from the kitchen. "Rach, this is Logan. Logan, my wife, Rachel." They exchanged greetings. "Our kids are in school."

"Yes, and looking forward to Thanksgiving next week and two days off. Speaking of which, if you don't have plans for the holiday, you're welcome to join us. We'll have members from both of our families here, the ones who still live in the area, so it will be a full house and lots of food."

"Um, well, thank you. I, uh, do have a tentative invitation already from friends at the church, but they haven't confirmed anything yet. I can let you know by the end of the week, if that's okay?"

"You can just show up if that falls through. And please, bring a friend. Adam told me you're not married, but he didn't say anything about a girlfriend. Or even just a friend. Sorry, don't mean to pry."

"No, no. That's fine. No formal girlfriend at the moment, but there is a friend I might ask. Thank you for the invitation."

"You're certainly welcome. My dad was military, and we

often had what my mom called 'Holiday Orphans' feasts for people in my dad's unit who couldn't get home for the holidays. I like that tradition."

Adam smiled at his wife. Her generosity and graciousness were but two of the many traits he loved about her. "Her folks carried on that tradition for years after he retired. Now, they come here, and we carry it on with them. We might have four or five other orphans next week."

"I'll let you two get on with things." Rachel excused herself.

"Follow me." Adam led Logan downstairs to his office. He pointed to a chair he'd moved there from another room. "We'll go out to the servers in a minute, but this is where I've been working, my control room so to speak. I'll be moving it to the other building, now that you're here. I also started setting up an office for you, but it's pretty sparse. I wanted to let you design and equip it as you see fit. But first, we have some paperwork to do. I take it you've reviewed the contract already."

"I have and it looks great. To be honest, I didn't expect such a competitive salary from a one-man shop."

"Well, I have a good feeling about our working together and want you to stick around. The Bible says we're to pay the hireling what he's worth. Or something like that."

Logan smiled. "Yeah, not exactly, but something like that."

They discussed expectations, from both sides, and completed the papers. Adam now officially had his first employee. They headed for the server building. Adam noticed Logan raising his brow as he pointed out the building.

"Don't let the appearance fool you. I designed it to look like a pole barn from the outside, to keep unwanted visitors guessing. Judge it from the inside. Also, there's extensive security along the perimeter of the property and throughout the woods. No one gets near this building or our house without my knowing about it."

Logan gave him a curious look.

"Yeah, I take security seriously. You learn to with the background I have."

They came to a massive door, not so much by its dimensions but by the gauge of steel that was clearly not your typical home, steel front door. Next to it was a keypad and biometric scanner. Adam looked toward the scanner and then keyed in a six-digit code. The door eased open on its own hydraulic power.

"The door will withstand anti-tank weaponry. It will only open and close on its own power. To get in, you will need to scan your face first and then enter a six-digit code that will be unique to you."

Logan gave him another but different look. Adam was going to have to learn what these looks meant. "Overkill?" he asked.

Logan shook his head. "Not at all. Have you ever been inside a major data center, like for Amazon or Microsoft? They're surrounded by 12-foot-tall fences topped with razor wire and inside the perimeter are armed guards with enough fire power to stop a small army. I've heard rumors that they even have anti-aircraft capabilities. What about the walls? I mean if someone is serious about getting inside, it doesn't look like it would take much to cut through."

"And that's where they'd be wrong, but we can talk about that later."

"What about if I'm inside and the power goes out? I figure you have a backup generator to power the servers. Does it handle the door, too? I mean, I can't get trapped inside, can

I?"

Adam smiled. "Actually, we're totally off the grid for power. 100% green. We'll never lose power."

"Never lose power? I didn't see any solar or wind turbines, and even those can go down. That's certainly not reliable enough to power servers, HVAC and ventilation, security, your home, and whatever else you're powering."

"C'mon, I'll show you." Adam led him to a room that was about the size of half of a shipping container. Inside was a box about the size of a large refrigerator. It hummed softly. "That is the generator of the future. 18-phase. AC or DC simultaneously. Scalable. Requires no special ventilation or HVAC. It runs 24/7 without any energy input, and the software controls manage its output depending on load requirements."

Logan appeared clearly impressed. "How? Where? Th-this seems amazing."

"Do you remember that Easter miracle out in California last spring? After the dam broke and LA went dark."

"Sure. Some small town without power lit up like a cross on Good Friday."

"Well, it was one of these that powered that town. I tracked down the company and became an investor and a customer at the same time. It's, well, I can't yet share the tech, but it has a solid-state alternator that is simply amazing."

Adam led Logan to their new offices, followed by open space for expansion, and then to the server room itself. Logan seemed duly impressed, but Adam suspected he would find ways to improve their service. Then it was if a dam broke, and questions came flooding from Logan's mouth.

NINETEEN

Werner's plan to work from their lake house on the *Starnberger See*, outside of the town of Münsing, was not going as planned. While the temperature was above normal for mid-November, Starnberg Lake looked dreary in the rain as the wind pushed fallen leaves across the water. The barren trees added to the desolate look.

Perhaps he should call his driver and return to the city. And yet, he sat in the great room and stared at the water . . . and stared . . . and stared. His mind replayed *ad nauseum* the report he'd received three days earlier, along with the physical items found at Yolina's apartment when he'd sent two men to escort "her" to his office. He picked up the short note she'd left behind and read it for the hundredth time.

In some ways, he hadn't been surprised that she had fled. Her bosses at Pozitiv Teknolodzhiz continued to profess her hacking and IT skills as among their best. And being among the best, the embarrassment of having been fooled, of having spent hours and days tracking down cleverly planted decoys, and of feeling so self-assured of those findings as to practically guarantee them, would be enough to leave town over.

She had been outplayed by a master, someone so intelligent that he could destroy their AlterNet program without so much as a trace of evidence leading to his identity or location. Werner remained convinced that he was searching for a single man. For a sole perpetrator to create a committee to "represent" him made sense, but it came across as a taunt. *Na-na-na-na-nahh-nahhhh. Where's Waldo?* For that matter, *who* was Waldo? The resources Werner had expended to search out and physically confirm multiple persons had been considerable.

He reread the note. Had it simply been a case of her having been deceived, he could have overlooked it. After all, as she stated in the note, she didn't have the resources to confirm her findings by physically locating and identifying the men. He had expected to perform that search—to do the necessary due diligence, so to speak.

No, it was what his men found along with the note and phone that occupied his perseverations. The small video camera appeared to be part of a typical nanny cam, like one you could buy at most electronics stores or online. However, when his people tested it, they found it offered much higher resolutions than those typical cameras. He could only begin to imagine what he, uh, she had recorded, and where that video might be? To date, she had made no demands of him and, in fact, had declined payment for her failure to find his quarry. What kind of blackmailer would do that?

Indeed, Yolina became an enigma. Her actions appeared to present no threat, but the potential existence of a video revealing his indiscretion—his momentary failure of the flesh, his lapse of judgment—posed a significant risk.

He retrieved his cell phone and typed in a terse text to one of his men. *Dieter, I have a task for you. Come see me in the great room.* He turned to stare at the lake again.

Shortly, the man he had summoned stood at attention next to him. Dieter Fuchs, age 38, had been a first sergeant in the 2nd Platoon of the 1st Commando Company of the

Kommando Spezialkräfte, the German Special Forces stationed in the Graf Zeppelin barracks in Calw, Baden-Württemberg. A knee injury during an air insertion exercise had taken him out of the 2nd Platoon, but his aptitude in intelligence gathering won him a spot in the 5th Platoon, which specialized in reconnaissance, intelligence operations and sniper/counter-sniper operations. A reconnaissance mission led to the re-injury of his knee and a medical discharge from the KSK. Werner had been quick to pick him up.

"Dieter, I want you to find Yolina Zhdanov. She is smart and has ties to the Russian FSB, so I have little doubt that she is now using a false passport and ID."

The man nodded. "*Ja*, Herr Koch. I will use facial recognition to track her down. False passport or not, she won't be able to get far. And when I find her?"

"Don't do anything rash. Just observe. Let me know where she is and what she is doing. Then I will decide what to do with her."

TWENTY

The family's Thanksgiving celebration had been particularly joyous. McFarland's entire clan had converged on the family's estate in Maryland, including their latest grandchild, one-month-old Angela, the third child of their youngest son, Anthony. With their three sons, two daughters, and 12 grandchildren—along with their oldest son's husband and the others' spouses—it had been a full house. For the first time in 30-odd years, the AG had had to sit out their traditional game of touch football after the early afternoon meal. He blamed it on his age but could not discount his wife's claim that the rigors of his job were taking a toll on his health.

Now, a day later, that job interrupted his long weekend's plans. McFarland sat in his home's study across from Special Counsel Jim Kerr. Each had a glass of America's own spirit—Kentucky bourbon. In this case, McFarland opened a bottle of E.H. Taylor, Old Fashioned Sour Mash. Released in 2011 as a limited-edition bourbon, its price tag of nearly $30,000 a bottle—if one was fortunate to find an available bottle—left few who could afford it. The bottle had been an early holiday present from an unnamed benefactor who had passed it along through several intermediaries in order to avoid the appearance of an improper gift to the Attorney General . . . and to circumvent the AG's requirement to report such pricey gifts. Ethics? That was for the middle and lower classes.

"Sir, that is one mighty fine whiskey. Thanks for allowing

me a taste."

The AG nodded. "My pleasure. Your report is going to do the country a big, big favor. And me, too."

He didn't have to spell out what that favor was. The man was bright enough to come up with his own conjectures, one of which was likely to be on target.

They discussed the counsel's upcoming report on the President's unfortunate retention of classified documents after his stint as VP, focusing on areas of nuance that required more direct language. They also discussed the timing of the report. The election cycle would truly kick off after the holidays, and this report needed to go public early in the cycle, but not too early. They hoped that several of the cases against former president Graham would be far enough along, perhaps even coming to a close, so that the report could not be used by him to bolster what should be a faltering campaign by that time.

The door to the study opened after a single knock, and the AG's wife poked her head in. "Honey, you'd better come see this."

McFarland raised his brow. She knew not to disturb them, so the interruption became all the more concerning. The two men hurried from the study and followed her to their den where a large-screen TV revealed scenes of chaos and destruction. McFarland was quick to see that the TV was tuned to Newsmax, with Fox News showing similar scenes in a smaller picture-in-picture frame.

"What's this?" he asked. He pointed to the Newsmax logo on the screen. Newsmax was not acceptable viewing in his house.

His wife looked sheepish. "I know, but it's not being carried by the mainstream media. I got a call from Carol alerting me to the incident. She said to check the conservative media if I couldn't find it on CNN or MSNBC. Well, I couldn't find anything on either one, or on ABC, CBS, or NBC. She was right. It seems only the conservative media is covering it, although a bunch of Republican congressmen are reporting being safe on Facebook."

He felt his face flush in anger. "And just what is *it*?"

"An assassination attempt on Bradly Graham. He was scheduled to attend a large fundraising banquet at the Four Seasons Hotel on Pennsylvania Avenue. He ran late, and as dinner was being served three bombs went off at three tables near the head table. A fourth bomb was discovered that was about to be served to the head table. Over twenty dead and three dozen injured. Survivors are saying that as waiters lifted the dome plate covers off several apparently rigged plates, bombs on the plates detonated. A number of the injured were hurt as people panicked to evacuate the room."

McFarland's face blanched as his knees began to buckle. He stumbled to the closest chair and sat down, shaking his head in both disbelief and dismay. "No, no, no, no, no," he mumbled.

His wife turned up the sound.

"Local police and the Secret Service have identified two people of interest. Security video showed these two assisting in the kitchen and then rushing away from the hotel just as the serving carts left the kitchen. Full-time kitchen staff, requesting anonymity, had the following to report: . . ." The screen showed a male in white kitchen garb whose face was blurred and voice disguised. "They were supposedly crew members of the part-time catering team hired to assist us with the banquet. One was clearly trans, but we were instructed to use *her* pronouns and make no snide remarks about *her* Y-chromosome. The other wore a ProChoice tee-shirt that she made no effort to hide under her whites. They helped prep plates and load the carts, and as soon as that was done, they bolted. That's what made us suspicious and report it to the Secret Service detail, but they had no time to stop the servers."

McFarland felt his heart begin to race upon hearing that. *From bad to worse*, he thought. *The conservative media will have a field day with this.*

Special Counsel Kerr's phone vibrated in his pocket, and he retrieved it. "Hello." The voice on the other end was not intelligible. "Yes, sir. Heading in now." He disconnected the call and turned to the AG, his ultimate boss. "Sir, I'm being called into the department. Thank you for your hospitality and that fine bourbon. I'm sure I'll see you downtown. I can show myself out."

McFarland, still feeling numb, nodded, but then it hit him. Why hadn't he been called? Why had he learned about this from the news media? The conservative news media at that. True, the Secret Service was not under his department, but as the chief law enforcement officer in the country, this incident would fall right into his lap. That a DOJ Special Counsel was being called into work made *that* very clear.

He checked his pockets. No phone. He stood and rushed to his study where he found the phone sitting on his desk. Maybe he had simply missed the calls. No. He found no missed calls recorded on the device. He called his Assistant Attorney General for the National Security Division, Mark Wilkinson.

"Mark, what in blazes is going on? Why was I not informed of a bombing at the Four Seasons? I had to learn about it from Newsmax of all places."

"Derrick, the DOJ is just now getting called into the loop. Lots of confusion and chaos at the scene, and the Secret Service took the lead. FBI is just now arriving at the scene. I've been in touch with Lacey, too. I thought she called you, and she thought I called you. You beat both of us to the punch."

Lacey McGrath was the Assistant Attorney General for the Criminal Division. McFarland was pleased to hear that both were in the loop, and he understood the confusion that such an incident could cause. Still, the director of the Secret Service should have contacted him directly.

"Okay. Keep me in the loop. It will take me a while to get there, but I'll be in the office as soon as I can."

The call disconnected. He didn't want to admit that he was a bit too "under the influence" of that excellent bourbon to drive, and to get his personal driver to pick him up at that hour on a holiday weekend would require time. After calling for the driver, he made another call . . . to Zhèng Jian. The White House switchboard required several redirected calls before connecting with the Chief of Staff.

"Derrick, I expected your call."

"I bet. Is this one of your ops, Jian? Did your people set up this bombing without coordinating it? Actions like this were supposed to be scripted, like all of the Antifa riots, and killing Graham was supposed to be a last resort if all of the criminal suits failed and he still moved ahead in the polls."

McFarland normally would not "attack" the Chief of Staff, particularly with his being handpicked by Werner Koch. The man could also persuade the President to find another AG. But he was livid, and maybe finding another AG wouldn't be such a bad thing. An attack like this against Graham so early in the election cycle was destined to backfire. All of the criminal charges were already beginning to propel his popularity upward and fuel both the conservative media's and his campaign's spins about the cases being "banana republic" political hit jobs.

"Not me. Not the WOC, Derrick. And from what I've been told, the CIA and FBI were both totally caught off-guard by this. No one saw it coming, and it's going to be a political disaster for the global movement generally and the Democrat Party specifically."

McFarland calmed down a bit. "Sorry. I'm pissed. I learned about the incident from Newsmax and Fox News. No one bothered to call me. I had to call them."

"Like I said, this thing caught everyone by surprise. I'm told it's still chaotic at the Four Seasons, but your folks are there now and will be taking lead from the Secret Service."

McFarland knew that much.

"How can I help, Derrick?"

"At this point, only the conservative media is reporting this. If our mainstream media allies remain silent, it's going to look like a massive cover-up and will confirm to America that the administration might be behind this. They need to get on it and come up with a realistic spin."

"Like what? I saw that kitchen worker blaming a trans female and a pro-choice, um, how did he put it? A pro-choice zealot. That was his description in one interview. That throws it right into the lap of the Democrat's base."

McFarland couldn't think. His mind continued to race. "I-I'm not the spinmeister here. Get CNN or MSNBC working on it and then get all of them to report the same things, like we usually do. And if they can't come up with something convincing, throw those two people under the bus. Like, the threat of another Graham presidency made them crack, become psychotic and homicidal. Or maybe w—" He started to say we. ". . . you have them publicly assassinated by some crackpot we can label a Graham supporter."

There was silence on the other end for a moment. "Who said you're not a spin doctor? I'm not sure that last idea is feasible. It could start a shooting war, and conservatives can still outgun us. I'll get the people at FromTheShadows and CNN to start working on it. We'll have our people covering it before midnight."

McFarland nodded in agreement. FromTheShadows was an excellent choice. As the current reincarnation of GameChanger Salon after its 2014 outing as a secret organization that controlled the news cycles, FromTheShadows members were the ultimate spin doctors for progressive, left-wing ideology. Several of those members were on-air staff at CNN where their first stories would test the public waters, so to speak, before passing them along to the other networks.

"Thank you. I have to go. My driver's on the way here."

McFarland knew that if Zhèng was on it, things would get done. Still, maybe his wife was right. Maybe this job was affecting him in a negative sense. After all, here he was, a former federal appellate judge and now the country's chief law enforcement officer, proposing the assassination of two people and pinning the blame on some mentally ill "recruit." He wasn't sure he wanted to continue into another four-year term should Charles Sidon, or his hand chosen successor, be elected.

TWENTY-ONE

To his mother's dismay, Aric and Jess spent Thanksgiving in Kenosha at her parents' house. In return, Jess had agreed to spend Christmas in St. Louis with the Aftons. Aric's mom had come to the realization that sharing holidays was likely to become the norm if Aric and Jess married, although recognizing that new reality didn't make accepting it any easier.

He and Jess spent that Friday visiting friends from the college there. They had one last stop to make before heading back to the house to join her family for dinner. No sooner had they pulled up to the house, than the front door flew open, and a spunky toddler came running out.

"It Ric-Ric and Jess. Yaaaay, time to play, Ric-Ric."

Aric smiled. At three-and-a-half years, little Joshua still hadn't quite mastered 'Aric,' but Aric found 'Ric-Ric' endearing. The boy's father, Lynch Cully, emerged from the house followed by his wife, Amy, carrying Carson the third. Aric had heard the story of how Amy tried and tried to get Lynch—who was legally Carson Cully, Jr—to agree to carry on the family name with their first born but hadn't succeeded. Upon learning they were having another boy, she had cajoled and harassed him enough to make it finally happen. That little guy had just begun to take his tentative first steps when Aric had left Kenosha the past spring.

"Welcome." Lynch walked up to both and gave them hugs.

"It's great to see you."

They greeted Amy as well, and then Aric looked at Josh and said, "Race you. I'm gonna get inside first." The boy laughed and raced to the door, with Aric right on his heels.

"I got here first!" Josh proclaimed as he spun around just inside the front door. Aric reached down and tickled him until the boy broke free and rushed away.

Aric and Jess followed the couple into their kitchen. Amy motioned toward a nearby counter. "We just opened a bottle of Riesling. Would you like a glass?"

"Sure. Thanks. We have time for a glass. We promised Jess' folks we'd be back for dinner."

With glasses in hand, they all settled down in the nearby family room where a fire crackled in the wood fireplace. The faint smell of wood smoke added a woodsy touch to the room. Josh came up to Aric and began to tug on his sleeve.

"Ric-Ric play." The boy handed him two wooden building blocks.

"He's into constructing things right now," said Amy. She took Josh's hand and said, "Honey, mommy and daddy want to talk with Aric and Jess, so why don't you go build something, and we can show Aric when you're done."

'Okaaay." Looking disappointed, the boy ran into the adjacent room.

"So, I hear you're doing quite well at UMSL."

"Um, thanks. I'll find out with finals in a couple of weeks."

"You'll do well. Is that a new car outside? Wasn't your car silver?"

Aric nodded. "Yeah, used to be. Same car. Had to have it painted." He told them about the incident with his car, and how it all started with pink-hair Toni tracking him down on campus.

Lynch shook his head. "Wow. The guy has become more of a problem here, too. A lot more aggressive, but I didn't expect that he would try to track you down and export trouble to UMSL."

"Well, I met Officer Jack Kenniston, and he had me do a real-life forensic work-up. With his help, we got all the evidence we needed, and they found the two guys who did it. Their parents agreed to pay for the damages, plus a little for the inconvenience it caused me, if their sons wouldn't get expelled. I received their checks last week."

"So, ol' Kenny is still at it. Good for him."

"Oh, and Jay from Brookes Auto Body says hi, too. He gave me the Cully discount."

Lynch laughed. "Good men there. Honest and hardworking. I was always happy to send them business."

Aric took another sip of wine and asked, "So what are you up to these days?"

"Same old, same—"

Just then Amy's phone sounded off with several alerts. She looked at the phone and rushed to the TV. "Something's happened in Washington." She flipped through channels until she came to Fox News, and there were scenes of chaos and confusion.

"We're at the Four Seasons Hotel on Pennsylvania Avenue, where just minutes before Bradley Graham arrived for a campaign fundraiser dinner, three bombs went off inside the banquet hall near the head table. President Graham had been late because of a problem with their car. At this time, we're told that 22 are confirmed dead and dozens have been injured."

Lynch let out a long sigh. "And so it begins," he said softly.

"What?"

"I talked with Graham just this morning and warned him to be careful. The beast isn't happy with him and his campaign. It won't relinquish power readily."

"The beast?" asked Jess.

Lynch nodded. "Let's pray for the people affected by this, and then I'll explain." Lynch led them in a prayer for the victims, their families, the hotel staff and all of those affected. He also asked God to give the investigators wisdom and to help them to uncover the truth and to find those responsible.

"And Lord, please don't let this incident get swept under the rug of government secrecy and media cover-ups. When the truth is uncovered, please make sure it becomes known throughout the world," said Aric.

"We also pray for protection over President Graham, his family, and his staff. Thank you, God," said Amy.

As four sets of eyes opened, three of them set their gaze on Lynch.

Lynch looked around at the others. "Okay then. I said I'd explain. All of you know that studying the Book of Revelation is something of a hobby for me."

"More like an obsession," said Amy, grinning. "Never a dull moment."

Lynch gave a non-committal shrug of his shoulders. "In chapter 13 there are two beasts, one from the sea and one from the land. These are modeled after the four beasts in the Book of Daniel, by the way. So, the beast from the sea is described as having seven heads and ten horns wearing crowns. It represents global government with the ten horns and crowns being symbolic of government and law, while seven heads represent its global nature. You know, like the seven seas and seven continents. Today, we would call it the Deep State."

Aric nodded. "I know a lot of the church thinks that beast represents a person they call the Antichrist, capital A, but this makes more sense. There are seven heads, not one."

"And one of those heads is wounded, but the wound heals. It came to me one day while praying that President Graham was the wound. He set back the globalists' plans by four years. When Sidon became president, the wound was healed, and a 42-month period of reign began."

"So, who is the beast from the land then?" asked Jess.

"That represents the mainstream media and corporate world, two heads. Both act as cheerleaders for the globalists and promote their policies. One example is when our government couldn't legally mandate COVID vaccines, the corporate world stepped in and did it for them."

Lynch stopped talking. For Aric, it was time to let his comments sink in.

"So, if there is no global tyrant called the Antichrist, what about the period of tribulation so many seem to be expecting?"

"Not found in the Bible. In fact, Jesus commented on this time period twice. Once He said it would be like the days of Noah, and the other time He mentioned it being like the days of Lot. In both, He said people would be buying and selling, marrying and being given in marriage, eating and drinking, planting and building. Does that sound like a time when the world is enslaved to some tyrant? Sounds like normal life to me. He also said He would be coming like a thief in the night. To me, a rapture, Antichrist, or seven-year tribulation period would be dead giveaways that His return was right around the corner. They would be like burglar alarms going off as the thief entered the building. No, His return will catch everyone off-guard except His people, whom He instructed to remain watchful and aware of the season."

"You mentioned 42 months."

Lynch nodded. "John tells us that the beast is given 42 months to reign. And Jesus, in the parable of the fig tree, tells us to be aware of the season, to understand when summer is coming. The parable of the ten brides tells us the same."

"So, when does those 42 months end?"

"Think about it."

Aric did a quick calculation in his head. Sidon became POTUS in 2021 and took a couple of months to get people into place. Three and a half years would take them into . . . "Whoa! The fall of 2024? That's less than a year away. Do you really think He's coming back next fall?"

Lynch shrugged. "I can't say so definitively. I have no 'thus saith the Lord' prophetic assurance, but if I'm interpreting Revelation correctly, that's a real possibility."

Werner found himself inside a room with walls of bare brick. He looked around, becoming more and more frantic as he looked for an exit. Yet, he saw no windows, no doors. The only exit seemed to be an opening filled with bright light in the ceiling 20 feet overhead. He scurried about looking for anything he could climb to reach that opening, but he found nothing. Everything he reached for—chairs, a ladder, boxes, tables—seemed to vaporize in a puff of mist as he touched them. His panic worsened as the distinct sounds of multiple smoke alarms broke the silence like klaxons announcing distress in dense fog.

He awoke with a start to the ring tone of his phone. A few moments passed before clarity of mind made him realize that the phone's ringing must have triggered the awful dream.

Yes, that was it. What other explanation could there be?

The phone call went to voice mail, but promptly started ringing again. Upon picking up the device, he discovered three things. It was 12:38 in the morning. No one dared call him at that time of day. The caller had been diverted to voice mail nine times already. And the caller was Ilse, his new aide. She knew better than to call him at such a time. It could wait until morning.

And yet, something must have happened that couldn't wait until morning. Why else would she be so insistent to have kept calling despite the multiple diversions to voice mail?

"*Ja*, Ilse? *Kann das nicht bis zum Morgen warten?*"

"Sir, I do not think you would want to wake up to this news in the morning. Also, Zhèng Jian has tried to reach you three times. I promised him I would keep trying."

Werner was fully awake now. "*Einen moment.*"

As he slipped out of bed, Liesl asked, "What is it? What's wrong? Are our children—"

"They are fine, *schatzi*. Something has happened in the U.S. Go back to sleep."

He donned his robe, slipped on his slippers, and padded his way to his study. He again put his phone to his ear.

"There. I can speak freely now. What has happened?"

"There was an assassination attempt on Bradley Graham."

Werner slumped back into his chair. "What? When?" This was not good news. Yes, the man was a thorn in their side, but an attempt on his life played right into the right-wing conspiracy theorists' talking points. The American conservative media will have a field day with this. Plus, the man's popularity grew with each indictment and civil suit launched against him. Werner could only imagine what this incident would do.

"He was to speak at a dinner to raise funds for his campaign. He was running late and was not at his table when three bombs exploded around the table and an unexploded bomb was later discovered next to his place at the head table." She went on to provide details on the casualties, the police response, and more.

As she talked, Werner turned on his American cable service and tried to find coverage on the main networks. There was none. Were they really going to ignore such an event? That would be a huge mistake. Their media friends could not be seen as attempting to cover up such an incident. He frowned upon finding on-the-scene coverage by both Fox News and Newsmax. As he had suspected, the Newsmax reporters were taking a hardline stance against the totalitarian, globalist cabal that could be behind such an act. Fox News toned it down quite a bit, but then, Fox Corp and News Corp had become far, far less conservative under the reins of Rupert Murdoch's eldest son, Lachlan.

"Zhèng Jian has talked with Attorney General McFarland. Mr. McFarland is expected to coordinate actions with the director of their FBI. Mr. Zhèng has already talked with our friends at FromTheShadows and CNN to develop the appropriate response by all of our people at the main networks."

"*Sehr gut.* If Zhèng calls again, tell him I approve. Also tell him to stress to the media their need to cover this story quickly and not leave it to conservative media alone. And one more thing, Ilse, we need to accelerate our plans for digital IDs and social credit scoring. Please pass that along to those working on the projects."

"*Ja,* Herr Koch."

Werner sat and ran through numerous scenarios in his head. The Republicans and other conservatives had been caught off-guard by the election maneuvers of the left in the previous election. They would be much more alert to possibilities for fraud. Indeed, numerous actions to ensure election integrity had already been implemented and more were likely prior to the next American election. The left would not so easily steal the next election.

In the majority of scenarios he considered, Graham would regain the presidency. This assassination attempt would be seen as a radical, last-ditch effort to keep him from that office. It would highlight the far-right's predictions that the left was so desperate to keep Graham out they would resort to killing the man. The depiction of Sidon's administration being a "banana republic dictatorship" would be bolstered by this failed attempt, and Graham's support would skyrocket.

As such, they needed to gain as much control as possible before he retook the office. Their digital IDs would give them such control, and once implemented, even Graham, as President, would not be able to turn back the clock. Their corporate partners would see to that.

TWENTY-TWO

Aric sat in church with Jess, his mind wandering, as he surmised many others' thoughts were doing as well. The bombing in Washington was being felt all across the country, across the globe in fact. Aric had checked just before church started, and still, over 48 hours after the incident, the mainstream media continued to ignore the incident, which did not look good for them, or the current administration. Reports were being published about airport waiting areas and lounges, bars, motels, and other establishments—where CNN had been the go-to viewing option for decades—now switching to Fox News, some to Newsmax. In fact, ratings for Newsmax had climbed 55% overnight according to some news sources such as The Gateway Pundit and The Epoch Times.

Politically, the ramifications were already a tsunami ready to wash the Democrats and far left out to sea in the outflow. The Squad in Congress, as well as some so-called Hollywood celebrities, had had the audacity to applaud the bombers and state that they hoped the next attempt succeeded. The swift backlash to those comments had forced them to close social media accounts and websites. Other members of Congress called for their censure.

Not helping the political left was the fact that, by dawn on Saturday, the two perpetrators had been caught, and reports of bomb-making materials being found in one of their apartments had been verified. As reported early on, one bomber was trans, having been a munitions specialist in the Army prior to leaving the service to transition. The other was a strident Pro-Choice activist who had been arrested on numerous occasions for violence against peaceful protesters outside abortion mills. Both were lifelong Democrats and supporters of the far left. Their motives had not yet been released by authorities, but it didn't take an astrophysicist to understand their dislike of President Graham and the policies he would likely reinstate upon returning to the office of POTUS.

However, what amazed and impressed Aric most was the religious impact. Not only had Pastor Larson, Jess' father, totally changed the morning's service from the scheduled teaching out of the Book of Romans to a prayer service for those affected, the country, its leadership, and more, but the auditorium was packed—SRO. Jess and Aric assisted in greeting newcomers and listening to their stories. Some felt a need to pray for President Graham and his family. Others felt the need to pray for the country or to reconnect with the Christianity of their youth. Others saw the incident as yet another sign that the world was coming to an end and figured they had better get back into church. The couple passed on such comments to Jess' father.

Moreover, their church was not alone. An already spreading revival among college campuses surged as if gasoline had been tossed on the fire. Churches across the country reported needing additional services to host all of those seeking solace and peace. Many saw this as the last great awakening, the revival leading to Christ's second coming.

"In Your name we pray, Lord. Amen."

Aric looked up as Pastor Larson finished the time of prayer.

"We want to give a special welcome to all of the newcomers this morning. We're pleased that you chose to join us this morning. However, I would be remiss to leave it at that. Simply coming to church isn't enough. We're aware that some of you see church attendance as what some call fire insurance, because you're not sure whether or not hell exists. Well, in the Bible Jesus tells us that it is real, and that's enough for me to believe it. The only way to avoid an eternity in torment outside the presence of God is not just coming to church but coming to Jesus. *He* is the way, the truth, and the life everlasting. *No one* can come to the Father, God, except through Jesus Christ. And a repentant heart is essential if you want to find your name written in Christ's Book of Life." He continued with his call for repentance.

"Many today believe in a god who is only loving and would never send anyone to hell. They continue to live unrepentant lives thinking they can do whatever is right in their own eyes. Perhaps that's you. But the Bible speaks twice as much about God's wrath as it does about God's love. Plus, the Bible tells us in 1 John, chapter 5, how God defines love .. . *'For this is the love of God, that we keep His commandments.'*"

Aric sat there amazed. He had never seen Jess' dad so fired up. Fire and brimstone. He minced no words. Aric was reminded of messages from Jonathan Edwards, C.H. Spurgeon, and a host of other great preachers over history. A dozen-plus people got up and left, but Aric recalled that the same thing happened to Jesus, too.

The service lasted over 30 minutes longer than usual. Pastor Larson looked spent, but he turned no one away who came up to him afterwards.

Aric, too, needed to talk with him, but not about the service or the short message and alter call that came at the end. No, his need was more personal.

Jess came up and tugged on his arm. "C'mon, we need to head home for lunch so we can leave at a reasonable time to go back to St. Louis."

Aric felt torn. She was correct that they needed to drive back, and light snow was in the forecast, so delaying wasn't a good option. But he really needed to talk with her father. The events of the weekend had superseded his opportunities to approach him.

"Can you get a ride back with your mom or brother? I want to stay and help your dad, so he's not stuck here too long."

She gave him a curious look. "Um, okay. I guess so." She caught the eye of her mom and scurried off to join her.

Aric went back into the auditorium and was able to help by answering some general church questions from a few of those who lingered. Fifteen minutes later, Pastor Larson waved bye to the last of those with questions. He stepped over to Aric and put his hand on Aric's shoulder.

"Thanks for helping out, but we need to get home for lunch. You two have a drive ahead of you."

Aric nodded. "Um, I, uh . . . could we talk in your office first?"

Jess' dad furrowed his brow. "Something wrong?"

Aric shook his head. Together they walked to the pastor's office. They were alone, so Aric saw no need to shut the door.

"What's up?"

Aric stammered. "I, uh . . . I didn't think this would make me nervous, but, uh . . . I've never done this before."

Suddenly, her father's face lit up and a broad smile spread

across his face. "Of course you can."

"Huh?"

"You're about to ask me for Jess' hand in marriage, aren't you?"

Aric nodded. "Yes, sir, uh, do I have your blessing?"

Her father laughed. "Of course you do. Susan and I couldn't have arranged for a better son-in-law. Not that Jess would have agreed to an arranged marriage. Actually, we've been expecting this moment for months now." He extended his hand and then pulled Aric into a tight hug.

"Um, please don't say anything to Jess. I want to surprise her at Christmas time, and I'd like to arrange for you all to be there, as a surprise. I haven't worked out any details yet, but I'll sure keep you all posted."

Pastor Larson pinched his thumb and index finger together and zipped them across his closed lips.

"Thank you, Pastor Larson."

"Hey, you need to get used to calling me Tom."

Aric smiled. "I will, but not until she says yes. If I start calling you Tom now, she'll get suspicious."

Tom laughed. "That's for sure. C'mon, let's meet back at the house and eat."

As Aric walked toward his car, Lynch's words from two nights earlier echoed through his thoughts. Like the days of Noah, marrying and being given in marriage.

TWENTY-THREE

Adam had looked forward to the Thanksgiving holiday providing a break. He and Logan had been setting up new accounts non-stop since Logan came on board. The new income allowed Adam to hire office help, which Rachel helped oversee, but he and Logan remained the sole tech support. Not that he wanted to keep such a personal rein on their equipment; he simply hadn't had time to advertise for or interview additional qualified IT workers.

While the onslaught of new account requests had diminished since the article in America News First, they had not stopped. Word of mouth alone among Christian circles had kept the demand for their services at an elevated level. He offered a suite of security services that no one else did, and for websites that were frequently targeted by denial-of-service, ransomware, and other viral attacks—simply for being Christian—those services were invaluable. All indicators pointed to their getting caught up with new accounts and having a breather for the holiday weekend. And then came the bombing . . .

The conservative media had become so focused on the bombing incident itself that it had been blind to other behind-the-scenes "attacks" on Christian and conservative groups. Various "black hats" had taken advantage of the bombing to up the ante with increased actions against Christian organizations and websites. Likewise for various conservative sites, not least of which was the Graham campaign's website. Following the bombing, the site went down with a DoS attack. Soon to follow was the website for the Midwest Justice and Freedom Defense Alliance. And by Sunday evening dozens of churches, pro-life family services, and Christian schools had suffered attacks on their websites and other online accounts.

"Hey, thanks for the weekend off. I—" Logan's eyes widened at the log for new account requests. "What in the world?"

Adam gave him a wan smile. "Yeah, these all came in after the bombing. I didn't start on any of them because we both needed a break, and I figured folks would understand that it was a holiday weekend. But the phone started ringing non-stop at daybreak today. I called Carol in early to begin working through the calls. Rachel will help when she gets home from taking the kids to school." He extended the tablet in his hands toward Logan. "These two requests take top priority today." He handed the virtual "paperwork" to Logan.

The man's eyes widened again upon reviewing the info. "Wow. Okay. I know we have the hardware to handle the law firm, but will we be able to handle the load of a presidential campaign that's just taken on a full tank of rocket fuel?"

Adam shrugged. "Maybe not right away. I've already talked with their IT manager, and he understands our situation. Their current service provider has grown tired of the continual attacks on their system because of the campaign. So, they are de-platforming them, giving them until the end of the month to find a new home."

"That's only three days from now."

Adam nodded. "I know. We need to get as much of their site transferred here onto our servers as we can and get the site up and running. On their end, they've already started shutting down hardware and will be moving those resources here in two phases. I've also got more racks and servers on order. Between their hardware and ours, we just might be able to pull this off without a major disruption to our own system."

Logan's brow furrowed. "But what about the black hats doing the DoS attack? They'll just follow them to the new servers, *our* servers. With the attack already in play, our system could take a while a stop it."

Adam smiled. "Already took care of them."

"Huh?"

The two had been so busy with websites and servers that Adam had spent no time on UltraNet. Until two days ago. Had he been more active with his software, he might have uncovered the threat to President Graham earlier. The Deep State was doing everything it could think of to get rid of President Graham, but the assassination attempt was proverbial straw on the camel's back, even if it was proven that the Sidon administration or Deep State had nothing to do with it. That was not the case, however.

"Logan, software is where I excel. You haven't really seen that side of me yet. When it comes to DoS attacks, my software typically back traces the attack and warns off the attackers. 90% of the time they back off, surprised at being discovered. These guys pissed me off, so I took care of them."

What Adam wouldn't share with his new friend and employee, no matter how much they thought alike, was the origin or the extent of the attack. The less Logan knew on that front the better. The cyberattack on Graham's campaign had come from their own government. CISA—the Cybersecurity and Infrastructure Security Agency under the Department of

Homeland Security—was responsible for cybersecurity and infrastructure protection across all levels of government. Clearly, they saw their mandate as being not only defensive but offensive, and with the weaponization of federal law enforcement under the Sidon administration, domestic "threats" to their power appeared to take priority over actual foreign threats.

With a security clearance several levels above Top Secret while he worked under government contract to develop the PysOps program that became the original AlterNet, Adam had a better understanding of the CISA networks than most, possibly even better than some of the higher ups in CISA itself. He had just taken down a quarter, perhaps as much as a third, of CISA's systems. His virus could have taken out the entire network had they been like the corporate world where everything interconnected. But someone at CISA knew better and had wisely insisted that they compartmentalize their operations.

Still, Adam suspected that the powers-that-be were hopping mad, and no doubt someone at CISA was being called to task this morning for their failure to protect their own system. DHS would soon be looking for the perpetrator. The FBI would be looking for the perpetrator. Just as likely, the CIA would be looking for the perpetrator, despite their legal lack of authority to operate on U.S. soil.

Naturally, as a patriotic American, the perpetrator felt "obligated" to help them. So, his virus left behind just a tiny fragment of code to be discovered by their forensics team. Actually, it was a small piece of annotation used by a programmer to describe the code. And that note was in Mandarin.

Werner's day had been most unproductive. Distraction after distraction took his attention away from not only his personal business dealings but also those of the WOC. His life, like those of so many Germans, had always been focused on order, and he didn't like this feeling of disorder. It was if some cosmic force was acting to subvert his plans and disrupt his life . . . if, of course, he believed in cosmic forces.

Yet another knock on his office door interrupted his thoughts. Ilse's head popped through the doorway.

"Yes, Ilse, what do you have for me?"

"You asked me to look into the American media reporting about the bombing."

He nodded. "Yes, yes. What have you discovered?"

He had been assured by Zhèng Jian that their media would start coverage of the bombing that night. Here it was, two and a half days later, and Werner still could find no media coverage by their friends in the mainstream media.

His aide walked over to his desk and sat in one of the chairs in front of it.

"Mr. Zhèng can provide no clear reasons for the delay in media coverage. It was a holiday weekend, and his contacts were all out of town. Inexplicably, none could be reached by phone. In one case a critical cell tower was down for maintenance and nearby towers did not pick up the load. Another told him this morning that his phone had been accidentally turned off, and he hadn't noticed until today. Other calls would go to voice mail, but no recordings were found. He finally reached them today, but now they all question the wisdom of covering an incident that's over two days old. They don't want to look like they're simply late to the game, as Americans would say. They would rather make the people think they don't see the incident as newsworthy."

Werner couldn't believe what he was hearing. Not newsworthy? The conservative media—indeed, the rest of the world's media—was covering it. Conservatives were making great gains in the arena of public opinion. He suspected that very few in the country had not heard about it and that all would be wondering why the mainstream media wasn't covering it. The accusation of bias would echo across the globe, and the media would be on the wrong side of that one.

"That is a grave mistake. It is because of attitudes like this that the American people are turning away from our friends in the media. CNN itself is in financial trouble and will likely have to fire several of its on-air staff to remain solvent. Being seen as out of touch with reality will not help them. Tell them that I think they're making a mistake."

"Yes, sir. Anything else?"

He nodded. "Yes, let Dieter Fuchs know I want to see him."

"He was here an hour ago. I will track him down." She rose and left the office.

Werner tried to focus on business, but his mind kept wandering. Despite the level of control he exerted over much of global governance, he was not solely responsible for all decisions. He could only advise in many cases, and this was one of those cases. He stood from his desk and again stared out the window, as he had for much of the morning.

The intercom on his desk phone rang. He picked up the handset. *"Ja?"*

"Herr Fuchs ist da."

"Send him in."

Werner greeted the ex-commando and offered him

coffee, which the man readily accepted. But then, Werner had yet to meet an ex-soldier who would refuse coffee. Werner pointed to the sitting area at one end of his office, and together they sat down.

After taking a sip of the strong coffee, the man looked at Werner and said, "I think I have found her."

Werner raised his brow. "Well, that is certainly good news compared to last week."

Two weeks had passed since Yolina Zhdanov's disappearance. At that time, her passport had not been used to leave the country, and facial recognition software had not found her at any airports, train stations, bus terminals, car rentals, or border crossings. The search had broadened and continued.

His desk phone began to ring again. His secretary knew better than to disturb him. The phone kept ringing. He rose, walked to his desk, and picked it up. "*Ja!*"

"Sorry, sir." It was Ilse again. "I did not wish to disturb you, but Mr. Zhèng is on the line and says it's urgent. He is on line two."

What was the saying? When it rains, it pours. He connected to line two. "Jian, I am in an important meeting. What can't wait?"

"Sorry, Werner. I've learned that one of our cybersecurity teams decided to take advantage of the confusion surrounding the bombing to start a denial-of-service attack on Graham's campaign website?"

Werner motioned for Dieter to step outside the office. The man complied, taking his coffee with him.

As the door closed, Werner returned his focus to the call. "What? Under who's authority? First the assassination attempt and now attacking his campaign. They're making

Graham look like a martyr and your administration like a totalitarian regime bent on political persecution."

"I understand. We didn't authorize it, and I'm still trying to find out who did. But the news gets worse."

Werner sat down behind his desk. He really didn't want to hear that.

"Someone traced the DoS attack back to CISA, countered with a virus we've never encountered, and destroyed 32% of their systems. They have no idea how that could have happened, but the forensics team looking at the hard drives found a snippet of code in Mandarin. I cannot believe that the CCP is behind this."

Could it be? This counterattack carried all of the hallmarks of the attack on AlterNet2. "More likely he's stirring up muddy water and trying to pin the blame on the Chinese."

"He?"

Werner still had no proof, just that gut feeling that he was dealing with one man. "Figure of speech."

"Blaming the Chinese makes no sense. The CCP is on our side."

Zhèng should know. He helped coordinate plans between the Sidon administration and CCP to bring down the U.S. economy and remove it as the world's leading superpower.

"CISA assures me that they will find whoever is responsible. We will deal with them, or him, accordingly."

While that last comment might be true, Werner found the former one unlikely. Perhaps they were dealing with two different people or groups, but he didn't think so. And if his people hadn't been able to locate their prey, who at CISA would succeed in doing so? They weren't even able to stop the attack.

"Well, let me know when you do? I might like to meet someone so capable."

After disconnecting the call, Werner went to his door and invited Dieter back in. His own coffee had grown cold, so as he poured himself a new cup, he offered a refill to his hunter.

"So, you believe you have found her?"

"*Ja*. The initial facial recognition search did not pan out. I then expanded our search to neighboring countries in case she walked across a border somewhere. She would need transportation in the next country. Still no luck, so this morning I started to look through new video from the airport while my men began reviewing bus stops and train stations again. That's when I noticed a woman that caused confusion with the facial rec software. It could not focus on her face because she wore a wild abstract tunic that stopped the software from isolating her face for matching. She wore a hat and sunglasses, despite being a cloudy day, and her hair was short and blonde, not long and black."

"Using the date and time, we were able to determine when she went through security, and I retrieved a photo of her passport. It is her. She took a flight to London and will leave from Gatwick airport for Antigua in the Caribbean on Saturday."

"Can you get to her in London before she leaves?"

The man shook his head. "I do not know where she is staying there, and to snatch her from the airport could cause trouble for you. I do not think you want that."

Dieter was correct. Without the government's permission to detain her, he could face serious blowback, particularly should the conservative media get wind of it. To get the cooperation of the British government, they would want to know why, and he was not prepared to tell them.

What would he tell them? That she was working with him to find a hacker who had disrupted plans for an all-consuming surveillance program that they knew nothing about and that he didn't want them to know about? That she was a lover who had fled, and he wanted her bedroom videos before she could blackmail him? Based on the degree of infidelity shown on British television, they might understand the latter before the former.

"Have you determined where she is going to stay on the island?"

The ex-intelligence officer shook his head. "The major hotels won't reveal their guest lists or upcoming reservations. We're trying to find credit cards in her name to see if we can find a useful charge. But there are too many small inns, rooms for rent, and the like for us to trace quickly and many don't accept credit cards. So, I might not be able to use a card to track her. I might have to go there personally to find her."

Werner nodded. If he did not know and trust Dieter so well, he might have thought the man simply wanted a tropical vacation.

"Then, do it. And when you find her, convince her that I need her skills now more than ever and tell her she is forgiven. I will pay her double." He paused. "And if you can get her back here before the Christmas holiday, I will pay *you* double. But do not harm or threaten her. I need her computer skills, and I need her to come back willingly."

Yes, forgiveness was needed. Perhaps the CISA attack offered her a new starting point from which to work.

TWENTY-FOUR

AG McFarland had heard through various sources that the entire WOC hierarchy, more specifically Werner Koch, was not happy that the American mainstream media continued to ignore the bombing at the Four Seasons Hotel. The AG could only imagine their reactions to the attack on CISA. In fact, he had been stunned to learn of it. How could the country's elite cybersecurity infrastructure and the brightest minds in the field have been caught off-guard like that? Clearly, there was at least one mind brighter than all of them.

McFarland walked into the conference room adjacent to his office suite. Already seated were Lacey McGrath and Mark Wilkinson. The FBI Director, James Hufham, and CISA director, Jolene Lattimore, were huddled near the coffee and pastries that McFarland's secretary had hastily arranged for this last-minute meeting. The Secretary of DHS, Miguel Rodriguez Saucedo, was running late and had the director of the Secret Service, Elizabeth "Libby" Constantine, with him. Only the seven of them would participate in this meeting. No assistants. No secretaries taking minutes. No recordings. In fact, this meeting would never officially exist so no FOIA requests or lawsuits could ever reveal it.

The AG addressed the group. "Folks, let's get started. Miguel and Libby will be here any minute." The five sat down around the table. The AG fought to keep his emotions under control. He was angry and frustrated, but the people in the room weren't responsible, and he needed to remember that.

"Mark, what do you have from the National Security Division?"

The Assistant AG shrugged. "Still early, but from our angle the bombing isn't so much a national security issue as much as it's a domestic criminal case. The bombers are pretty much what the few news agencies reporting on it are saying, distraught activists for their causes. As Jim can attest to, they wrote a manifesto outlining their concerns and motives. It's really pretty cut and dried."

The FBI director nodded. "We have the manifesto. We have them on security video, and we found bomb making materials in one of their apartments. What we don't have yet is actual proof of them planting the bombs."

"Have you released any of this to the media?"

"No, sir. The right-wing media discovered their names from workers in the kitchen, followed up by talking with neighbors, and then scoured social media to put together profiles and such. They've actually done a pretty good job profiling."

The AG shook his head. "Yeah, well, don't tell them that. We need to keep everything close to the vest, downplay their activist roles. Try to find a twist that we can pin on Graham's people or supporters. Something like Graham supporters taunted them, attacked them on social media. We need to distance their ties to our side. Lacey?"

"Well, despite the obvious criminal action, I'm not sure this falls under our jurisdiction. I know that Jim has his agents handling the crime scene and assisting the metro police, but it seems this is more of a District of Columbia matter. Our violent crimes section is tied more to organized crime than something like this, and I don't think we want our capital case section handling it. Might send the wrong message." She paused. "The CISA case, on the other hand—"

McFarland cut her off. "We'll get to that when the others get here. The big thing is putting the right spin on the bombing case, if and when our media friends cover it."

At that moment, the Secretary of DHS and director of the Secret Service entered the room. Both grabbed a cup of coffee and sat down.

"Sorry we're late. Busy morning, as you might suspect," said Miguel Saucedo. "What have we missed?"

"We were talking about the bombing." The AG turned toward the USSS director. "What the . . ." McFarland remembered to be civil. "What happened, Libby? How in the world did you guys miss this?"

The Secret Service director sighed and wrung her hands as she shook her head. "Straight outta Hollywood. The bombers were screened and approved. We're still looking into that process, since their social media postings have come to light. They should have been flagged since they were rabidly anti-Graham. Anyway, they were on the approved list and allowed to work in the kitchen. The two agents assigned to the kitchen area were drugged—over-the-counter Benadryl in their coffee. Enough to put a horse to sleep. Everyone was so busy, no one noticed they were gone. Afterwards, they were found in a supply closet sleeping it off."

The AG wasn't alone in shaking his head in disbelief. "Lacey was saying this would be a DC case."

Libby shook her head. "No, we'll be referring this to the local U.S. attorney as a federal case. It was, after all, an attempted assassination of a former president and candidate for the office under USSS protection. Not to mention that two of our own were among the fatalities." She nodded her head toward her DHS boss. "We were talking on the way over. This could go to your Capital Case section, if for no other reason than public perception. The public would see the DOJ taking it seriously enough to consider it a death penalty level case, and yet, the District finally abolished the death penalty in 1992 in a referendum where it was two to one against capital punishment. You can look tough while knowing a death penalty will never happen."

Other details of the bombing and its aftermath were discussed. There was one thing, though, that the AG did not understand.

"So, Libby, why was Graham late? And don't tell me something like DC traffic."

She smirked. "No, not traffic. Would you believe his car wouldn't start?" She nodded. "Yeah, the car wouldn't start. Our agents had to bring in another car and that took about 15 minutes. Funny thing is right after the bombs went off, that first car started right up for the tow service. They didn't have to tow it in."

McFarland didn't know how to respond, so he moved to their second topic. "Okay, next item on the agenda."

All eyes turned toward Jolene Lattimore. She shrugged and frowned.

"What can I say? We have no idea how this happened. All we know is that a quarter of a million dollars' worth of hardware was fried. Even more valuable, however, was what was on those computers. It will take us months to rebuild."

"So much for your EINSTEIN intrusion software to protect you."

She nodded. "I have no excuses. It didn't and that, too, is

going to take time to inspect, line by line of code, to figure out why."

"What do you think happened?" asked the DHS boss. "We haven't had time to talk about this ourselves."

"The intrusion software looks for hackers coming from outside. All we can surmise at this time is that the virus traveled back on one of our own pings and EINSTEIN let it through thinking it was one of ours. Like our military air defense systems that identify our own drones and let them through, but act against anything they ID as an outside threat."

Jim Hufham asked, "What do you mean, one of your pings? Rumors at the bureau say you guys tried to take advantage of the bombing to kick Graham while he was down and launched a denial-of-service attack on his campaign."

The CISA director frowned. "I wouldn't say 'you guys.' It wasn't an authorized action, and they certainly didn't have *my* approval. Miguel and I still need to discuss appropriate disciplinary actions against the three who did that. Their excuse was that they thought the bombing would trigger a wave of sympathy for Graham and a major uptick in donations to his campaign, which they hoped to stop. They were correct about that. His online donations have skyrocketed since the DoS attack was stopped and his campaign went back online."

Jim did not look mollified. The AG couldn't say that he was either, but he was happy to let his FBI director take point.

"Yeah, too bad Graham's campaign won't pay to replace all that hardware." The sarcasm was clear.

Jolene's brow furrowed, and her eyes glared at Jim. "Yeah, well, to my people's benefit, there was no way they could have anticipated what happened. Oh, and by the way, one of those guys used to be one of *your* guys. Guess you didn't train him well enough either."

Despite his own emotions, the AG saw that this was becoming counterproductive. "Okay, look, we need to deal with it. Jolene, do you have any idea who did this? Do you have a way to track him, her, or them down?"

She shook her head. "No idea and no way to track. At least, not that we've discovered. There was one bit of code that our forensics team found on a hard drive. It points to China, but that makes no sense. Whoever it was appears to have acted in Graham's favor, and our friends at the CCP wouldn't do that."

"What about Iran?"

She shrugged. "Maybe, but I can't see them acting on Graham's behalf."

"No," said McFarland. "But I can see them wanting to attack CISA and blame it on someone else. Maybe they were just waiting for CISA to go after Graham and saw an opportunity."

"Fair point," replied Miguel. "We can look into that. All I can say is I'm glad our systems are compartmentalized. That virus could have wiped out CISA entirely."

"Which would have pleased the ayatollah no end."

Lacey spoke up. "One way or the other, our Computer Crime section will work with you on this. However, tell me, why don't you think someone directly on Graham's team could have done this?"

Jolene shook her head yet one more time. "No way, we've looked at the personnel on his team. None of them have the education or skill sets needed to pull that off. A state-sponsored hacker remains at the top of our list."

By the end of the day, Adam and Logan had succeeded in re-establishing the MJFDA website and about half of the Graham campaign's site. Adam had focused on the donation features as that was considered the most critical feature, even above the ability for volunteers to sign up. His main worry was that the credit card processor would turn off that spigot. He had seen several conservative causes denied credit card processing. In fact, the MJFDA had been one of them. The resultant lawsuit had put fear into the hearts of such companies, but Adam had little doubt that they would become emboldened again.

As dinnertime approached, Adam hoped Logan might stick around for a meal and a little work afterwards.

"Hey, if you're available, would you want to join us for dinner?"

Logan laughed. "Why do I sense there's more to that invitation than just sharing a meal?"

"Touché. You've gotten to know me too well over these past couple of weeks. I was hoping to put another hour in after eating to get a couple more websites transferred."

Logan smiled. "On any other day, I might say yes, but tonight I actually have dinner plans. Speaking of which, it's later than I thought. I need to get going."

Adam nodded. "Okay. See you in the morning."

"Hey, before I leave. Were you serious about frying the hardware of those hackers?"

Adam now questioned his having said that earlier. He realized he said it in what some would call the heat of the moment. Perhaps he should have been more discreet. After all, he'd only known Logan for a few weeks. Although he had discovered that they shared similar thoughts about many topics, including politics, he should have handled this one differently. He hoped his disclosure wouldn't come back to bite him.

"Why? Does that idea bother you?"

"To be honest, I'm not sure. It is, after all, the destruction of someone else's property even if that someone was acting criminally. I'm not sure how to look at this biblically."

"Well, I look at it this way. In Deuteronomy, Moses said that if person A is found to be giving false witness against Person B, then what Person A wanted to do to Person B would be done to him instead. So, if hackers are caught depriving someone of their ability to raise capital, then they should be made unable to raise capital. That's in essence what I did."

Logan looked thoughtful. "Okay, I'll look that up and think about it. So, just *how* did you do that? I've never heard of anyone else being able to do that."

Adam paused to consider his response. "I think that might be a topic for a different day. In the meantime, please keep that confidential. I mean it. Mum's the word. I used to have to deal with some seriously bad people, and if that were to become known by the wrong people, it could endanger me and my family. I'm trusting you."

TWENTY-FIVE

Aric's emotions were torn. He should be happy, nervous, and at times giddy as he prepared for the surprise engagement party. And yet, after dropping off Jess for one of her last finals of the semester and heading toward the jeweler's, the news reported another bombing.

The 26-year-old Christian social media influencer was well-known for her strong position against abortion and so-called reproduction rights. Reproduction rights—the latest oxymoron of the progressives, where the "reproduction"—a baby— had no rights, but others claimed the right to kill the "reproduction." The woman, along with her four-month-old daughter, had fallen victim to a car bomb right outside their home and the incident was witnessed by her husband and several neighbors. She had just backed out of their garage and stopped at the curb to check for traffic when a man wearing a balaclava ran up, tossed something under the car, and started to run away. A moment later, the car blew up to the horror of her husband. The explosion knocked the killer to the ground, which gave two neighbors the opportunity to subdue him for police. A second explosive device was found in the man's car after it had been identified and located.

The man was later identified as an illegal alien from Venezuela who had been flown into the U.S. on a flight chartered by the Sidon administration under some sort of amnesty program. The man had been processed in the Darién gap between Panama and Colombia by NGOs raking in millions of taxpayer dollars. He had been arrested three times since his arrival into the U.S.—twice on felony charges—and released without bail by progressive district attorneys. As with the Graham event bombing, the mainstream media had yet to report on this incident or the individual.

Aric's heart ached for the family. They had been in his prayers repeatedly since the news broke on conservative media.

Yet, what he had to push out of his mind was the recollection of Lynch telling him that pink-hair Toni had become more aggressive on campus in Kenosha and wondering if the guy could ever become so unhinged as to do something like this illegal alien. Was Toni's visit to UMSL a precursor to something worse? He refused to dwell on that idea and chose to trust in God instead. Even should something happen to him, he knew he was in God's hands and did not fear death. It was Paul who had written in Philippians that *"For me to live is Christ, and to die is gain."* Aric, as well as Jess, fully understood that sentiment.

Aric resisted the urge to speed, but he had an appointment at Mama's on The Hill where his family, her family, and various friends would collect to celebrate her saying "yes." His parents were footing the bill for Mama's private room, but he needed to confirm the menu and numbers.

He parked about a block away and walked to the restaurant. Once inside, he approached the hostess.

"Hi, I'm Aric Afton. I'm here to confirm plans for an engagement party Friday night."

"Sure. Let me get the manager."

The aroma of authentic Italian food wafted throughout the restaurant. Aric had missed lunch because of his tight schedule while Jess took her exam. He wondered what he might be able to get to go, but then thought better of it. Jess' acute sense of smell would no doubt detect it in his car when he picked her up.

"Hi, Aric. I'm Marc Campisi. Let me show you the room, and then we can review the menu."

Aric followed him to a side room. It wasn't anything fancy but seemed quaintly Italian. He glanced about. It would handle the 40 or so people expected to attend, and the food would definitely make up for any deficiencies some might find in the setting.

"This'll work." He grinned. "And I'm getting hungry already just from the aromas from the kitchen."

The manager smiled. "Great. Here's the menu."

"What do you typically do for a buffet for 40 to 45 people?"

"Usually, our house salad and homemade dressing, three or four different classic pasta dishes, garlic cheese bread, a dessert, and, of course, our famous original toasted ravioli."

Aric laughed inside. He knew all about the three claims to inventing toasted ravioli, of which Mama's was one. It didn't matter. He loved that St. Louis classic. He wondered if he might get "lunch" by tasting some samples.

"Is it possible to sample some of the pastas?"

"Sure is. Be right back."

Aric wanted to pump his fist in the air and scream "Yes!" but held back. A few minutes later, the manager was back with a plate of several pasta dishes . . . and two toasted raviolis. It didn't take long for Aric to satisfy his hunger. "Ummmm. Those are delicious. Let's do lasagna, fettuccine

Alfredo, pasta con broccoli, and tortellini ala Pappa . . . and your tiramisu for the dessert."

"Sounds good. We can also put out a couple types of pizza. Adding that simply reduces the amount of pasta we put out by a bit."

Aric nodded. They settled on two types of pizza and beverages.

"That about settles it. All we need now is the deposit. That would be $600."

Aric had anticipated that and had his mom's credit card. "My folks are footing the bill, so here's their credit card, if that's okay."

The man nodded. After confirming the billing address, the charge was placed, and Aric was on his way. One last stop. The most important one, and he barely had enough time to complete it before needing to pick up Jess on the Wash U campus. He prayed there would be no complications.

Despite accusations on occasion about being a typical, college-aged male, at the point when he began to seriously see Jessica as his future spouse, he also started to take notes. Mental notes, but notes nonetheless. Comments she would make about this person's ring or that woman's jewelry registered in his brain. He hadn't forgotten. Early in the semester, he had managed to get hold of one of her rings to get the right size. Then, when he went to a jeweler highly recommended by several people whose opinions he trusted and valued, he described her likes and dislikes. The week after Thanksgiving, they had emailed him with a final design. And now it was ready.

He entered the small jeweler's shop on time for his appointment. "Hi. Aric Afton. I have an appointment."

"Right on time. Let me go get it."

Aric watched as the man retrieved the ring from his vault. Back at the display case, the jeweler opened the small box, and Aric gasped.

"It-it's beautiful. She's gonna love it." The set included white, rose, and yellow gold with a central one-and-a-half carat diamond flanked by two smaller stones. The design was sleek in its simplicity and highlighted the stones.

"I've created a lot of rings in 30-plus years, but I think that's become one of my own favorites. So few people ever include rose gold. This one was fun to create." The man repackaged the ring and handed it to his assistant who tied a ribbon around the box and placed it in a bag for Aric.

Aric followed the man to the register and pulled out his own credit card. He had cleared his account and knew he had more than enough in his credit line to make the purchase.

The man ran the card through the machine and frowned. He tried again. "Uh, this is unusual."

Aric grew concerned. "What's wrong? I just paid the account off two days ago. There should be enough credit."

"It says this card is no longer valid."

TWENTY-SIX

Yolina stood on the desolate beach braving the polar winds and looking out to the Baltic Sea. The seaside resort town of Heringsdorf, one of the three resort towns of Germany's Kaiserbäd, was largely closed for the season. True, the large hotels remained open year-round, but few of even the heartiest of souls wanted to brave the beach with temperatures just above freezing and wind chills of 21°F from the 20-knot winds from the north. And that was on a relatively calm day. Still, compared to Siberia at this time of year, Yolina thought it quite tolerable.

She scanned the horizon to the northeast, along the Polish coast. Sergei had promised to find transportation back to Russia that would not require her passport. She checked her phone. It was time.

Yolina had worked her way north from Munich by hitchhiking. She knew better than to use public transportation, which would expose her to widespread security cameras and facial recognition. She also knew to make her travel unpredictable and her hours outdoors irregular. As such, she required over three weeks to reach her destination. Using cash for cheap rooms and meager food along the way, she had managed to make it to Germany's northeast coast undetected by those she suspected were hunting her.

She checked the time on her phone again. She scanned the sea, getting anxious that she'd be stuck in Germany. Any attempt to cross over into Poland would require the use of her passport, and that would alert Koch to her whereabouts. She and Sergei had decided that her chances were best to get to Kaliningrad, a Russian state nestled between Poland and Lithuania. Although separated from the rest of the country by Lithuania and Belarus, she would be able to fly directly to Moscow without alerting Koch's people.

Was that the boat? A small speck of dark against the gray skies had appeared. Fifteen minutes later, its outline was clear and getting bigger. A series of light flashes from the bow confirmed it was Sergei.

Yolina walked cautiously toward the Heringsdorf Pier, which at 508 meters was the longest in Germany. At the end of the main pier sat a tall, glass pyramidal structure that housed a restaurant, but just beyond that the pier stepped down to water level and provided a place for boats to tie up while their owners ate or shopped. This was where she was to meet Sergei. Her caution was rooted in the extensive use of security cameras around and on the structure. Fortunately, the wind and temperature justified her being bundled up with head and face covered.

She eased along the pier, pretending to take photos with her phone. By the restaurant, she made a point to keep looking seaward and away from the cameras. She circled the building twice before noticing that the boat was almost to the pier. She hurried past the eatery, down the stairs, and onto the dock. A few minutes later, the boat sidled up to the dock and Sergei emerged from the enclosure, smiling. He extended his hand to her and helped her jump aboard.

With her belongings safely stashed away and the two of

them secure inside the enclosure, the captain of the vessel pulled away from the dock and throttled up. However, instead of heading back along the way she saw them approaching, he headed north-northeast into the open waters.

"привет, котик. Я скучал по твоей улыбке."

She had missed his smile, too. She hugged him tightly before easing into a full-mouthed kiss.

"How was your travel?"

She explained in fair detail how she traveled from rural town to rural town, sometimes in farm trucks but mostly in private vehicles. Her benefactors had been courteous and more than happy to assist a struggling student hoping to surprise her family for the holidays.

"No problems? You were not followed?"

"No, I do not think so. They would have taken me before now if that were so. If my plan has gone as I hoped, the WOC thugs are trying to find me in sunny Antigua right now."

She had chosen Antigua because it had direct flights from London. She had used such a flight in the past to transfer to St. Kitts and then Nevis to set up her account there. However, with three times the population of St. Kitts, Antigua offered a better chance for her "friend" to disappear in the tourist scene.

"What? The Caribbean? How did you do that?"

I met a young woman at the takeaway restaurant I frequented. We could have been twins except for her short blonde hair. In fact, a few people who saw us together asked if we were sisters. I saw her as a possible decoy if I ever needed one and befriended her. After you told me I had been fooled, I knew I needed help to get away, so I told her that I could get her a free trip to Antigua, except meals, but I would need her passport and a credit card to make it happen. It took some convincing, but I succeeded. I prepaid her flights to and from London and the island and a week of lodging there." She wrapped her arms around her chest. "After standing out on the beach for almost an hour, I wish we could change places. Do you think she would have taken me up on a free trip to Kaliningrad?"

Sergei laughed as he shook his head. "Not if she had a brain in her head."

As she glanced outside, she saw that they were already almost out of sight of land. "Where are we headed? I thought the boat would stick closer to shore."

"Ah, yes, well, this is a Polish charter. A friend of a friend you might say. I am making it worth his while. He is taking us to a Russian trawler based in Kaliningrad, where we will join the crew heading back to port. He will then return to his home port of Ustka. A trawler might not sound comfortable, but this one is, you might say, specially outfitted, different from most fishing boats. It will be much easier on us both for the almost 450-kilometer trip."

Yolina smiled. She could not imagine traveling nearly 300 miles on the Baltic, in December, on the boat she now sat in. A storm could rush in within hours, and this was not the vessel she would want to be on should that occur. Yet, she now wondered what Sergei meant by "specially outfitted." Antigua definitely sounded better.

TWENTY-SEVEN

Aric looked at the jeweler. He wasn't quite sure what to say. His charge for the down payment had gone through without an issue, and he had already paid off that balance.

"I, uh, I don't know what's going on. Your charge for my down payment came through, right? And I personally went into my bank two days ago to pay off the balance. I wanted to make sure there'd be no hiccups in making this purchase."

The jeweler nodded. "Yes, your down payment went through without a hitch. Perhaps you should call the company."

Aric couldn't quite think straight. In so many ways this was the biggest purchase of his life, and until now, all of his plans were coming together as well as he could expect. How could he propose without the ring?

"Yeah. Thank you. I should have thought of that. Give me a minute."

He stepped away from the counter and walked to the front of the store where he dialed the 800-number on the back of his card.

"Bank services. How can I direct your call?"

"Um, hi. Yeah, I'm trying to use my card to buy an engagement ring, and you folks are denying the charge. My balance is paid in full, so I know I have enough credit in my credit line. I'm—"

"One moment please."

The last thing Aric needed at the moment was their Muzak. He worked on being patient while on hold.

"Fraud and card security department. This is Angela. With whom am I talking?"

Aric introduced himself, answered the requisite security questions to validate that he was who he said he was, and then explained the issue.

"Oh, I am so sorry. That's an important purchase."

"It sure is. One that I only plan on making once in my lifetime."

"Give me a minute to check your account."

Back came the Muzak. Aric sighed as he listened to *"raindrops are falling on my head . . ."* for the third time.

"Okay. Mr. Afton, are you still there?"

"Yes."

"It appears you called in to report your card as being lost or stolen. This card number was deactivated, and a new card has been issued. You should get the new card within a week or so."

"I never called about such a thing. My card wasn't lost or stolen. I . . ."

"Again, I am soooo sorry, but we can't reverse this action. The new card has been issued. Is there someone else with access to your card? Perhaps they thought it got lost or was stolen."

Aric shook his head as he replied, "No one else. Not even my girlfriend at this point."

"Well, sounds like that'll change soon."

Aric couldn't help but laugh. He could practically see Angela grinning. "You are probably right about that."

The woman laughed. "No 'probably' about it." She paused. "As I said, the new card has already been issued, and you should have it in a week or less."

Aric realized there was little he could do about it now. He thanked Angela and disconnected the call. Returning to the jeweler, he explained what he had been told.

The man shook his head. "I've heard of being swatted before, but I've not heard of someone calling in a fake lost credit card report before. When is the big day again?"

"My last final is tomorrow, Thursday, and hers is Friday morning. So, we plan on celebrating Friday, and that's when I want to surprise her."

For some reason, pink-hair Toni's image flit into Aric's mind as the man compared this situation to being swatted. But the guy never had access to his credit card info, had he?

"Hmmm. Doubt the new card will arrive tomorrow, and that would be cutting things close if you have a final tomorrow."

Aric had one choice. He pulled out his mom's card. She wouldn't care, would she? He could Zelle the money into her account that afternoon. "This is my mom's card. I just used it without trouble at Mama's on the Hill. Under the circumstances, I don't think she'll mind."

With that tragedy avoided and the purchase made, he realized he was running late. He ran to the car, stashed the ring box in his backpack, and hurried to pick up Jess.

After over two weeks of 12-hour days, Adam saw light at the end of the tunnel that he felt he'd been buried in. Once again, he and Logan—a pair of like-minded workaholics—had pulled through. The crush of new accounts was behind them as the day neared its end.

"Wanna beer?" asked Adam.

Logan shook his head. "Thanks, but not a beer drinker. Now, a glass of Chardonnay or Riesling and you have a taker." He smiled.

"We can do that, too. Take your pick."

"A nice Riesling would be great."

"C'mon over to the house."

The pair left the server building and walked the 50-plus yards to Adam's home. Adam ushered him into their den. "Have a seat, and I'll be right back."

He hurried to the basement where he stored a selection of Missouri, Ohio, and California wines. He rummaged through the whites in their small wine fridge but found no Riesling or Chardonnay. Then he recalled opening the last bottle or Riesling over the Thanksgiving holiday. He grabbed a few bottles of white wine and walked back upstairs to find Logan playing GraviTrax with his son, Arthur.

Adam smiled. "Looks like he roped you into his favorite pastime."

"Are you kidding? This is an amazing toy. Great for STEM education."

Adam smiled. He couldn't argue with that assessment. "Regarding wine, guess I spoke too soon. Don't have either one. We've got some local whites. Steinberg White from Stone Hill Winery. Chardonel from Adam Puchta Winery. Vignoles from Hermannhof. Oh, and a Trebbiano from my favorite Wisconsin winery, Spirits of Norway."

Logan looked contemplative for a moment. "Well, I've tried the locals before, so how about the Trebbiano?"

"Don't think you'll be disappointed, Trebbiano is the number one white table wine in Italy."

Adam decided against a beer and poured himself a glass of Trebbiano as well. He handed Logan his wine tumbler and sat down. Logan peeled himself away from the table holding Arthur's latest marble run and sat across from Adam.

"So, I have another question for you. How in the world are you able to afford all of this—the house, the property, the servers, fiberoptic connections? All of it. Every ISP I've ever encountered was covered by investors. You don't seem to have anyone looking over your shoulder."

Adam was actually surprised that it had taken this long for Logan to ask. His company certainly was an anomaly for the industry. And yet, he still wondered how much he could entrust to Logan. Perhaps it was time. This much he could divulge.

"Among my first programming jobs was an ultra-top-secret project to be used in Afghanistan. Heavy on PsyOps. The company who developed it for the military managed to snag all rights to it afterward, and my job continued with them. They paid very, very well, and I invested in real estate in Maryland and northern Virginia, since we were based in DC."

Did he want to leave it at that? No, his new friend needed to understand that there was more to the story.

"Then, one day I was at the park with our kids. Our daughter, Carolyn, whom you've met as Grace, was kidnapped. It destroyed me. She was gone, on my watch. I used alcohol to cope and became an alcoholic. It destroyed our marriage, but I never gave up looking for Carolyn."

"But you're drinking wine. If you were an alcoholic, should you be doing that?"

Adam smiled. "Ah, that's part of what God has done in my life. He removed that addiction from me. Totally. I know better than to overdo it, but a glass or two, or a beer or two, on occasion doesn't entice me at all. I do steer clear of the hard stuff though."

He took a sip. He knew other Christians who had once been alcoholics but now totally abstained—even communion wine. He would never drink around them because he would never want one of them to stumble, to fall back into that addiction. For him, God had truly worked a miracle. It helped that the cause for his drinking, the loss of Carolyn, had also been restored back to him, to them. God really was a miracle worker.

"Back to the story. I never gave up on Carolyn. It drove me to develop software that could help me track missing kids online." That much was true, but understated what UltraNet could do by a zillion miles. "Since I had no family to keep me busy, I also learned to invest in the stock market, to trade options, and select stocks to short. Again, I put my talent to software that helped me analyze companies for this, and it paid off very well. I ultimately sold my properties in the east for very handsome gains, which I ultimately put into this property."

"But what about your daughter. Obviously, you found her."

Adam nodded. "My software led to the discovery of a child trafficking ring. The FBI got involved, and the ring was taken down. It ended up that a man involved in that, well, he and his wife were childless and took a fancy to Carolyn. They took her in as their own and renamed her Grace. She was one when she was kidnapped and five when I found her. That trafficking ring was involved in some truly horrible things with those kids, but she was spared from all of that, through God's grace. And it was His grace that led me to her, and finally to Him. So, we kept the name she had grown up with."

"Wow. I will never look at her the same way after this. She

is a walking miracle. Where is she, by the way?"

"At dance class. Rachel should be home with her within the hour."

Logan appeared to be scrutinizing him. "So, do you think you could teach me what you know about the stock market and your software?"

Adam smiled. "Sure. I might have to update the software a bit, but, here, let me show you."

He grabbed the laptop he had brought in with him from the server building, opened it, and called up that program. He was glad he had developed it separately from UltraNet. The program tried to log into one of his brokerage accounts, an account he didn't mind showing to Logan, but failed. He tried again and failed.

"That's weird. I had no trouble with it last week."

He went directly to the brokerage house's website and tried to log in. No luck. He became concerned. He still had over three million dollars spread across several accounts with that firm and would need to access some of that soon.

"Give me a minute." He walked into his study and called customer service at the brokerage. As soon as he connected with a representative and explained his situation, the rep passed him off to a supervisor, who passed him on to yet a higher-level manager. Now, Adam's concern elevated.

"Hi, Ms. Reardon, this is Adam Afton, account 2232-9992-98-1. I'm having trouble accessing that account as well as my other accounts there."

"Yes, Mr. Afton." Her tone was curt. "I'm sorry, but you have been determined to be a high-risk customer, and your account has been closed. You have thirty days to find a new firm where we can transfer your—"

Adam's anger flared. This was uncalled for. Were they

truly willing to lose the millions of dollars they held for him there?

"Were you intending to notify me or is this how I was to find out? You do realize how large my account is there."

But then a new thought struck him. A British politician involved in Brexit had been debanked, his funds frozen and no other bank willing to take him on because of his politics. The public uproar over this made it to conservative members of parliament who took up his cause and got the decision rescinded. The MJFDA had had something similar happen to them when their credit card processing company closed their account, leaving them unable to take credit cards for donations. Public pressure and a lawsuit quickly reversed that decision, too.

The MJFDA had just moved their website and donation page to his servers. Was this a renewed attack on them through him? But then, the Graham campaign had also just moved to his servers. Was this an attack on it? Or was this a direct attack on him personally because of his willingness to support conservative, Christian groups? Perhaps all of the above.

"Yes, Mr. Afton, we're aware of what's in your accounts. Again, please find a new brokerage, so we can expedite the transfer of your funds and stock positions."

"And there is no appeal process I take it."

"Not on this."

"Then please be advised that a lawsuit will follow soon and understand that my ability to expose this to the public may very well cost you more than my accounts. Have a great week." He hung up before hearing a response.

Adam felt like throwing the phone across the room but knew that would only cost him a phone. He allowed his anger to subside before looking up a number in his business contacts—his contact person at MJFDA. It was after hours, so he left a detailed message and hoped for a quick response.

"Wow, Logan, you are not going to believe this." He went on to explain the situation to the man. "Good thing, my business accounts have money in them and a steady stream of income now."

Logan looked concerned. "Do they? You'd better check them as well."

TWENTY-EIGHT

Yolina climbed aboard the trawler with assistance from a crew member. No sooner had she and Sergei found their sea legs on deck, the smaller boat raced away toward what she assumed would be the Polish coast. She had lost her bearings with respect to the compass while on that boat. The sun's position low on the horizon didn't help her though she knew it to be midday.

A second crew member grabbed her gear, led her below deck, and ushered them to a small cabin with two berths positioned like built-in bunk beds. She looked about. The room appeared as if it had been hurriedly cleaned for a female guest. Overall, however, she saw that she would have no issue with staying there for the next day or two.

The crew member looked at them. "The head is to port, the left, at the stern of the boat. There is no separate head for women, so you will need use care if you want privacy. The galley is to the starboard, right, second door down. The cook will serve dinner in four hours, but coffee and fruit are available all day. The captain wishes to see you after you are settled in and available. He is above in the pilothouse. Only after you see him are you allowed into other parts of the boat. You will be watched until he gives you clearance." He pointed to a camera in the ceiling of the passageway outside the cabin. Turning back to them, he tipped his hat and left the room.

"Bottom bunk," she said to Sergei.

"I was hoping we could share," he replied as he wrapped his arms around her.

She giggled and shook her head. "Not if we're being watched." She pointed to the camera in the passageway. She kissed him on the cheek and pulled away. "We'll have time for that when we get back home. Right now, I'd like you to escort me to the head and guard the door."

He nodded and led the way aft toward the stern of the vessel. After he made sure the head was empty, she entered, relieved her bladder, and led him back to their room. She thought it odd that while she smelled the distinctive odor of diesel fuel, there was no stench of fish. She thought for sure she had seen a partially opened hatch up top on deck with fish on ice visible. But then, she also noted that the fishing nets hanging on each side of the boat appeared dry. Sergei had said that this boat was specially outfitted. She began to have thoughts as to what that might entail.

"I'd like to take a short nap. It's been a long day already for me," said Sergei. "Should we visit with the captain now or after my nap?"

"Now. If you start snoring, I want to be able to escape to someplace quiet, and the galley might not be far enough away." She laughed and poked him in the ribs.

He looked offended. "What? Snoring? I don't snore."

"Yeah, and foghorns sound like a toy horn on a child's bicycle."

They bundled up and climbed the stairs, er, ladder—she needed to remember her nautical terms—to find the pilothouse. Two men were there. She assumed the one looking at the weather radar to be the captain. He turned upon their entering his space.

"Welcome aboard. Sorry I couldn't be there to greet you

at first. We have a weather front moving in and I've been trying to lay our best course to avoid the worst of it while you're with us."

"*Спасибо*, sir," said Sergei.

"Yes, thank you, Captain."

"This is Yolina." He looked at her. "I've known Captain Vasilyev for several years. I served with him before joining Pozitiv."

Yolina raised her brow. Sergei had only hinted at his previous work, but she was pretty good at deducing what those hints meant. "Oh? So, this is—"

The captain nodded. "You both have full clearance, so yes, I can say that we are not a real fishing vessel. We fish for and catch information." He grinned. "You could say that we are a *spy ship*, to use the terms of a novel or the movies." He laughed. "It is not so glamorous or intriguing as the movies make it out to be. It is often boring, and quite dangerous when a storm appears out of nowhere. But we live in a dangerous world, and our government must stay informed of what our neighbors are doing."

Yolina understood. She faced a specific danger, and now that she was safely out of German territory, she needed to deal with that. By now, her "decoy" was back in London, if not home in Munich. As such, she could only presume that her ruse had been uncovered. She had determined that her homeland would be the safest place for her. Werner Koch and the WOC were not welcome in Russia, although she held no illusions that they had no agents there. Still, to make sure no such agents paid her a visit, she had decided to deploy her insurance policy.

"If you wish to see the life of a typical *spy . . .*" Again, he used the term laughingly. ". . . use the door marked engine room. It will take you to our communications center. You might find it quite interesting in your line of work."

"*Спасибо*, Captain."

"Good to see you again, Sergei. You can show her how we do things. Perhaps we could then recruit her to join us." He smiled.

The duo returned to their assigned cabin. "Now for my nap."

"Now to explore this boat." Yolina smiled.

She stopped first in the galley and found a clean mug and the coffee maker. With that in hand, she headed toward the "engine room." Inside she discovered a suite of electronics gear that made her usual computer console look like a first run Apple II, which, of course, she'd only seen in pictures. She hadn't even been born when that early computer was popular.

"Ah, our guest," said one of the three men manning their various stations. "I am Nikolai. That is Valentin, and that is Artem." The others nodded in greeting and turned their attentions back to their work. "So, where is our old friend, Sergei?"

"He needed a nap."

Artem laughed. "And you need to escape his snoring, *da*?" The others laughed with him.

Yolina laughed as well. "So, you all know him." Again, they nodded.

Nikolai pointed to the various stations. "I am monitoring the internet right now. Over there, Artem is gathering microwave and radio communications, and Mikhail is working on cable transmissions."

"Cable?"

"Yes, we have taps into several undersea cable lines here

in the Baltic."

Yolina could only envision how that might be done, but she did not ask for details. She had no need to know.

"You wouldn't happen to have a secure internet access I could use for a minute, would you?"

Nikolai nodded. "Sure, use that terminal over there." He pointed to a monitor and keyboard to her left.

"*Спасибо*." She sat down in a nearby chair and scooted it up to the terminal. She signed into a remote server that took her to a secure—and secret—internet mail app. From there she called up a specific contact and sent a message. She smiled upon receiving confirmation that her message had been read. *One small package on its way*, she thought.

She also checked for new messages sent to her. Nothing. Her hacker friends expected her to still be in the employ of Werner Koch and tied up with that project. She reached out to one friend. *Back online. What's new?*

The response was fast. *CISA attacked. A third of their systems taken out. Otherwise, same old same old. Welcome back.*

That news took her by surprise. She wondered if the men on this boat knew about it.

"Nikolai, do you know anything about an attack on the American's CISA?"

He nodded but continued to watch his monitor. "You won't find anything on the web or in the media about it. The *Amerikantsy* think they're keeping it secret, but I'd be surprised to find any major intelligence agency that hasn't heard about it."

"What happened?"

"Word is they launched a DoS attack on the campaign of their current president's opponent right after someone detonated some bombs at a campaign dinner."

"What? A bomb?" She had been out of touch for much too long.

He nodded again. "Word is also that someone used their own DoS attack to send them a virus that totally wiped out a third of their systems. How they could do that, I have no idea. Maybe you can understand how such was done."

She didn't. Not yet anyway. But what caught her attention was how the attack was accomplished . . . just like AlterNet2 had been destroyed. The person she hunted for Werner Koch just became much more interesting to her.

Werner had rested easier knowing that Dieter was on the trail of Yolina. He would not fail to find the woman.

Yet, one thing puzzled him. Dieter had "avoided" a trip to sunny Antigua after discovering that the woman had already booked a return flight to London. Why would Yolina return? He could understand Dieter not wanting to go to the island. Trying to find one woman on a tropical island with a population of 96,000 and four times that many tourists trying to escape winter weather would be a longshot at best. He would have had no time to enjoy the sun and beach and was likely to be unsuccessful in his quest. But Yolina? Why return to London when she could fly to any number of American cities from which she could escape to anywhere in the world?

One possibility bothered him. Perhaps she felt no need to escape because she did not fear him. And there was only one reason she would not fear him. She had "insurance."

As he paced in front of the windows, his private phone rang. Caller ID showed it to be Dieter.

"Yes."

"I just intercepted the woman at Gatwick Airport."

"And?"

"It is not her. She could be her twin, but it is not her."

Werner's knees buckled, and he hurriedly sat down at his desk. "How?"

"I showed her a photo of Yolina, and she admitted that they had met in Munich. It was Yolina who arranged the free trip to Antigua. Yolina told her that she'd won the trip through work but for family health reasons, she couldn't go."

"Anything else? Anything helpful?"

"Nothing. I am sorry, Herr Koch. Even as she entered the baggage area, I was convinced it was Yolina."

Werner sighed. "I understand. Come home. We need to regroup and perhaps start again."

He disconnected the call and stood to resume his pacing. Werner could not blame Dieter. He, too, had fallen into the assumption that Yolina had a false passport. The woman was possibly an FSB asset, so why wouldn't she have one? The resemblance in the two women's photos was uncanny, and that had worked to confirm the false passport premise.

Still, this threw everything up in the air. His earlier deduction seemed wrong now. She clearly did fear him, so much so that she set up a carefully arranged ploy to throw him off her trail. Did that mean she did *not* have "insurance?" Why go to such effort? And yet, her leaving behind the stealth camera in the apartment's bedroom seemed intended to send him a message. And worse, if she was an FSB asset, was there more to her seduction than met the eye? This latter question was the most troubling for him.

His desk phone rang.

"Sir, there's a courier here with a package for you. He says he's not to deliver to anyone else but only to you personally."

Werner huffed. He did not want to be bothered by such mundane things. "Tell him I said you could accept it."

After a moment, his secretary replied. "I did, sir. He's insistent that it's for your eyes only. That's the phrase he used—your eyes only."

Werner remained miffed, but his curiosity was aroused. "Very well."

He walked to his office door, opened it, and identified himself to the courier.

"May I see some ID, please?"

Werner took a deep breath. *If only Dieter was here. He'd show this guy some ID*, he thought. The audacity of the man to walk into his office, insist on a face-to-face delivery, and then ask for an ID. And yet, Werner complied if for no other reason than to get rid of the courier.

"*Danke*, Herr Koch. Please understand that my instructions were explicit. Have a good day." The courier handed him a small, padded Kraft envelope.

Werner carried it into his office and began to tear it open. A small flash drive fell out. *What?* he thought as he picked it up from the floor.

He inserted it into the laptop on his desk. Auto play started a video on the flash drive immediately. His face blanched as his heart plummeted into his gut. As for Yolina having insurance, he had his answer.

TWENTY-NINE

The following morning did not bring good news to Adam. Logan's words proved prophetic, and as with his investment accounts, he learned of the problem second-hand.

"Good morning, Adam. This is Tim Harden at Cisco."

Tim was his account rep at the network computer company. Something in the man's voice told Adam this wasn't a courtesy sales call. Adam had placed an order for four Cisco UCS C240 M7 servers with eight terabytes of memory for each. These would support a total of 112 new hard drives and enable him to more easily support the influx of new websites. The thought hit him that maybe this wasn't going to be such a "good" morning after all.

"Hi, Tim. What's up? Is there a problem with my order?"

"Yeah, there is. Your bank won't honor your payment for the order. We'll have to put it on hold until the payment is cleared."

Adam's gut churned. At Logan's suggestion the previous night, he had checked his bank accounts online and all seemed in order.

"What? I was online at my account just hours ago and discovered no problems. There's plenty of capital there to cover this bill. Let me get hold of my banker and get back with you."

"Okay, but again, we won't be able to move ahead until payment is made."

"I understand. Wouldn't expect otherwise. I'll give you a call as soon as I find out what the problem might be."

As soon as he disconnected the call, he had his suspicions about what he was going to hear. He still had half an hour before his local branch opened. What to do in the meantime? He tried to access his account online, and unlike the previous night, his account was now frozen. He tried to kill time working on setting up a new website, but his mind wasn't on it. He decided to quit before botching it up and to restart the process after his thoughts had settled.

As soon as the clock ticked to the top of the hour, he was on the phone.

"Good morning. May I talk with the manager please? This is Adam Afton from Pelethites Cybersecurity."

After five minutes, the manager came on the line. "Mr. Afton. I, uh, I was expecting your call. Actually, I was going to call you this morning, but you beat me to it."

"Okay. So, about my accounts there—"

"Yes, I'm sorry. But someone much higher up on the food chain has decided you're a high-risk account and has closed it. It was not a decision we made locally, and I'm, well, I'm not happy about it. You have one of our fastest growing businesses, and I was hoping to develop a long-term relationship with you. My opinions and plans, however, apparently pull no weight with corporate. Again, I'm sorry."

"Is there any appeal process?"

"None worth exploring. They all start at managerial levels well below where this decision was made. Oh. And, please, you didn't hear this from me. There was a note in your file that no one was to talk with you or give you any explanation. I could get fired over this, but I'm pretty sure you were canceled because of your Christian views. Your file doesn't say that explicitly, but that's the pattern we're seeing. You're not alone, and all of the canceled accounts are Christians or conservative organizations." She paused. "Again, you didn't hear that from me."

Adam felt torn. He didn't want to put her job at risk, and yet, he might need her testimony in a lawsuit.

"I won't say anything, but if this leads to a lawsuit, my lawyer might contact you about testifying. It'll be your decision at that point. You can't be forced to testify."

"I-I need my job, Adam. P-please don't say anything."

He could hear the fear in her voice, and that's exactly what these people, the misnamed progressives, wanted. They used fear to control the population. Fear of a virus that had a 98.5% survival rate untreated. Fear of losing a job. Fear of politicians whose ideas didn't mesh with theirs. Fear of climate change. Fear of the future.

Social credit scoring. Cancel culture. See it our way or be swept from the roadway. Well, he wasn't one to give in. And as tempting as it was, he would not resort to using UltraNet to make *their* lives miserable. That would be stooping to their level, and he lived by a much, much higher standard now.

As he pondered his next move, he recalled scripture from Revelation 13: "*Also it causes all, both small and great, both rich and poor, both free and slave, to be marked on the right hand or the forehead, so that no one can buy or sell unless he has the mark, that is, the name of the beast or the number of its name.*"

Are we seeing the beginning of this? he wondered.

"Denton, you might want to see this."

His legal assistant, Twila, caught him in the hallway on his way to his office as he got off the elevator from the parking garage. He was grateful he'd had his first cup of coffee on the way to work. She wouldn't catch him growling at her. She kept talking as they walked.

"I got this from our IT guys, of all places. You'll recall that we just moved our website to a new internet service provider, Pelethites Cybersecurity." She pronounced it pee-lee-thites. "I'll never pronounce that right. Anyway, I think you signed off on the move and expenses."

He nodded. "I do recall that."

"The owner, an Adam Afton, contacted Ron in IT. They've been working together on the move. Seems the owner had his personal brokerage accounts canceled yesterday. He discovered it just by happenstance. Sound familiar?"

He stopped walking and turned to her. "Adam Afton? Why does that name sound familiar?"

She furrowed her brow. "I . . . I don't know. Maybe from a contract for web hosting services and security packages?"

He shook his head. "No. That was a simple agreement done online. I don't remember an individual's name associated with their side of it." He took the paper she was holding and resumed walking to his office. "It'll come to me."

As he entered his office, she turned back. "I have the morning briefs ready for you."

He turned back to her. "Give me 15 minutes."

"Sure."

He walked to his desk and unloaded his briefcase. *Adam Afton. Adam Afton. Why is that name familiar?* he wondered. He glanced again at the notes Twila had given him. The address was in St. Louis. He poked his head out the door toward Twila's desk.

"Twila, this Afton guy, your note says St. Louis, but could

you check and see if he's lived or worked elsewhere?" She nodded. "Thanks."

Twenty-plus minutes later, he wondered where she was. He needed to go over the briefs before settling into several meetings. This time he picked up the phone and dialed her intercom extension. "Hey, I'm ready for the morning briefs. I have a meeting in half an hour."

"Be right in."

And she was. She handed him the usual stack of potential cases culled from inquiries the previous day. He screened the top ten or so and handed them back. "Move these out to our affiliate attorneys." She nodded. The next five were more intriguing. "Okay, pass these along internally for review." The next two seemed interesting as well, but they didn't seem to fit into their current caseloads. "These two can go out to affiliates, too."

"Okay, I must be slipping. I thought for sure you'd keep those. These last four, though, I'm pretty sure you'll want to keep."

He leafed through the last four, three representing a Christian organization and one a Jewish non-profit, all of which had had their bank accounts canceled. He noted a disturbing trend. Three years earlier, the debanking issue had affected mainly conservative groups. Then, a handful of Christian organizations joined that "club." However, since the Hamas invasion of Israel, the wave of antisemitism now caught an increasing number of specifically Jewish groups, and the number of Christian organizations grew logarithmically. Curiously, the Adam Afton case fit as well, but Denton saw no specific tie to the others. They lost bank accounts, while his case involved brokerage accounts. Was his case simply some form of retaliation for taking on the

MJFDA website?

"Twila, have you found out anything more about Adam Afton?"

She nodded. "We found out about his company through a client. It seems he caters to Christians and conservatives, offering not just website hosting but also a suite a security packages to prevent various attacks from hackers, like the recent denial-of-service attack on the Graham campaign website."

He had heard about that, not that the mainstream media had covered it. Conservative media and X had made it widely known, along with the fatal bombing of the campaign banquet. There were even rumors that the attack had come from the U.S. government itself—another example of a weaponized federal government.

He shook his head in dismay at what the country had devolved into. It was no longer conservative versus progressive or right versus left. It was now sane versus insane. How anyone could think that man would "evolve" into a higher state just amazed him. All they had to do was look at how low mankind now stooped to eliminate *ideas*—not actions—they disagreed with.

"After that attack, the campaign moved their servers to Afton's company, too. In fact, from what I'm deducing here, he got both of our website transfer requests over the Thanksgiving holiday weekend."

"And now, just two weeks later, he's had his brokerage accounts canceled? Doesn't sound coincidental. What about his bank accounts?"

She shook her head. "I don't know."

"What about his whereabouts? Was he based somewhere else before St. Louis?"

"Again, I don't have that answer. Yet." She smiled. "It has been all of thirty-seven minutes since you asked me to find out. I might be getting close to becoming superwoman, but I'm not there yet."

He smirked. "Okay, okay. Put on your cape and find out. And if he's available, I want to talk with him personally when I get out of this meeting."

Adam spent the morning researching the debanking issue. It seemed to have run into the headlights of conservatives in June of 2023 when the UK's Nigel Farage, leader of the Brexit Party, was debanked by Coutts Bank, part of the NatWest Group. Dame Alison Rose, CEO of NatWest, leaked to the press that his account had been closed for "commercial reasons," that is, not meeting minimum deposit requirements. However, Farage provided proof that such was not the case, including a document from Coutts that suggested his accounts were closed because his political views did not mesh with the values of the bank. Once the conservative press and various members of Parliament exposed the issue, Dame Rose was forced to resign, and NatWest had to retreat and reinstate the accounts. Yet, the financial regulator in the UK concluded it had found "no evidence" of politicians being debanked for their political views.

No evidence. Gee, where had Adam heard that before? Oh yeah. The lack of efficacy and safety with the COVID-19 vaccine. Collusion between the FDA, CDC, NIH, and Big Pharma. Claims of election fraud. The CCP's quiet invasion of the U.S. The weaponized federal government coordinating the "lawfare" against ex-President Graham. "No evidence"—

the left's favorite phrase when it came to debunking claims from conservatives, particularly as used by progressive politicians.

Adam found numerous other examples of conservatives and religious groups having bank accounts closed or credit card processing accounts terminated besides the MJFDA case he was already aware of. He hadn't come across anyone whose investment accounts were closed. In that, he alone seemed to have crossed a new threshold. Lucky him.

The "no evidence" claim could also apply to a central bank digital currency. The Federal Reserve Chair had publicly stated, ""People don't need to worry about a central bank digital currency, nothing like that is remotely close to happening anytime soon." And yet, Adam found real evidence that the Fed was moving ahead full steam on that project, having hired software developers. The implementation of a CBDC would make his current hassles seem like nothing. The federal reserve, aka Deep State, would control everyone's money. There would be no cash, only virtual "credits" that could be applied to or removed from an account at will.

The "bankers" would be able to employ AI software to implement any number of mandates, policies, and rules, and be able to enforce them completely. Such mandates could include "digital health passes" aka vaccine passports, climate-change related restrictions, and where and when you could spend your credits. They could lower retirement benefits with a keystroke and end property rights. Imagine being evicted from the home you have totally paid off because your social credit score was lacking. The WOC's goal of "owning nothing and being happy" would come to pass. Well, it would come to pass if you accepted that there was no evidence of anyone owning nothing and being *un*happy.

Logan knocked on his doorway. "Any success?"

Adam looked up. "Sure, if an education on the banking industry was my goal. Not so much when it comes to solving my banking issue."

"What about your investment accounts?"

"Oh, that one wasn't as much of a concern for me. I have an investment in a private equity offering, which the big brokerages won't touch. So, I have a company that handles that, and they also handle real estate, precious metals, and all sorts of investments the big guys won't deal with, along with everything they do handle. I didn't move everything over to them when I made the private equity investment because they still charge some significant fees. But I've opened new accounts with them and will transfer everything to them ASAP."

"That's great, what about—"

Adam's phone rang. Lisa, his new front office assistant, had forwarded the call to him. He saw the ID stating that it was the MJFDA. He pointed to the phone, and said, "It's the lawyers. I need to talk with them."

Logan nodded and eased out of Adam's office, shutting the door behind him.

"Pelethites Cybersecurity, this is Adam."

"Adam, this is Denton Pierce with the Midwest Justice and Freedom Defense Alliance."

Adam was surprised. He hadn't expected a call from the main man himself. He doubted that the CEO of the MJFDA would remember him.

"Yes, Mr. Pierce, it's nice to talk with you again, but I didn't expect *you* to call me."

"Um, we've talked before? Your name seemed familiar but, sorry, I don't recall from where. I had my assistant check other St. Louis area cases, but your name didn't come up."

"Not a problem, sir. Actually, I was in Wisconsin at the time. I gave you folks some data for Anson Hardy's parental rights case." He heard a sigh from the other end.

"Of course, now I remember. I still don't know how you found those documents, but they proved instrumental in winning our case against the school district. Thank you again."

"Welcome." He almost said "happy to help anytime" but thought better of it. He didn't want to become the source for hard-to-find documents, even if finding them with UltraNet was practically effortless.

"My assistant passed on your message from our IT folks. I have to say I hadn't yet heard of brokerage houses closing someone's accounts. Banks accounts, yes."

"Well, sir, all of my bank accounts have been closed down as well." He couldn't tell just what the sound on the other end of the call was, but it wasn't a happy sound. "I have a resolution for my investments, but I've just started trying to figure out the banking bit."

"Which bank?" Adam told him. "Adam, you're not alone. In the past month, we've had over two dozen non-profits, companies, and even individuals who have contacted us about being debanked. All of them are Christians, Jewish, or conservatives. Not a single case of a left-wing, progressive group being debanked. This issue is growing, and I'd like to take it to the Supreme Court. Of course, we can't just start there, so I want to start with a lawsuit against your bank. We have 14 others from that bank, but I'd like you to be the lead plaintiff."

"Do you think we'd win?"

"Doesn't matter. This is one of those issues where no

matter who wins, the other side will appeal. And whoever loses the appeal will appeal again to the next level. That's how we get to the Supremes."

Adam shook his head. That wasn't an answer to his immediate problem.

"All respect, sir, but that will take years. How does it help me now?"

"True, we're looking at two to three years at best, unless some judge helps fast-track this a bit. And you're right, it doesn't help immediately. So, what you need to do is find a state bank, one certified and licensed by the State of Missouri, and move your accounts there. Most of them are also FDIC insured. It's the top ten or twelve banks, all federally certified, that are doing the debanking because it's pressure from federal regulators and their woke mindsets that are working against us."

"Okay, I can do that. There are a couple of state certified banks that come to mind already. I just figured the big banks would offer more services as my accounts grew."

"Maybe, maybe not. I think these regional banks would love to have the accounts of a growing business, like I'm told your company is." He paused. "We have a game plan that we're putting some final touches on. It involves flooding social media and a conservative media blitz to expose these banks. I sincerely doubt the mainstream media will cover it at all, but if the splash is big enough, and the target too big to fail, we might just force their hand."

Adam liked that idea. He could help with a blitz like that, even in ways he wouldn't divulge.

"But I have to warn you. As lead plaintiff, you might find yourself with a target painted on your back."

THIRTY

Aric awoke that Friday morning after exams with his gut grumbling with hunger, but he couldn't eat. Why was he feeling so anxious? Yes, today was the *big* day. Everything was set. Family members and friends from Kenosha and even more distant places had arrived the night before to make sure no travel snags hindered their attendance at the party.

And he was sure she would say "yes," wasn't he? Why did he have doubts? She *had* followed him to St. Louis for their final year in college after all. True, both came to better programs in their respective fields, but that wasn't the main reason she came to St. Louis, was it? It was because of him, wasn't it?

No, he had to cast away the doubts. He had to remain positive, or his own actions could jeopardize his plans. He took several deep breaths. *She will say yes. She will say yes*, he thought over and over.

Jess had an early final that morning, her last, and the plan was for him to pick her up from Wash U and grab a bite to eat in the Central West End. While there he figured he could kill some time browsing the eclectic shops that would be decked out for the holidays. After that, they planned on taking in the holiday poinsettia and train display at the botanical gardens. The show had always been a childhood favorite of Aric's. He'd mentioned it several times to Jess over the past few years, but this was the first time for her to be in St. Louis during the holidays. She was the one to suggest going there to celebrate the end of finals. How could he not take advantage of the opportunity?

He walked into the kitchen and poked his head into the refrigerator. Why did nothing look good to him?

"Hungry?"

He grabbed the orange juice, straightened up, and turned to face his mom. "Yes . . . and no."

The butterflies had regrouped and resumed their attack in his stomach. He had the morning to kill. What was he going to do to take his mind off the doubts?

She smiled. "Don't worry. She'll say yes."

Was he that obvious? "I hope so."

She laughed. "Oh ye of little faith."

That comment hit him. Yeah, where was his faith, in Jess that is?

"If you're looking for a distraction, go see your brother. He could use some encouragement right now. I don't know the details, but he's facing some financial issues and could use cheering up."

Aric nodded. He hadn't seen or even talked with Adam for the past three weeks. They could encourage each other.

Yolina's time on the trawler neared its end. Captain Vasilyev had informed her at breakfast that they would reach port in Kaliningrad within five hours. They had succeeded in skirting the storm that the captain had told them about at their first meeting. So, despite some rougher seas, they had avoided the worst of it. Yolina was glad to have missed it.

Sergei sat in the galley drinking coffee with Mikhail. As she joined them, a wave tossed the vessel to starboard, and her attempt to grab a clean mug missed the mark. She corrected for the yaw of the boat and grabbed the mug, but she waited for steadier footing before trying to fill it with coffee.

With her mug half full—she had learned not to fill it full in such seas—she sat down next to Sergei. Another swell hit them, and all three grabbed their cups, lifting them in unison to avoid spilling their drinks.

"What are you talking about?" asked Yolina.

Sergei took a sip before answering. "They have learned more about the attack on CISA."

"Oh?" This was just what Yolina wanted to hear. "First, can you tell me what kind of DoS attack they launched against their political foe?"

Mikhail nodded as he, too, sipped his coffee. "We have no confirmation of this. I doubt anyone does, but the chatter among other security agencies says it was a distributed attack using numerous computers from within various points in their government. Some are saying it was a HTTP flood attack, but the Israelis are claiming it was a SYN flood attack."

Yolina nodded. A SYN flood attacked the accepted protocols of connecting on the internet. A computer sends a request to connect to a website, the website responds, but the first computer never accepts the "handshake" to complete the connection. It was much like a warehouse worker getting a request to find an item and gets it, but never gets confirmation of where to deliver it. He gets another request, and another, and another, all without getting confirmations. He becomes flooded with requests to the point where his cart is full, and he can't accept any others.

The HTTP flood, however, attacked the basic application of an internet connection. The standard model of a connection consisted of seven layers with layer one being the physical transmission of raw data packets over the physical medium and layer seven being the actual app, the human user interface. The type of DoS attack, or DDoS since it was distributed among numerous computers, affected that seventh layer by exhausting the resources—calling up image files, accessing databases, and so on—needed to reply.

"So, why use a SYN flood? The HTTP flood is much harder to defend against. The system can't tell a legitimate request from a malicious one."

"We were talking about the same thing just before you came in. Why not use both?" asked Mikhail.

"And why wasn't the website protected? It is politics. The website is a major tool in communicating with supporters, collecting money, and more. Anyone with a basic knowledge of internet security would have anticipated the potential for disrupting their website and the need to protect it."

She shrugged. "Eh, Americans. They have experts on everything, yet they know so little."

All three laughed, yet Yolina's interest went beyond the DDoS attack. It was the aftermath that she wished to know more about. That was not a laughing matter. If it could happen to CISA—and it appeared to have happened to Koch's AlterNet2—it could happen to Pozitiv Teknolodzhiz, the FSB itself, or any other major cybersecurity agency. The man with such capabilities could disrupt the internet worldwide, bring down governments, bankrupt international corporations. No wonder Werner Koch kept looking for him.

She wanted to meet such a man.

THIRTY-ONE

After spending the morning with, and helping, his brother and Logan, Aric's mind had more to chew on than being nervous about proposing. While he wanted to say that what his brother was dealing with was unbelievable, it wasn't. Aric had seen enough between the Antifa riots in 2020 when he and Adam had reunited after three years apart, the pandemic fraud and mismanagement, and the stolen election of later that year, followed by the growing antagonism he personally faced from the LGBTQ+ minority on campus between 2021 and 2023. Anything the progressive left proposed or did was suspect from the beginning.

Lynch's readings of Revelation, where he saw the Deep State as the beast with seven heads and ten horns wearing crowns, rang truer and truer. Representing the Deep State, the WOC's publicly stated goals of reducing the global population to less than half a billion people, of eliminating private property with everyone happy to own nothing, and of totalitarian control over the remaining population were steadily coming into being. And those who fought it were being "hunted," placed on domestic violent extremist—DVE—lists, being denied basic constitutional as well as human rights, and more. Christians and Jews would be among the first to be taken out.

One didn't need more than two brain cells to rub together

to see what was happening, where the world was heading. God's judgments were all around them, but the world couldn't see them for what they were. Instead, they saw it as climate change. And as the world marched closer and closer to Armageddon, all it heard was a cry for peace where there was no peace. The world saw evil as good, men as women, and insanity as common sense. They heard only their desires echoing within their minds. As the Lord kept reminding him, the world had eyes but could not see and ears but could not hear.

Aric had gotten so carried away with Adam that he now risked being late in picking up Jess. Still, as he climbed into his car, he couldn't help but wonder if the credit card issue he had encountered was the result of being Adam's brother. And before starting the car, he used the banking app on his phone to check his own bank account. *Phew, still there*, he thought. *So far.*

He pulled up to the curb outside Seigle Hall just as Jess came out the door. Seeing her made him flustered again, but now he could blame any changes in his behavior on his brother's predicament.

"Hi." She leaned over and kissed him on the cheek.

That simple act helped ease his jitters. Why would she do that and then say, "No?"

"How'd it go?"

"Fine. The visual media presentation went well, I thought, but the evaluation team didn't seem to interact with me very much afterwards. I expected more, but then, I'm not sure what I should have expected."

"I'm sure you did well. Where to for lunch?"

She was up for Mediterranean food, and he was up for Mexican. After three rounds of "Your choice - No, your choice," they settled on Medina Grill, a well-liked spot for Middle Eastern food. While eating, Aric explained Adam's latest crisis. While doing so, he noticed his inside pocket felt empty. Panic ensued—where was the ring?—but he tried hard to hide it. Where was it? Had the box fallen out in the car? Would she spot it? Or worse, had it fallen out walking to the grill?

After finishing their meal, he encouraged her toward some shops away from the car. Upon entering one cute boutique, he looked at the clock inside and said, "Hey, I'll be right back. I want to make sure we put enough money in the meter."

She gave him a funny look. They both had contributed change to feed the meter upon arrival. He knew they had enough time, but did she?

He ran to the car and checked the meter. Sure enough, they still had an hour. Glancing back toward the shop, he quickly opened the driver's door and checked inside. He sighed in relief. Sure enough, the box had fallen to the floor, but it had rolled under the edge of his seat. It was unlikely she had seen it. Looking back toward the shop again and not seeing her outside, he grabbed it and placed it into the inside pocket of his coat. Satisfied that it was secure, he hurried back to the shop in time to see her checking out with a cute top that was on sale.

"We're good."

She smiled and held up the top. "Like it?"

He nodded. "Yeah, that's pretty. You'll look great in it."

She frowned. "It's not for me. It'll be your Christmas present to your sister, Mabel."

"Oh. Okay. She'll look good in it, too."

She shook her head as if wanting to say, "Really?" What

was he going to say? She had been after him to start shopping for his family, but he'd been procrastinating. Kinda. He couldn't very well tell her why, that he'd been busy putting together the rest of their day.

By the time the end of the hour neared, he had managed to get gifts for his other two sisters, one niece and both nephews. What to get his mom and dad, whether separately or jointly, still eluded him.

"Hey, we need to get going. Our admission to the gardens gets us into the Holiday Flower and Train Show, but the show itself closes at four."

They headed back to the car in time to see a meter maid, or rather, the parking violation officer, scanning the meters for expired time. He opened the trunk to place their purchases inside and opened his door just as the red violation flag popped up. He looked at the officer and smiled. "Just in time. We're outta here."

He pulled away and 16 minutes later pulled into the parking lot of the Missouri Botanical Gardens, MoBot for those in the know. As he climbed out of the car, he double checked his pocket. *Still there*, he thought.

Once inside, he purchased their admissions. While she looked the other way, he handed his phone to a volunteer who agreed to assist him. As they moved beyond the counter, he said, "I need to use the bathroom. Meet you outside the Emerson Conservatory. That's over there." He pointed.

"Okay, I need to go, too. Meet you there."

Well, that went better than expected. He did use the urinal, but his real purpose for going to the restroom was to transfer the ring to his pants pocket. Check!

They met up outside the conservatory where the show took place, and she grabbed his hand. "I hope this lives up to your childhood memories."

"Oh, I'm sure it'll be memorable. You'll love it. I hope." He hoped the inflection in his voice didn't give anything away. Again, she gave him a strange look.

The conservatory seemed much like he recalled, or did it? This wasn't where they held the show the last time he'd been there. The new multi-million-dollar visitor center was so unlike the old one that he felt as if he were in some other botanical garden. It was beautiful and open. No longer were there two floors but one expansive area that opened onto a new plaza. He did miss the large Chihuly glass sculpture that hung within the atrium of the old center. He would have to ask about it.

The show itself was what he recalled more so than the conservatory, which he realized was new, too. Over two thousand poinsettias from over 600 varietals filled the space. The G-scale trains ran throughout to-scale towns and scenery amidst the brilliant flowers. They walked hand-in-hand among the displays. Jess gazed wide-eyed at everything about them. He could tell she loved it.

"As a kid, I always liked the trains, of course. I would stand and watch them, time how long it took each train to run its circuit, and wonder how they made the villages and everything else to scale."

They came to an arch made of flowers.

"This is beautiful," she said, as she reached out to touch the flowers.

Aric knew this was his opportunity. As she let go of his hand and looked the other way into the flowers, he retrieved the ring and dropped down to one knee.

"You certainly are."

"Huh?" She turned back toward him and the look on her

face was one he would never forget. Tears filled her eyes as she realized what was happening. She looked from right to left before settling her eyes on him. Aric followed her gaze. A dozen people had stopped to watch. He looked up into her eyes.

"Jessica Larson, I once asked God to find me the perfect mate, a bride that loved Him and placed Him first, but who would love me and dedicate herself to our marriage. He showed me that you are that woman. I love you, Jess. Would you do me the honor of marrying me?"

She seemed stunned. What was she thinking? Why didn't she respond immediately?

Then that broad smile he loved so much spread across her face. "Yes, yes, yes. I love you, too, Aric."

She helped him stand up, and he noted that for the first time she really noticed the ring. As all the people around them began to applaud, with a few whistles, he slipped it onto her finger.

"Aric, it-it's perfect. It's beautiful."

Then she wrapped her arms around him and gave him the most passionate kiss he'd ever shared with her. The whistles and applause increased. Then a melancholy look crossed her face.

"What?"

"This was perfect. I just wish we could have shared the moment with, well, with our families."

He smiled. "We will." At that moment, the garden volunteer walked up and handed him his phone.

"Thank you."

The volunteer smiled. "You're quite welcome. Glad we could help out. The video should look great."

He looked at Jess. "We can share this with everyone

later." He noted the time on the phone. "Hey, this place is closing down. We need to celebrate. You've been wanting to try Mama's on the Hill, so I made us reservations."

"That sounds great. A cozy Italian restaurant with a secluded table for two. Champaign. Oh, I think I'm going to love it." She turned and kissed him again before grabbing his hand. "Let's go. And then I can't wait to call my parents with the news."

Now she seemed to be in hurry to get out of there. The restaurant was only five minutes away, but he wasn't supposed to show up before 4:15. He needed to kill time, and he had one more thing to do there.

"Hey, let's stop in the gift shop and find something, a memento of today."

"Okay. I know just what I want, a book on the flower show and trains."

"Sounds perfect. You go start looking at the books, and I'll find a clerk in case they don't have one."

"Um, I can go with you to ask."

Well, that ruse didn't work. "Okay."

They quickly found just what she wanted, paid for it, and left the gift shop.

"Sorry, but I need the bathroom again. I think I was so nervous, my kidneys worked overtime." That sounded plausible.

"Okay. I'll be right outside here."

In the men's room, he quickly doffed his coat and outer shirt. He peeled off the tee-shirt he'd been wearing beneath, donned the outer shirt again, but put the tee-shirt on over it. He looked in the mirror and nodded, pleased with it. He put on his winter coat, zipped it up, and exited the restroom.

At 4:20, they entered Mama's. "Hi, reservations for

Afton."

The hostess grinned. "Yes, sir. We're all set for you. Right this way."

Jess looked at him. "What did she mean, they're all set?"

He didn't answer. The woman led them to a private dining room that was dark except for a small table right in the middle that was lit by two candles.

"Oh, Aric, really? You set this up?"

He helped her with her coat and then slipped off his coat. She looked at his shirt and began to laugh. It said, SHE SAID 'YES!' At that moment, the lights flashed on, and their family and friends yelled, "Congratulations!" from the edges of the room. The tears of happiness that filled Jess' face assured Aric that he had succeeded in making her day memorable.

THIRTY-TWO

Christmas was but days away, and yet Werner had found little joy in the season so far. As an atheist, Christmas per se meant nothing to him, but the traditions of that time of year surrounding family and friends were ones that he looked forward to each year. Plus, they offered solace from the dreary, gray, and cold winter weather.

But not this year. This year was not business as usual.

Sitting in his study at their home outside Munich, he thought about the obstacles he faced. Yolina had yet to be found, and until she was dealt with, the video evidence of his "moment of weakness" remained as a Damocles Sword over his head. The debacle in the U.S., particularly the attempt on Bradley Graham's life, held the potential of derailing all that the WOC and their fellow progressives had patiently striven for over the past five decades. The man's popularity grew with each effort they made to stop him, but the assassination plot had made his poll numbers skyrocket. The delay in passing the WHO's International Health Regulations had stalled their ability to usurp sovereign rights of member nations for pandemics still in the planning stages. Yet, he had to admit that the release of that last virus, the enterovirus that had wreaked so much damage, had been premature. It had also cost him the life of Edvin.

And then there were regional wars that some said could lead to World War III—the Ukraine-Russia war and the

Hamas-Israel conflict. While he had not been directly involved in any aspect of those wars, he saw the potential spillover from those struggles as leading to the possible collapse of western culture itself.

As he watched the wood fire crackle and burn in the room's fireplace, he shook his head in a feeling of inadequacy. He was proclaimed to be one of the most powerful men in the world, and yet, there was little or nothing he could do to alter the issues he now pondered . . . except for one.

He pulled out his secure phone, dialed the sole number in its directory, let it ring once, and hung up. All he could now was wait.

Yolina glanced again at the room in which she sat. To call the structure 55 kilometers outside Moscow a dacha seemed to stretch the definition. The cabin must have been built during the czars and expanded by some Bolsheviks with no fashion sense. However, she had noted two redeeming qualities so far. The cold December winds were no match for its thick timber walls. She suspected bullets would have little effect as well, should it come that. The second feature was its large natural stone fireplace. The fire Sergei had built was large enough to cause climate change all by itself. And she loved it.

The intelligence trawler had been an experience, but Captain Vasilyev would find himself hard pressed to try to talk her into joining the crew, even if she had a private bath. The constant yaw and pitch of the vessel, the wind, and the confinement to such a small space had made her want to kiss the ground as they disembarked in Kaliningrad. She didn't want to try to imagine what boat life could be like in a sudden

Baltic Sea gale.

"привет, котик. What do you think of it?"

She didn't want to say what was on her mind.

"You said this has been in your family for how long?"

"Two centuries. Czar Alexander the first awarded the land to my ancestor for actions in the Russo-Persian War in 1812. He built the first dacha here after that war, but it was burned in the Decembrist Revolt in 1825. The nobility killed that ancestor for siding with the czar. His son rebuilt, but I was told as a child that it was a simple cabin. A number of structures were built here over the next century, and this current home was built during the reign of Nicholas the second, just prior to the Bolshevik Revolution. It was reinforced and used as a family refuge during that uprising. My grandparents updated the utilities 40 years ago, and my parents hardly used the place, so they saw no need to spend money on it."

Yolina could see that such was the case.

"But they gave me permission to do whatever I wished with it. So far, I have updated the well and water supply, upgraded the electrical service, and added a small vertical wind turbine and some solar panels to provide some of the electricity."

She walked into the kitchen area and noticed new appliances. She nodded in approval. "This looks nice."

Sergei nodded. "My latest project. I am happy with how it turned out."

She looked into several cabinets and found a healthy supply of food stuffs. "I will make you dinner tonight." He smiled.

She continued her tour. The place consisted of the main room, kitchen, bath, and two bedrooms. It would do, but as she had thought earlier, it hardly qualified as a dacha, a villa.

"It is not as big as I anticipated. Where will I set up to work? Where is the российский Интернет? I see no wireless or cable connections. I thought you said you sometimes worked from here."

The российский Интернет, or Russian internet, called Runet by some, was well established. Almost 90% of the population was online, and social media—Odnoklassniki and VKontakte—was very popular. VK was the 6th most popular site in Russia, followed by OK at the 7th position. VK was, in fact, the 56th most visited site in the world according to Alexa rankings prior to its closure in 2022.

He grinned. "да, любимый." He stroked her cheek with his fingers. "Follow me." He led her to the larger of the two bedrooms. "Watch what I do."

He walked up to the bookcase and pointed to two books. She did not understand the titles but saw that as he pulled on each, they tipped forward, and the bookcase moved maybe two centimeters away from the wall. At that point, he slid the bookcase to their left and exposed an opening. It was like something in a British mystery movie.

"I told you the family used this as a refuge during the Bolshevik Revolution. Most people think of castle dungeons as prisons, but they were really the very first safe rooms, where the family could hide if an enemy made it into the castle. My great-great-grandfather built this to hide from the revolutionaries. Come."

He turned on the lights, and they descended to a well-lit, modern-looking suite of rooms. She glanced about and noticed the space seemed twice as large as the home above ground. The main room contained a large screen television and comfortable seating for nearly a dozen people. A kitchenette, three more bedrooms, and two bathrooms added to those above ground. One room held an array of monitors and multiple computers."

"*This* is where I've spent most of my money on this place. Watch this."

He flipped another switch and one wall lit up with built-in monitors that mimicked a large picture window overlooking the grounds to the back of the dacha. It was like looking outside in real-time. He pressed a key on one computer and the scene changed from real-time to the same area in mid-spring. He pressed the key again, and it was summer.

"I wanted to avoid feeling confined to a basement, so I added virtual windows and recorded weeks' worth of video during each season. There are terabytes of video stored on hard drives connected to this computer. It also handles security for the house."

He pressed another key and images of all the rooms upstairs, as well as multiple views outdoors, appeared. She had not noticed any cameras, but then she hadn't felt the need to look for them.

"The computers are connected to the internet by cable, and there's an additional satellite uplink should you need it. Those accounts are all listed under a name and identity provided by the FSB. I think you will find my setup every bit as good as at Pozitiv."

Yolina was impressed. "This, you, I . . . I-I do not know what to say." She scrutinized the computer setup. "Who else knows about this?"

He shrugged. "Until now, only my parents. They helped cover the costs of this remodeling, but they don't come down here. They like the rustic coziness of the home above ground.

You can go to ground and be safe here. I will bring food as we need it, but I will also have to spend time at Pozitiv. The neighbors are used to seeing me come and go here. But if you wish to go outside, it would be best to limit that time to after dark. The other dachas have cameras, and you could be spotted and questions asked."

That made sense. She had wanted to find a location where she could disappear from Werner Koch and his people. This seemed to fit that criteria. Then she wondered. She also felt a need to hide from the FSB, but now she understood that Sergei's ties to that agency were deeper than she had understood. Just how deep were Sergei's connections to the FSB? He had spent time on the trawler and now had cover from the security agency for his work here. Was he hiding her here because he cared for her and wanted her safe? Or was he only protecting her as an asset to the FSB?

As Werner climbed into bed, he still had not heard back from Yuri. That in itself was unusual but not alarming. One couldn't expect clandestine operatives to drop everything at one's beck and call. However, Werner's patience was dimming. The issue of Yolina Zhdanov was one that he wished removed from his plate sooner, not later.

As he drifted off to sleep, the secure phone buzzed and vibrated on his bedside stand. He grabbed it as he arose from bed and walked to his study so as not to disturb Liesl.

"Ja."

"I apologize for the timing. I was not in a good place to return your call. I am still not, so we must be fast."

That suited Werner. He wanted to get back to bed.

"I want you to look into one Yolina Zhdanov from Pozitiv

Teknolodzhiz. Can you confirm that she is an FSB asset? If so, find out who her handler is. She has a sensitive video of, shall we say, a minor indiscretion of mine that needs to be destroyed. If her handler has a copy, it needs to be dealt with, and he needs to be eliminated. Same with her if she will not cooperate. I am trusting in you to be discreet, and upon proof of everything being finalized will pay you handsomely."

"How handsomely?"

"What do you want?"

"This is not a minor job. I can already confirm that she is sometimes used by the FSB. I cannot confirm she was tasked by the agency to compromise you. Finding such a video will take a little time but is not impossible for me in my position there. However, arranging an accident for her handler, and others if there are more than one involved, will take more time. I cannot guarantee a quick resolution."

As much as Werner wanted this dealt with yesterday, he understood. One did not deal with FSB agents carelessly and the fates of all personnel were investigated with suspicion.

"What do you want?"

"100,000 euros down and 400,000 more upon completion."

Werner did not expect that much. He did have the upper hand in this negotiation, as he could out Yuri that minute as working for him. Yet, he had taken too much time and spent too much capital to position him within the FSB to risk losing that now. Plus, Yuri was the one taking all of the risks.

"Agreed. The down payment will be sent to your account tomorrow. Keep me informed."

He frowned as he heard voices in Yuri's background and the call disconnected.

THIRTY-THREE

Aric was amazed at the energy Jess put into their betrothal. He had figured they would start wedding planning after graduation in the spring. Au contraire. Her father had to return to Kenosha to oversee a variety of church functions related to the holiday, but her mom—now officially "Sue" or "Mom" to her new almost-son-in-law—had stayed behind. Together, with and sometimes without Aric's okay, they found a venue, caterer, and photographer for a mid-July wedding. Despite the wedding's taking place in Kenosha and Sue's having contacts all over the city, they declared it a miracle to find all three open on the same day in the peak wedding season there. Jess had already planned to wear her grandmother's wedding dress so only alterations would be needed. Aric was offered no opportunity to see pictures of it, but he did sneak a look online at some examples of 1970s wedding gowns to get an impression of the style then.

Now, with the holidays behind them and classes resuming, he was determined to buckle down and get through his final semester. It felt strange not having the uniquely intense January, or J-term, of their previous college, but he took that in stride. His car was parked across from a security camera, and he suspected that those involved in the earlier incident had spread the word that he would take any further vandalism seriously and that the law was on his side. As he walked across campus toward his first class, he kept an eye out for anyone who might have issues with him. He entered the Express Scripts building without incident.

Likewise after class, but this time he headed for the Campus Security Department.

"Hey, Aric. How were the holidays?"

"Hi, Monica. They were fantastic."

Monica was the receptionist in the department. He had met her and several other officers, as well as the chief, when he worked with Officer Kenniston on his car vandalism case.

"I proposed to my girlfriend, Jess, and she said 'yes.' So, yeah, the holidays were great."

"Well, congratulations." She gave him a huge smile. "What can I do for you?"

He leaned across the counter in front of her.

"Officer Kenniston has twice offered me a part-time job here. To do forensics work, I guess. I wondered if he was serious and what it would entail. I need to start saving money for a honeymoon."

She smiled again. "Any thoughts about where that would be?"

He laughed. "Not yet. We'll figure that out." He had his own thoughts about where, but he wasn't going to discuss that with a near stranger.

"Let me see if Kenniston is in the back. I thought I saw him come in a little while ago." She picked up the phone and dialed an extension. She hung up and smiled. "He'll be out in a moment."

The moment turned into several minutes, but Aric was seated at the officer's desk shortly.

"So, I want to learn more about this job offer you made."

The man nodded. "I talked with the chief, and he's good with it. By the way, I hear congratulations are in order."

"Thanks." Aric wondered how he knew. He hadn't heard Monica say anything. "So . . . the job?"

"Yeah. We don't have that much need for forensics, but the occasional break-in in a dorm, vandalism of cars, that kind of stuff, and we don't really have the manpower to do a forensics work-up. So, I thought maybe we could start an O-J-T kind of program with the criminology seniors. You would be the guinea pig to try it out with." He laughed.

The idea intrigued Aric, but it couldn't interfere with classes. "How many hours a week? How would we be credentialed? What kind of pay?" He had lots of questions.

Kenniston nodded. "Good questions. To be honest, we're still working out some of the details and looking at the budget. With our current load, we're looking at maybe ten hours a week, but some weeks there may be no hours. On-campus crimes aren't exactly scheduled like classes." He smirked. "At first, you'd be with an officer, like we did for your car, but eventually you might work on your own. That's our goal, so we can free up an officer. We're thinking that starting with a senior student in the fall could get him going solo before mid-terms. You would be starting now, so we're not sure how we're going to handle it. We also have to work this out with the state and county folks. Anyway, as for pay, we're thinking, like, $20 an hour with a potential for a raise based on merit for anyone working solo."

Aric liked that idea. He could manage ten hours a week, especially if it was giving him experience and paying him to boot.

"That could work."

"So, we would need you to get the new state digital ID. The state has made it available as an option for drivers, but they're requiring all police departments and security groups to use it for chain of custody, training, and credentialing purposes."

Aric had read a little about the digital IDs being proposed in multiple states. There were two formats, and Missouri was considering the Apple Wallet-proposed ID that would incorporate the mDL, or mobile driver's license, with Apple Wallet for buying and selling. The idea sounded great, but there were still significant privacy concerns. While the companies stated that the biometric data would be secure and the "property" of the individual, Aric had read of concerns about the government taking control of the programs. TSA had already started using the technology in several airports. Should that become widespread . . . well, the government's recent track records on privacy and an individual's rights made that prospect daunting.

"So, that just entails facial recognition, right?"

The man shook his head. "That was the initial plan, but AI deep fakes threw that concept a curve. Now, the IDs will require a retinal scan and right palm print. Either one could then be used for ID purposes at banks, car rentals, stores. It's really a neat idea and pretty much eliminates identify theft."

"Retinal scans?"

He nodded. "Yeah, most of the commercial scanners have you place your forehead on a pad and scan your right eye."

Apprehension flashed through Aric's brain. Scripture from Revelation 13 flashed through his mind. *Also it causes all, both small and great, both rich and poor, both free and slave, to be marked on the right hand or the forehead, so that no one can buy or sell unless he has the mark, that is, the name of the beast or the number of its name.*

Lynch's comments about the beasts of Revelation already having control became more real.

THIRTY-FOUR

They had a saying in Missouri—well, it fit most states actually: if you don't like the weather wait an hour. Adam wondered what the latest wintry front had brought with it.

In the past month, since signing on with the MJFDA to fight for banking and financial rights, his once thriving business had gone from meteoric rise into a tailspin. Yes, he had successfully placed his bank accounts in a regional, state accredited bank. That wasn't the immediate problem.

"Pelethites Cybersecurity. This is Adam." This was the third call forwarded to him from Lisa that morning. The first two reported banking issues and said their payments would be delayed until they worked out the problems. He fully understood.

"Hi, Adam. This is Ron Edwards at Cup Runneth Over."

Adam had personally redesigned the coffee shop's website several months back, before the deluge of hosting requests. It was a local company, one of his first customers, and he had enjoyed more than one latte there since their opening. They also had great hot chocolate, which made Adam crave one just thinking about it on that chilly January day. Besides their coffee and cocoa, they were known among various Christian non-profits for their philanthropy.

"Hi, Ron. What's up?"

"Our website's not up. No, I shouldn't say that. It's just really, really . . . really slow. It's like we're on old dial-up connection speeds."

Adam understood what the man meant, although he had never personally experienced "dial-up." Ron, however, was old enough to have persevered during those early days of the internet.

"Are you on your site now?"

"Yep. Took me like over a minute to go from the home page to the iced mocha page. Same with moving to any other page. It's painful, and our online orders have dropped to next to nothing."

"Okay, let me check into it. Can you hold, or do you want me to call you back?"

"I'll hold."

Adam called up the site. The server was working well. Internally, the site worked at blazing speeds. He switched to his phone so he could see what was happening outside his own network. He called up the site and waited . . . and waited . . . and waited. Ouch! Like Ron had said, it was painful.

"Ron, your site works as designed on our network, but when I tried to use it on my phone, I got just what you described. I need to check some things, and I need to do that off-site, outside of my own network. If I come over, can I use your internet connection to run some tests? I can be there in about ten minutes."

"Sure. Happy to have you. Chocolate or latte? I'll have one waiting for you."

"Ooo, on a day like this, hot chocolate for sure. Be there shortly."

He found Logan at his desk. "Hey, our local coffee shop account is having problems with their website, and I can't find any issues with it here. So, I'm heading over there to see what might be going on. Want anything when I come back?"

"Oh, yeah. One of their large cinnamon lattes. Thanks. What do you think is happening?"

Adam shrugged. "Eh, at first I thought it was probably something on their end, but when I used my phone, I could reproduce what he said. They were one of my first clients, so I figured I'd give then some extra attention and go over there."

"Yeah, yeah, yeah. You just want a coffee break." He laughed.

Adam smiled. "Hot chocolate break. Back soon, I hope."

Minutes later, Ron greeted Adam at the counter and ushered him to the back office. A tall cup of cocoa goodness sat on the desk. Adam took a sip.

"Thanks. So, when did you notice the problem?"

"Had a couple of customers at the drive-up who said they tried to order ahead and couldn't. That's when I checked it."

"And I take it you tried restarting your modem and router."

"Of course. But that wouldn't affect customers outside the building."

"True."

Adam plugged his own laptop into the modem and called up the website. It took over a minute for the first image to appear and almost four minutes for the home page to fully load. That was clearly not acceptable. Out of curiosity, he tried another website that they hosted. Then a third . . . and a fourth. All were painfully slow.

He called Logan.

"Hey, could you check the AFN, Oasis Ministries, and Run to Win websites? They're all underperforming here."

"Sure. One sec."

Adam could hear his friend tapping the keys.

"They all check out fine here. What's up?"

"I don't know."

Yet, as he said that, a sinking feeling washed over him. He tried a handful of other sites hosted on their servers, including the Graham campaign and MJFDA sites. All ran like turtles, or as Ron had said, like they were on dial-up.

Adam then did one of the most basic tests he knew. He performed a simple ping to one of his servers. It hit the server within milliseconds but took over four seconds to return.

"Logan, can you switch us over to the backup fiberoptic line?"

"Sure. You think the cable's failing?"

"Not sure yet."

"Okay, done."

Adam repeated his scrutiny of the websites he had already tested. No change. He pinged the server. No change.

That sinking feeling felt as if it hit the ocean's floor . . . in the Mariana Trench.

"They've throttled us, Logan."

Ron's brow furrowed as concern crossed his face. "Throttled you?"

Adam nodded slowly. "Our telecom company, the one that provides our fiberoptic internet connections has cut our speeds. Significantly. Every site we host is affected. They've joined the crowd that wants to put us out of business."

THIRTY-FIVE

AG McFarland sat with DHS Secretary Saucedo in the grill room of The Washington Club. As one of the city's oldest and most exclusive private clubs, its Renaissance revival building housed an ornate lobby, the casual grill room, a lounge and bar, barbershop and salon, a more formal dining room, sleeping quarters for the occasional out-of-town members, exercise rooms, racquetball courts, and more. During its first 150 years, only prominent white males were allowed membership, but in the early 1970s, its rules were changed to allow black members. Another 16 years were required before female members were accepted.

Two rules had never changed, however. No note taking was allowed at any table within the building. And with the advent of cell phones, they were not allowed to be used within its confines. These rules made the club a favorite for the backroom deals known as "private discussions" among the politician members.

"Miguel, thanks for joining me for lunch."

The DHS secretary smiled and nodded. "Always a pleasure, Derrick."

They scanned the menus, although both men frequented the club and knew its offerings well. After ordering and the delivery of their drinks, the AG got down to business.

"I've been wanting to know how the digital ID rollout with TSA has gone."

Secretary Saucedo smiled. "Quite well. As you know, we started testing it at three airports a few months ago. It was well received and a significant reduction in security screening times was noticed very quickly. The business fliers have embraced it because it practically eliminates their time in security lines."

"Great. I understand you've expanded the program to 40 more airports now."

The man sipped his bourbon and replied, "That's right. And by summer, we will have it in every airport."

The AG nodded. "I take it you've been coordinating this with Zhèng Jian."

"Yes, at the president's directive, we're expanding quickly, will give it a month or two for people to get accustomed to it, and by the election, it will no longer be optional but required for flying. What's happening through the DOJ? I haven't heard much about your plans."

At the president's directive? McFarland knew where the marching orders originated, but of course, the talking points included the president despite his failing health. But did they truly need to keep up the charade among themselves? *I guess the walls have ears in this place, too,* thought the AG.

Their food arrived and both began to eat. After several bites, McFarland said, "We're pushing ahead with the mobile driver's license. We've required all police authorities to use it now for their officers and staff. It'll be used for chain-of-custody, certifications, and the like. We've also moved ahead with standardization of the IDs, requiring retinal scans or palm prints instead of allowing facial recognition. Thirty-two states, plus D.C., are already moving ahead with the mDLs for all new licenses and renewals. The other 18 states have legislation pending to require them. Once a state has over

50% coverage with mDLs they'll move to make them required of all drivers, instead of being optional as they are now."

Saucedo looked serious. "So, when do you think that conversion level will take place? Seems slow to me."

The AG nodded. "I agree, but there's still significant blowback by various ideologues and first amendment rights groups. We're moving ahead with several large corporate partners who will link the IDs to shopping in their stores and banking at their banks. As more people see how convenient this is and how it protects against stolen identities, we think the momentum toward acceptance will greatly outweigh the naysayers."

"Okay. I know you have a much bigger population to deal with than we do with fliers and airports. I thought the goal was to get this all in place before, you know, the election. In case you-know-who wins."

McFarland leaned forward and said, "That's not going to happen. I know it looks like a real possibility right now, but I'm hearing rumors that the power brokers will set off something to allow Sidon to call for martial law before ever letting the election take place. Zhèng hinted at such in one of our conversations, but he refused to say anything more."

"Speaking of which . . ." The DHS Secretary pointed with his head toward the door.

McFarland turned to look and saw the President's chief-of-staff in the entrance to the grill. He waved and motioned for the man to join them, but the CoS waved and shook his head. A moment later, three members of the Joint Chiefs of Staff joined him, their uniforms bristling with ribbons and awards. They were seated across the room at a larger table. The still-empty seats indicated that three more people were expected.

The AG harrumphed. "Well, that certainly appears to corroborate my statement."

THIRTY-SIX

Yolina sat at the computers in Sergei's hideaway staring at the monitor directly in front of her. She didn't mind the isolation of the place, and Sergei's outdoor viewing screen went a long way in preventing claustrophobia, if such were possible in an 800-square meter underground bunker with just about every possible modern convenience.

The only drawback to the viewing screen was that she tended to focus on the summertime video footage with its sunshine, a mother deer and her fawn that came by regularly, and the wildflowers that carpeted the forest's floor. Then she was shocked to step outside for fresh air in the evening and rediscover that it was January with its bitter cold and polar winds.

As she stared at the closest monitor, she reflected upon her first direct conversation with Sergei after staying at the dacha for a week.

"I think I've figured out how he did it."

"How who did what?"

"The hacker who attacked CISA. He figured out a way to use a SYN flood to return the attack. He must have written programming to recognize the DoS attack, add code to the original pings, and complete the handshake to allow that virus to infect the attacker's computer."

"Ingenious, if that's what happened." He shook his head. "Way above my programming skills."

Then she spent a week trying to figure out exactly how he accomplished the feat. Writing viral code to wipe out a network was fairly straightforward. Perhaps a lot more sophisticated coding was needed if your plan was to attack another cybersecurity agency, but the basics were the same. Still, doing so without leaving traces of the virus behind was a level above even that type of sophistication. That would be like using an explosive that left nothing behind to identify its chemical makeup. She wrote samples of such a virus to test, but she could never get the connection to complete itself in order to introduce the virus into the system. The more she tried, the more she wanted to meet the programmer who had done that.

Her phone's ringing startled her. When he wasn't with her, Sergei communicated only through secure email. No one else had the number of the burner phone she had purchased en route to Heringsdorf. She had first planned to leave it turned off and its battery removed, but the need for it in an emergency overrode that thinking.

She debated answering it. The CallerID number displayed was unfamiliar to her. Was it simply a wrong number? Was Sergei calling from a number unknown to her? Was he in trouble? If so, then she, too, was likely in trouble.

She let it go to voice mail but then decided not to check the in-box. No, she needed to let whoever called believe the number was not in use. Even to check for voice mails would leave proof behind of someone using the number, should anyone inspect the phone's logs.

The phone began to ring again. Same number. Now anxiety began to engulf her. If it was Sergei, his insistence on reaching her meant trouble. If it wasn't Sergei, well, the possibilities there seemed infinite. Again, she let the call go to voice mail.

After the ringing stopped, she waited to see if a notification came through about a new message. Nothing. Maybe she was becoming paranoid. Living in a bunker without real human contact for days at a time could do that. Still, the old saying—just because you're paranoid doesn't mean they aren't out to get you—didn't apply. She was sure Werner Koch was out to get her. 100% sure.

She and Sergei had talked about contingencies. She always kept the opening to the basement closed and latched, even when she was upstairs in the main kitchen or sneaking outside for a break. The last thing she needed was an unexpected intruder to discover the building's secret. Tied closely to that was to reduce the energy signature of the place. For anyone snooping around, to see a seemingly unoccupied building using energy like a large family home would set off alarms that something was amiss, that there was more to the structure than met the eyes. That only required a look at the home's electric meter outside.

She walked through the main room to the stairway, climbed the steps, and confirmed that the hidden door was secure. While walking back through the main room, she turned off all but one light. Back inside the workroom, she turned off the outdoor viewing screen. Now the place seemed claustrophobic.

She forced her emotions to settle down and resumed her work. For the past week, she had been working through her work for Werner Koch. Step-by-step for each false identity. She scrutinized each employment record, property deed, credit card account, school history, and more. She looked into each and every alleged family member and their respective records. She found nothing out of place.

It all appeared perfect and that's when she realized it was too perfect. There were no typos. No corrections to any records. No updates or changes.

She needed to look at the actual code beneath the records, but were her binary coding skills up to speed to do this? It was one thing to use modern scripted coding and such to accomplish a task. It was something else to be able to use actual machine code, or even just the ones and zeros of a pure binary system.

She pulled up the college records of Igor Karamazov and switched from the customary HTML code to the machine code behind it. There. At the beginning of the record was a short string of code that marked it. She looked at another individual's records. That code was different. She checked a third and fourth record. Their records matched that of the second, but not that of Igor.

She studied both strings of code and realized that the host computer and record-keeping software of the university would not see them differently. Yet, for a hacker, the difference would allow the rapid removal of the fake record. In fact, such a removal could be automated so that many such records could be deleted effortlessly. They could also be added to a database quickly the same way. When Sergei had called the man's reverse coding ingenious, he had been correct.

She inspected the college records of the others—Dormán János, Danil Kiselyov, Arno Prinsloo, and Christopher Solovyov—only to find the same thing. Next, she checked employment records. She smiled on discovering that the same technique had been used for them all. And since almost all record-keeping software was based on SQL database programming, a standard, he had little or no need to vary his coding. Her respect for this hacker increased with each minute she spent looking for him.

But now she faced a dilemma. Yes, she had uncovered his technique for adding and deleting such data. How could she use this to locate the man himself? Where would she even start?

The monitor to her right suddenly flashed on—a secure email from Sergei. Her heart rate accelerated as she read: *I'm being watched. Be careful. Do not go outside. Be there as soon as I can.*

THIRTY-SEVEN

Werner paced along one wall of his office as Ilse laid out papers along a folding leg table she had set up there. He rubbed his temples as he watched her. Clearly, there had to be some other way to organize the topics to be covered in this year's WOC meeting in Davos. The conference was but five days away and still she hadn't fully laid out meeting room plans and schedules. The program was supposed to be at the printer's shop a week ago.

"Ilse, could this have been done electronically a lot faster?"

She seemed flustered for the first time since he had taken her on as his assistant. Had something happened to her? This did not seem like the same woman he had hired.

"I am so sorry, Herr Koch. I thought I had this finished last week, but two of the hotels called at the last minute saying that bad weather had damaged portions of their buildings and that at least six of the rooms we had planned to use were out of commission. One of them called again yesterday to inform us that two more room were unusable."

His eyes widened. He had not heard about this unfortunate turn of events. "But this?" He waved his hand toward her makeshift whatever it was.

"Sir, I have tried and tried to work this out on my computer, but I am going cross-eyed. I need to see the big picture. And I need your input because we may have to cancel some sessions."

He edged closer to her table and now saw what she had done. The hotels to be used were drawn to scale along with which rooms they held. Also to scale were the hotels' proximity to each other, with walking times noted along the routes between them. It was like a mocked-up version of Davos where she could delineate which sessions were being held where and how long it would take to move between them.

"This lets me really *see* what is going on. I can get a better perspective of the overall layout and note how long it will take to walk from one venue to the next. We may need—"

A phone ringing from within his desk interrupted her.

"Excuse me, Ilse. I will need to take this call privately." He waved his hand toward the door.

She nodded and left the office but looked none too happy for the disruption. He could tell that she was under pressure to complete the task.

He reached his desk, pulled the phone from his desk, and answered. "*Ja*, Yuri."

"Herr Koch, I have obtained a flash drive and have been assured it has not been copied here or given to anyone else. Please forgive me, but I had to view enough of it to verify that it was the one you sought. It is."

That displeased Werner, but he understood the necessity for doing so. He believed he could trust Yuri to keep secret what he saw.

"Please destroy it."

"*Ja*, Herr Koch. I will do so after our conversation. As for Yolina, she has two handlers. Sadly, one of them, Kostya Raskolnikov, had a fatal hit and run accident while jogging yesterday. The other, Sergei Agafonov, will take a bit of time to deal with. I am told he is romantically involved with Yolina, although she does not know he is also one of her handlers. If I am to find her, I must let him live for now."

That made sense. At least he had secured the FSB copy of the video.

"Yes, yes. She must be found."

He still preferred to convince her to come back but considering the extent to which she had deceived them about her travels, he came to suspect that her cooperation would not be gained. Could her boyfriend be used as leverage?

"And am I still to eliminate them both?"

Werner remained torn between the options.

"Could her boyfriend be used to get her to cooperate?"

"*Nein*, Herr Koch. He is too well-trained. I do not believe he will give her up easily. I think he has her well-hidden, so I will have to track him to find her. However, I must be very discreet, so I don't blow my own cover."

Werner nodded in agreement. Yuri was much more important to him inside the FSB than her services. Besides, she had failed in her task once. Was he unrealistic to think she might succeed if given another chance? Yes, unrealistic.

"Find her and then take care of them both."

THIRTY-EIGHT

Denton looked across the conference room at the lawyers and assistants gathered there. The debanking issue had grown faster than any other civil rights case they had handled in the thirty-plus years since he started MJFDA. He had "poached" these people from other groups within the firm to help him handle the load.

"Okay, folks, what do we have? Jerry, you first."

The attorney nodded. "Well, we're now up to 115 separate cases. My assistants and I have been talking with them all. While they naturally want their individual cases handled, they are all in agreement to become joint plaintiffs in whatever we put together."

One of his aides raised her hand. Denton nodded to her to continue.

"Of these, all but four had accounts at one of the big ten national banks. We've contacted those banks on behalf of these account holders, but so far, no response from a single one of them."

Jerry took back the conversation. "And I don't think they will. They have the protection of the federal government, if you want to look at it that way. Of concern, however, are those four banks Tina mentioned. They're all state accredited banks, like those we've been pointing our clients to. I called each one. It took some cajoling to get someone to talk, but the gist of it is, they've been threatened with losing their FDIC insurance coverage if they fail to fall in line. It appears the Fed, as in the Federal Reserve, is starting to pull no punches."

Denton furrowed his brow in concern. "What do we tell our clients?"

"Well, so far, the state banks affected are all in blue states where the state banking regulators tend to enforce whatever the federal regulators tell them to do. The banks in red states, so far, haven't been threatened or, maybe, they're resisting. We'll start looking into that more closely, to see if we can find a group of banks to specifically recommend."

Denton shook his head. "We have to be careful about making specific recommendations. That could blow back on us, too. In a variety of ways."

Jerry nodded. "We understand. I hope to have more for everyone at next week's meeting."

Denton nodded to another lawyer at the table. "Amanda, what do you have?"

"As everyone knows, all of the groups affected so far lean conservative . . . no, lean's the wrong word. They *are* conservative in social and political ideology. And the majority are Christian groups. Not one of them, however, is explicitly political in nature. They can't be as 501(c)3 non-profits. We've talked with a number of them about becoming private associations or 508(a)1(c) non-profits. Of course, as members of the bar and officers of the courts, we have to be careful how we advise them. We're staying withing our bounds."

"Thank you," said Denton.

She nodded. "My team has also been scouring what records we can get hold of, and so far, we haven't come across a single left-leaning or progressive group that has been debanked."

Denton frowned. "Should we be surprised?"

As a 501(c)3 non-profit itself, the firm was based upon biblical principles and its staff all understood that they would be facing down an enemy whose goal was the elimination of God's people, whether Jews or Christ followers. That the Book of Revelation foretold this persecution was not lost on the group gathered in this room.

The discussion continued as to whether or not to use class-action suits against the involved banks, individual suits using only those plaintiffs they already had, and other possible actions. The problem with class-action suits was that they tended to end in settlements that earned the plaintiffs little and restricted further legal actions. Such a case would not give him an avenue to the Supreme Court.

Denton's preference was to sue in federal court over constitutional issues such as freedom of speech and religion. Someone had thrown out the idea of looking at the Constitution's commerce clauses as well. With several of the plaintiff organizations having a national or even international presence, that approach was considered worth looking into.

On his way back to his office, he asked, "Twila, where are we with the Pelethites Cyber case? I need to update Adam Afton soon. It's been three weeks since we notified his telecom carrier of the issues and the potential of a lawsuit."

Although the debanking issue affected Pelethites Cybersecurity as well, the matter of his services being throttled down was a separate case. The law and case precedence fell clearly in favor of Afton and his company. Even his contract with the telecom clearly stated the service levels and speeds he was to get from the fiberoptic lines he leased from them. For the telecom to slow down those speeds and break their contract made no sense. Had the company's DEI policies led to a legal department of diverse but less-than-competent solicitors?

"The paperwork is on your desk."

They entered his office and Twila made a beeline to his desk, retrieved the papers, and handed them to Denton.

"What? How in the world can they . . ."

"That's what I thought, and I figured they were trying to delay things. But when I talked with the tech guys, they insisted the problem wasn't on their end. I have to say, they sounded sincere." She pointed to her handwritten notes at the bottom of the page. "They went so far as to go to the Pelethites building and test the fiberoptic cable. The problem is within the building, not the outside from the building to their relay."

Denton was puzzled. Adam had explained his security setup to him, so how could someone have gotten inside to sabotage his cables? Unless . . .

Adam sat at his desk feeling desperate. From the high hill of the roller coaster straight down to its subterranean tunnel, running at 60 miles per hour, he wanted to get off but wasn't able. Over three weeks had passed since they had been alerted to the slowed speeds of their fiberoptic cables. Three weeks and there was nothing he could do to change the problem. Logan was far more expert in the systems side of the work, and he continued to assure Adam that their network was operating at peak speeds and efficiency.

Adam had contacted Denton Pierce at the MJFDA, who promptly fired off a letter to the telecom company. Was the company stalling? Or were there serious problems on their end? From his last communication with Denton, the company had yet to respond to the letter. If they were out to destroy Adam's business, they were succeeding. Most of his clients understood the problem, and were willing to give some grace, some time to resolve the issue. But three weeks stretched their limits. He'd lost 63 clients within the past ten days, clients he had bent over backward and worked overtime to get up and running after they had been removed from AWS and de-platformed.

Adam understood their side of it. They needed websites running at optimal levels to stay in business themselves. They had jumped at his service because of the AFN article, but his company wasn't the only internet service provider they could turn to. His business *was* the only one who offered such a suite of security features and cloud services like that of Amazon at prices that non-profits and small businesses could readily afford, but what good was that, if no one could access their websites. He refunded all unused fees and wished them God's favor as they moved to the greener grass on the other side of some virtual fence. Perhaps in time they would migrate back . . . if he could get the bandwidth and speed issues resolved.

"Hey. I'm heading out for the day. Call if you need me." Logan waved goodbye before turning toward the exit.

Adam only nodded and waved back. He debated heading up to the house, as there wasn't much for him to do either. Lisa, too, had agreed to cut back her hours until, and hoping that, the situation was resolved. Even Rachel used the slack time. She was off to school with the kids for a field trip to the St. Louis Art Museum. As such, the entire staff consisted of just him for the afternoon. He stood as he acknowledged that it made little sense for him to sit there in his office in the server building and headed toward the main exit. At least in his house he could watch TV or raid the refrigerator or even catch up on home repair tasks he'd been putting off. Something.

As he neared the front door, the phone rang on his company number.

"Pelethites Cybersecurity. This is Adam."

"Oh good, got you directly. This is Denton."

Adam perked up. The man didn't sound cheerful or excited in a clearly positive way, but he didn't sound down either. Adam didn't know what to expect, other than he hoped the telecom company had finally replied.

"What's the name of that guy you hired, the systems engineer or whatever?"

Adam furrowed his brow. What? Why would he ask about Logan?

"Logan Mathias. Why?"

"How well did you check him out?"

"Thoroughly."

"Did you call and talk with any of his previous employers?"

"Yes ... and no. The local church where he worked before coming here. I tried two others but never received a response. I was so swamped with work that I never took the time to try to get back with them. Why?"

He didn't like where this was going. He liked Logan. They worked well together and had many of the same thoughts on business and customer service, as well as politics and religion.

"The telecom folks got back with us. They insist that the problem is internal to your system. They even came to your facility and tested their cables between your building and their equipment. Said they worked as contracted. Now, I know you wouldn't sabotage your own business, so I can only conclude that your guy is up to something."

Adam turned around immediately and began to run back to the building. "Thanks, Denton. I'll get back to you."

Back at his desk, he tried logging into the modem equipment that handled their fiberoptic connections. No luck. The username and password had been changed.

He tried calling Logan. The call went straight to voice mail. Should he leave a message? If he did, would he ever see the man again, to confront him face-to-face?

He had but one choice. He needed to pull the plug, to do a factory reset of that gear. It would take down access to all of the websites that he hosted, but he expected that period to be brief. Even the big guys went down from time to time, so he felt no hesitation in acting. He just hoped that none of his remaining clients were in the middle of anything critical with their sites.

Within five minutes, the modem was functioning, and he had full control of it again. He changed the username and password so that Logan could no longer access it. He also altered his security system to deny Logan access to the building. Next, he tried a number of their websites. They all worked as expected.

He let out a long sigh of relief. Now, what to do about Logan?

THIRTY-NINE

Kenniston had told Aric that it might take a week or two to iron out the wrinkles in their plan. They still needed state and local approval, as well as university approval. The delay now exceeded three weeks, but Aric saw their dawdling as a blessing of sorts. As much as he needed to earn some cash, the idea of needing the digital ID for processing evidence and more did not sit right with him.

"What's up, Aric? I can see you're unsettled about something," asked Colonel Southworth.

Aric didn't realize he was pacing in the man's front hall as he waited to Jess to come downstairs. He was slated to take her to class as well as pick her up for another round of shopping. Well, it was more like hunting since they were just looking at things to add to their bridal registry.

The colonel waved him into the adjacent sitting room and pointed to a chair. "I think you have time. Have a seat."

He stopped, glanced up at the older man, and nodded.

"Thanks."

They each took a seat.

"So, yeah, I've talked about it with Jess, but haven't really mentioned it to anyone else. The security department at UMSL wants to start an O-J-T program for senior forensics students, and I was offered the first position."

"That's great. Sounds like it'd be good experience and a nice addition to your resume."

"True, and I'd get paid as well. I need to start earning some money for a honeymoon."

"Sounds like a win-win. So, what's the hang-up?"

"They're requiring the new digital ID for everyone in the department."

The retired officer shook his head and frowned. "I see. Um, I don't think I'd be taking that job either."

"Yeah, right? The bigger problem is that *all* police departments are now requiring it. I'm a criminal forensics major. Any job I try to get will now require it. We can't establish chain-of-custody for evidence without it."

The colonel continued to frown. "I see. That is a problem. I still wouldn't take it."

"I tend to agree and that's why I'm unsettled. What am I going to do? My entire college education is suddenly flooding down the drain."

"I suggest you talk with Lynch, get his advice."

Aric nodded. "That thought crossed my mind, too. Have you talked with him recently?"

"Well, over the holidays, if you define that as recent. Actually, we talked about this seemingly sudden push for digital IDs."

"What'd he say?"

"He won't get one either. It might cost him his position, too."

Aric took a deep breath and sighed. "Mark of the beast, right? That's what keeps coming to my mind."

The man nodded. "They've consolidated the different formats of the IDs to all use a retinal scan or palm print to identify a person. They're pushing them as improving your security, reducing identity theft, or making shopping easier. Forgot your wallet? Buy your gas or groceries by using your palm print. Just saw where Amazon is increasing its push for Amazon One. You can now photograph your right palm and submit it to them virtually to enroll in the program. Once enrolled, all you need is to use your palm print for your purchases."

Aric's eyes widened. "Wow. And once Amazon gets it going, you know the other major retailers will push for it, too."

"Agree. I can see Sam's and Costco adding palm scanners very quickly and tying them to their shopping apps."

Aric didn't want to think about it.

"Lynch believes the big push is because of politics. The Dems think Graham is going to win the election. So, if they can get their digital ID programs into the mainstream before the election, whoever gets the presidency won't be able to stop it."

Aric heard Jess' footsteps coming down the main stairs and stood. "Will we even get to the elections? I don't think the elites will even allow us to get there."

The older man stood to join them. "Well, there's that talk, too. Lots of speculation about that, and only time will tell."

Jess looked at both men. "Hmmm, I think I know what this conversation has been about. Good thing is, Christ is still on His throne. He's still in control, whatever happens here."

Aric nodded. "Amen to that."

Jess grabbed him by the arm and pulled him toward the door. "C'mon. I'll be late for class."

Yolina started pacing the bunker from one end to the other the moment she awoke from a short and restless sleep. Once upon a time, in what now seemed like a land far away, she could look at the sun in the sky and guess the time of day within half an hour. Now, she couldn't recall when she'd last seen the sun. And her Prince Charming, too, seemed to be a distant memory.

She longed to leave the bunker, but Sergei kept telling her it was not safe to do so. He was being watched, so he could not join her for fear of exposing her location. For the past three weeks he had been able to get groceries to her via a friend who delivered them to the doorstep in the belief that he was self-isolating from a recurrent episode of COVID. No questions were asked, so no answers were required.

After dark, she would cautiously open the door to retrieve the deliveries, but the thought of venturing outside caused her heart rate to accelerate and her lungs to hyperventilate. Just wondering when the next delivery might take place led to a panic attack. At least Sergei knew the limitations of the downstairs kitchenette and could order food appropriately. All of her meals—if one could call them meals—were being prepared there, not in the main kitchen that was so wonderfully equipped.

Her sole measure of time came from the clocks on her phone and computer. That kept her grounded as to date and time. Yet, she could no longer enjoy a normal sleep cycle. Worry kept her from sleeping at night, which led to falling asleep during the day. That pattern became more and more erratic.

This was her new normal . . . and she didn't care for it.

After a brief period of grazing from the miscellaneous foodstuffs remaining from the last delivery, she sat down at the computer and resumed her "work." Having found that unique piece of code—her prey's trademark, so to speak— she had begun searching the dark web for examples of it. At

Pozitiv, she could have unleashed one of the large mainframe systems for such a search. In the bunker, all she had were Sergei's computers and her own laptop, and she refused to boot up his systems for fear of ramping up the energy use of the house. Likewise, she refrained from using his viewing screen of the outdoors.

To date, she had found nothing on the dark web. She had moved her search to the known worldwide web a couple of days earlier. Searching that vast virtual universe could take an eternity with the equipment she had. Perhaps even that Pozitiv mainframe would struggle with this task. There was no way she could search every possible website for the presence of that data string in the background coding, so she placed "traps" on the main servers of multiple ISPs. Not really traps like most people think of a trap that captures and holds something. They were more like parsing screens through which everything going in and coming out of the provider's servers would pass through for analysis.

She searched those screens once again, found nothing, and began to pace again. Clearly, she had not hit upon the right internet provider yet. She didn't want to think that her prey had stopped using his trademark code. That thought would have overwhelmed her fragile spirit at that point because it would again mean that she was wasting her time.

As she paced, the recollection hit her that the CISA attack had been the result of their DDoS on the Graham campaign in the U.S. Could she get into the CISA network without detection? Was this code there? She had learned that a fragment of code had been found that was meant to implicate the Chinese. What if this man's trademark code was there?

Then reality hit her. Those computers would no longer be available. They would be offline somewhere in a forensics lab totally isolated from the internet. That is what Pozitiv or the FSB, or any other intelligence agency would do.

However, where was the Graham website hosted? It seemed a longshot, but if someone at that hosting company was also responsible for the CISA attack, maybe . . .

Yes, truly a longshot. Wouldn't the authorities at CISA have wondered the same thing? Wouldn't those people have been thoroughly investigated?

What did she have to lose? She wasn't getting anywhere with her current efforts. Why not add another ISP to her list?

FORTY

The sunny skies of the previous day had yielded to increasing clouds but at least the temperature promised to reach the mid-50s. Adam recalled that the day he met Logan for lunch at Sugarfire was much the same. Had that only been three-and-a-half months ago? With the deluge of work that they had overcome together, it seemed like years had passed.

He sat in his office waiting for Logan to appear at the door and have trouble accessing the building. He wanted to give the guy the benefit of doubt and an opportunity to explain his actions. The man had done a lion's share of good work for Adam. Giving him this chance was the least he could do.

08:30 rolled around. Then 09:00. By the time Adam's clock hit 09:30, he wondered if the man would show up at all.

He dialed Logan's number. He was startled to get a recording: *We're sorry you have reached a number that has been disconnected or is no longer in service. If you feel this is in error, please check the number dialed, and please try again.*

But then, maybe he shouldn't have been surprised. All that was required to learn that his hack of the company modems had been discovered was to monitor any one of the websites being hosted or the company's website itself. To find the website operating at normal speeds was a dead giveaway.

At 10:00, Adam had arranged to call Denton Pierce with an update. He still had some time, so he decided to make another call first, one that Denton had asked about the previous day. Logan had listed Aragon Systems as one of his references. Adam found the number and contact's name.

"Aragon Systems. How may I direct your call?"

"Bryce Knapp, please."

A moment later, another woman came onto the line. "Mr. Knapp's office. Can I ask who is calling and what this is about?"

"Hi, my name is Adam Afton, with Pelethites Cybersecurity. I'm calling again about a reference for a previous employee of yours, Logan Mathias. Mr. Knapp was listed as the contact."

"One minute."

"This is Bryce Knapp. What can I do for you Mr. Afton?"

"Please, call me Adam. I'm with Pelethites Cybersecurity."

"Paylay-what? Can you spell that?"

Adam shook his head questioning why that was needed but complied. "I called a few months ago about a past employee of yours named Logan Mathias, wondering what you could tell me about him."

"Okay, yes. I recall the inquiry. We never had an employee by that name, so I never called back. Sorry."

"You're sure? Can I send you a photo of him?"

"I'm sure, but here's my email for that photo."

Adam quickly sent off the photo. There was a pause on the other end.

"Ohhh, that guy. I hope you didn't hire him. He was known as Keith McGuire here. He did all kinds of damage to our networks. Set some of our work back by six months and nearly cost us the business."

Adam took a deep breath, shaking his head. He had just learned a valuable lesson.

"Don't get me wrong. The guy knows his stuff and could put in a long day's work. He just didn't work for *us*."

"Huh? What do you mean?"

"After he bolted, one of guys did a photo search for him. We discovered he's closely tied to the World Order Council and has been going around sabotaging various types of companies. We found at least a dozen names affiliated with that face, all put up online by companies he'd worked with and nearly drove under. A few he did take down."

Adam kicked himself again. He had used UltraNet to search for the name, but not the photo. He was slipping.

"Well, we're another one. His education seemed sensational. Maybe it was too good to be true."

"No, not at all. His training is just what you found. He somehow changes all of his records to match whatever new name he decides to use. Guess that's easier than making up new records."

Adam's face flushed. What could he say? He thought they were very much alike. He just hadn't recognized how deep the similarities went.

"So, these other businesses . . . you mentioned various types. Can I ask what types?"

"Hey, wait a minute. Now I know where I've heard your name before. You guys were brave enough to take on the Graham campaign website after that DDoS attack they suffered. Knowing how much the WOC and feds are trying to take Graham down, you guys have guts. You're just the type of business McGuire, or Mathias, or whatever name he's using, is working to take down."

They talked some more, and Adam learned that fellow believers owned Aragon. Besides that, they discussed setting up an alert system for Christian and conservative tech companies to warn them of individuals like "Logan." That was a project Adam looked forward to spearheading.

Adam saw that it was already several minutes past ten, so he called the MJFDA and was put through to Denton Pierce.

"Good morning. I've been told that our website is up and running smoothly. I guess you found the problem."

Adam proceeded to inform the attorney about what he'd discovered and corrected on his network. He also relayed the info he'd been told by Bryce Knapp about his saboteur.

"Good idea about the alert system. Sorry you had to learn about this guy the hard way."

Adam wholeheartedly agreed. "Me, too. I learned a hard lesson. So, do you think I have a case against him, a civil suit for damages? He cost me a lot of money."

"You would, if we knew where to find him. But I suspect that he's protected by very powerful people, and we'll never find him."

Adam thought about that for a minute before rebuking the idea that came into his mind. *Vengeance is mine, says the Lord.* The guy would pay for his actions before the ultimate judge, the King of Kings.

FORTY-ONE

AG McFarland sat at his desk, preparing for the flack he knew was coming. This time he expected it from all sides.

Special Counsel Jim Kerr had released his report on the president's mishandling of classified documents while vice-president. The report stated the counsel's belief that the mishandling was unintentional, but also detailed the memory lapses, time disorientation, and mental deficiencies of his old friend, Charles Sidon, which had been observed during interviews. The statement also detailed how the president had given classified documents to his auto-biography ghost writer without clearance for the man. The bottom line was that the president was an old man with memory issues that would make a jury sympathetic and unlikely to convict him, so no indictment would be forthcoming.

He could hear the arguments now. From the White House protesting the depiction of the president as a senile old man. From Graham's campaign stating that the ex-president was being politically targeted and the subject of selective and vindictive prosecution for having documents that he was permitted to possess under the Presidential Records Act. From Sidon personally proclaiming that his memory was fine. From Graham saying that Democrats are given a free pass while he's fighting a corrupt federal government and its weaponized law enforcement agencies.

His personal phone rang. CallerID revealed Werner Koch

on the other end. When did the man obtain his personal phone number?

"Hello, Herr Koch."

"*Guter tag*, Mr. McFarland. May I call you Derrick?"

"Certainly, Herr Koch."

"Then, please, call me Werner."

Well, this is an interesting turn of events, thought McFarland. He was now to be on a first name basis with Werner Koch?

"I received a copy of Special Counsel Kerr's report. Have you received any feedback yet from the president? Will he still insist on running for another term?"

McFarland raised his brow and shook his head in surprise. The man's information network was astounding if he'd received and had time to read the report already. The only way that could have happened was for it to have been sent to him before its public release.

"Werner, I have not yet heard from the White House, neither Zhèng Jian nor Charles Sidon himself, but I don't expect their feedback to accept the report's findings. That would acknowledge that Charles is senile and shouldn't be president even today."

"But isn't that what we want? Did we not talk about removing him and getting someone younger into office?"

The AG simply did not see that happening. Not yet.

"We talked about pushing him gently into not running again. As for removing him under the 25th Amendment, I recall telling you that the vice-president is not ready. Putting it bluntly, she is not capable of being president and moving her into that position would only prove it to the world. She cannot come close to beating Graham in an election, despite whatever poll data we create and publicize."

"But this report? Will it not create a firestorm of controversy?"

"It will, but we need it to give it time to play out. The report was distributed here less than an hour ago."

"Very well. I am counting on you and Zhèng to make this happen. We need to secure your government for another term."

The man did not sound happy. McFarland couldn't put his finger on it, but Koch did not sound as in touch with the world as he had the previous time they had talked. Could he truly have expected this one report to bring about the results he sought? And so quickly?

He took that opportunity to call the White House, Zhèng Jian in particular.

"Jian, this is Derrick. I just took a call from Werner Koch."

"You, too? He must have called you right after hanging up with me. What did you tell him?"

McFarland repeated the conversation he'd had with the WOC founder.

"Sounds pretty much like what I told him."

"How did he seem to you? You've had more of a relationship with him over the years."

There was a pause on the other end. "I'm hesitant to say, but he seemed distracted. He gets that way prior to the annual meeting, but that's over, so I'm not sure what he's dealing with right now."

"Okay. Well, I'm sure there's a lot on his plate all the time."

They discussed the situation for a few more minutes before ending the conversation. McFarland did not feel more confident about the outcome. He knew Charles Sidon well enough to know that the man was unlikely to back down. And the polls continued to show rising approval ratings for

Graham. It was time to implement Plan C . . . to "convince" enough Republican congressmen to resign or not run for re-election to allow the Democrats to return to power as the majority in Congress.

Then should Graham win, they could refuse him the presidency using the insurrection clause of the 14th Amendment. Never mind that he had been impeached for that once and acquitted and that the Supreme Court had ruled that it did not apply to him and could not be used to keep him off several states' ballots. The law was whatever the party in power said it was. That was *their* rule of law.

FORTY-TWO

Denton took to the pickleball court with a vengeance. The welcome rain of the past two days had cooled off Scottsdale's typical February temperatures from the upper-60s to the mid-50s. Yet, today, the sun shone brightly and made it a perfect day for outside exertion. It wouldn't be too long before the daytime temps rose into the 80s, 90s, and higher, making pickleball exclusively an early morning activity.

Yet, it wasn't the cooler weather alone that made him aggressively attack that perforated, hollow plastic ball, and he had nothing against their opponents in the current doubles game. No, he needed to work off the annoyance he felt as he and his people delved further and deeper into the growing number of cases of debanking, de-platforming, and the closing of credit card processing accounts. Conservative and Christian accounts were being systematically removed from the "public square" of the internet.

He and his partner were up by six points and the serve had passed over to them.

"Fourteen, eight, two" announced his partner as he prepared to serve.

Just then Denton's phone began to ring inside his bag at the side of the court. He held up his paddle and moved to the line between the two service courts.

"Hey, guys, give me a minute."

He ran to his bag, retrieved the phone and turned away

from those he played with for a bit of privacy.

"Hello."

"Denton, sorry to bother you. You sound out of breath."

He recognized the caller's voice. "Hi, Adam. You caught me playing pickleball. What's up?"

"If this is a bad time, I can call back."

"Not at all. Go ahead."

"I may be in big trouble."

"Oh?" Having worked with Adam on his company's financial obstacles, he wondered what Adam might be referring to when he said, "big trouble."

"Yeah. I was reflecting back on the time Logan was here and remembered the morning after the bombing of the Graham banquet. The Graham campaign website was suffering a denial-of-service attack after the bombing and came to me for help and to start hosting their site. That Monday morning, Logan was surprised to see that we had the campaign's account and needed to get it up and running ASAP. He also commented about your account at the same time. Logan was concerned the DoS attack would just follow the campaign and cause problems for our servers."

"Okay. I can see that concern being legit."

"Well, I said something off the cuff about my taking care of the attackers already, implying they would no longer be a problem."

Now Denton could see where Adam's story was heading. If what's-his-name was indeed a WOC operative, he could pass that on to whoever had perpetrated the DoS attack. That could make Adam a target.

"What exactly did you say?"

"Something to the effect of I already took care of them."

"Did you say exactly what you did to them? Did you know

who it was and mention their name?"

There was a pause on Adam's end. "Not that I remember. That was over two months ago, but I'm pretty sure I didn't. I do know who attacked the campaign, however."

Denton didn't like the tone or hesitancy in Adam's voice.

"Who? And what did you do?"

"Maybe it's best I not tell you either."

"Nonsense. I can't help if I don't know. Plus, we're covered by attorney-client privilege."

"The Graham campaign was attacked by our own government, the Cybersecurity and Infrastructure Security Agency." He paused again. "And I hit back with a virus that took down a third of their network, the group doing the DoS attack."

Denton's knees buckled. This wasn't just big trouble. It was *huge* trouble.

FORTY-THREE

Two more days had passed according to her phone. Yolina couldn't personally corroborate the time as she refused to venture upstairs into the main house, much less open any doors or step outside. And when she did turn on the viewing screens, she preferred the peaceful summertime scenes recorded by Sergei. Two more days, and no further contact from Sergei. She longed for his physical touch.

She hadn't been able to sleep and existed on caffeine. She hoped that whoever might be following Sergei and looking for her—her logical conclusion—wasn't monitoring the water meter for the house. With all of the coffee and tea being expelled by her bladder, she felt sure the meter was running rampantly with the continual toilet flushes.

She had pursued the lead that came into her mind earlier about looking at the ISP hosting the Bradley Graham campaign website. Curiously, discovering that host had been more difficult than usual. Any number of domain name registrars utilized the WhoIs database, regulated by ICANN, the Internet Corporation for Assigned Names and Numbers. The database held mainly redacted information if queried by anyone in the public, but she usually had no trouble penetrating the redactions. Yet, for this account, she could not find what she wanted.

Her alternative was to utilize the nameservers which were not hidden. These led to Cloudflare name servers.

However, Cloudflare was a cloud and security service, not a hosting company. She needed the specific IP address of the server, or servers, hosting the Graham campaign. Cracking the security of Cloudflare had been a challenge. Her old hacking tools had not worked. Their lava lamp random generator was ingenious, but she found a way to hack that setup's camera and generate the random code for her own use.

As she stared at the monitors in front of her, her eyes began to blur. She needed a break. She needed Sergei, his touch, his lips, his embrace . . . his intimate presence. Since those wouldn't be forthcoming, she wanted to at least touch base with him. She had sent several messages to their secure chat, but to no avail. This time she took a chance and sought him directly at Pozitiv Teknolodzhiz, AO.

"What?" she spoke out loud to the empty room. *Kostya Raskolnikov is dead? s*he thought. She knew Kostya, but not well. He and Sergei were close friends. She delved into finding out more about the man's death. Out for his daily cycling and victim of a hit and run. There had to be more than that. Had they caught the driver, identified the vehicle? She turned to sources outside the mainstream channels for news in Russia.

Her eyes bulged wide in what she discovered. Kostya was FSB, and the hit-and-run was not believed to be an accident. She also found that Sergei and Kostya often worked together, and that revelation made her heart race. Had Sergei become a victim as well, but one whose body had not yet been found? Was that why she no longer heard from him?

She decided to take a chance and hack into the FSB servers. But she used Sergei's credentials from Pozitiv, which she had discovered on one of his computers there in the bunker. Minutes later, she wished she hadn't.

Tears welled up in her eyes and the initial shock was displaced by a sense of betrayal. Kostya was one of her handlers, but so was Sergei. Together they had pressured her to seduce Werner Koch. *Sergei* had forced her to do that. Had that less-than-an-hour-long tryst not occurred, she would not be in hiding, on the run, fearing for her life. How could he? How could he have betrayed her like that? Her desire to see him had devolved into a need to throttle him to within an inch of his life. She . . . she . . . she could only imagine what she would do to him when she saw him next.

Suddenly the monitor to her right flashed on. Their secure chat. It was Sergei. She was going to give him a piece of her mind, but his messages stopped her fingers from typing.

Yolina, what have you done?
Using my creds has triggered an alert.
They will find your location within minutes.
Turn everything—everything!—off right away.
I am coming to get you.

Fear gripped her very soul as she rushed to power down the entire system. Her own laptop was last, but as she started to type, her programming popped a message onto the screen. It had found the servers for the Graham campaign.

She couldn't power down yet. She needed to know. She needed a name. She ran another short program. Yes! The telltale code was there. The ISP was a company named Pelethites Cybersecurity. She wrote Pelethites down in a note on her phone. The owner, and apparently the only tech staff at the moment, was a man named Adam Afton. She added his name to the note.

She looked at the clock. If Sergei was coming from Moscow, she still had 15, maybe 20 minutes, until he arrived.

She had to know. Had she found the man she'd spent months searching for?

She found a phone number. First, she composed a short text: *I have finally found you. I admire your brilliance in destroying AlterNet, outwitting Werner Koch, leading me on chase for wild goose, and attack on CISA (which I assume was you). I do not wish to expose you. I hope to meet you—kiber-tsaritsa (the CyberTsarina)* She pasted the message into her text screen and sent it to the number she had uncovered.

With satisfaction that she had finally succeeded, she reformatted the hard drive on her laptop, wiping it clean of everything she had on the drive. Then she powered it down.

As she completed the task of turning everything in bunker off, the alarm upstairs began to sound. Was it Sergei? She needed to see what was going on. She turned on the system that gave her security video of the main house. A minute later, she saw that it was indeed Sergei who had entered the house. Why hadn't he turned off the alarm system?

Because he wasn't alone.

"Where is she? Where is Yolina Zhdanov? I know you've hidden her somewhere."

The man and the voice were unknown to her.

Sergei didn't answer. The man broke a finger, then another. Sergei still said nothing. The man used his handgun to fracture Sergei's right kneecap. Pain filled Sergei's face, but he remained silent.

Tears welled up in her eyes and began to run down her cheeks. Despite what he insisted upon her doing for Mother Russia, he loved her. *Ohhh, Sergei, what have I done?*

Sergei turned his head to look up at the nearest camera. Tears filled his eyes. He tried to blink them away, but the pain he now experienced appeared clearly on his face.

The man noticed Sergei's attention turn to a corner of the room. He glanced up and grinned as he saw the camera. He pointed to it.

"Ah, the red light goes on. It is active and that means she is here somewhere." Again, he faced the camera. "Yolina, I know you are here. Werner Koch sends his condolences."

With that he pulled a syringe from an inner pocket and injected Sergei. Within minutes, he collapsed from the chair to the floor. The man undid the bindings from Sergei's wrists and ankles. "There. No bullets to be traced. No bindings to suggest anything other than an accident."

She watched him move into the bedroom. Standing next to the hidden doorway, he lit a candle and placed it on the table. He then walked into the kitchen and turned on the gas range but did not ignite it. Just one burner. The largest. The house would fill with gas quickly, which upon reaching the candle would ignite and engulf the entire building.

She grabbed her coat and ran to the emergency exit. After unlocking it, she pushed and pushed, but the door would not budge. A trace of snow found its way inside on one of her tries. The exit had become blocked by a snowdrift. Sergei had mentioned the need to keep that clear, but he hadn't been there to do so, and she had been fearful about going outdoors.

She was trapped.

A loud roar filled the air as the entire bunker shook. She ran back into the main bunker and into the bathroom. Maybe she could immerse herself in the tub and escape any flames. She turned the knob. No water. The water pump was already gone.

Smoke began to fill the bunker. She realized now that she would be joining Sergei . . . if there was really an afterlife.

Coughing, she decided to fulfill one last act of retribution. She grabbed her phone and called up the number for Werner Koch. She typed, *I finally found him. You were right. One man. A genius hacker. His name is* and she left the remainder blank as she sent it off to the man responsible for her inevitable death. Coughing uncontrollably with tears from the smoke clouding her vision, she did one thing. With great effort, she opened her phone and removed the SIM card. She had told the man, Adam, that she wouldn't out him. With the last of her strength, she threw it toward the wooden cabinets in the bathroom, hoping it would be consumed by the fire that now filled the bunker.

Werner paced within his study at home. He had received a text from Yuri that Yolina's location had been found. Sergei Agafonov was now involved in an unfortunate house fire, and Yolina's body would also be found in the rubble, unidentifiable with a little luck.

And yet, he felt unstable. Was this the end of the threat she posed?

He walked to the small drink cart in one corner of the room. He lifted up a decanter of Asbach Uralt and filled a snifter with the unique German brandy. It should be time to celebrate, but he sensed that something was off.

At that moment, he heard the ping of a message arriving on his phone. He did not expect an additional communique from his man.

Surprise was not an emotion he felt accustomed to, but it caught him fully. A text from Yolina.

I finally found him. You were right. One man. A

genius hacker. His name is

Where was the remainder of the message? Where? He threw the glass into the fireplace, and the alcohol flared up in the flame.

He sat down at his desk and buried his head in his hands. She had succeeded. She had found the man he'd been hunting for years. And he had ordered her death, a death that occurred too quickly.

FORTY-FOUR

Adam sat at his bench working on a new server. The racks and hard drives had finally arrived after straightening out his banking issues. Of course, the demand for his services had leveled off. He no longer had clients abandoning ship, but he also wasn't seeing an influx of new accounts. It was both a curse and a blessing. He needed the business in order to grow, but he couldn't handle it all by himself, so the slowdown afforded him the family time he needed to stay sane.

As he reached for another hard drive to install, his phone rang. He picked it up instead.

"Pelethites Cybersecurity. How can I help you?"

"Hi, Adam. It's Denton. Sorry to call you on a Saturday."

Adam laughed. "No problem. I'm a one-man band again, on duty 24/7. Call me anytime."

"Yeah. Again, sorry that's the case, too. I know you got along with Logan pretty well."

They had agreed to continue to call the man "Logan" since his real identity remained a mystery.

"Yeah, well . . . so, what's up? Sorry to see you working on a Saturday, too."

"Yes and no. I'm at home, and we have family plans a bit later. But I was thinking about our last conversation three days ago. Is there any way that CISA can trace the attack on them to you? Any way at all, other than testimony from Logan that implies your involvement."

Adam had been thinking about that very issue over the past few days.

"I've been reflecting on that. I realize that what I did was wrong and that I acted impulsively in anger over what they were doing, particularly when their attack on the Graham campaign followed right on the heels of the bombing. I've asked God for forgiveness about that."

He truly felt remorseful, despite his belief that the federal government should never be involved in attacking a political opponent. His way—taking down a third of the agency's computers—could result in successful future cyberattacks, strikes that could be prevented, on the people and businesses of the country, folks who had nothing to do with the DDoS attack on Graham. Perhaps he should have simply exposed them for what they were doing and let public opinion take its course.

"As for their being able to track me down, no, they have no trail to follow. I do not believe they will ever find real evidence to use to indict, much less convict, me."

As he said that, doubt entered his mind. After all, *someone* had found him, a Russian hacker named CyberTsarina.

"Okay, good. I agree you shouldn't have done that, at least not that way. But if all they have is Logan's word, we can quickly and effectively discredit him as a witness just through his use of multiple identities aimed at damaging the businesses he worked for. What was our last count? Five identities and five businesses?"

As they spoke, Adam noticed his brother entering the room. He turned toward Aric and pointed to the phone, holding up his hand to keep him from saying anything.

"Yes, five. I have a message out to a sixth but haven't

heard back from them yet."

"Okay. We just need to make sure we have good documentation on all of that and pray that nothing comes of it. If something does come of it, I'll need to refer you to another firm. We don't handle criminal defense."

Adam nodded. "Understood. I'll keep you up to date. Promise."

Upon disconnecting the call, he turned toward Aric and said, "Hey. Here to help, I hope?"

Aric smiled and nodded. He had helped Adam build new servers on several occasions. "Sure. Where do you want me to start?"

Adam pointed to the cables still needing to be attached to several hard drives. "If you could do the cabling, that will speed this up."

Aric did as asked. "So, five, maybe six what?"

Adam waggled his head. Aric was already aware of the Logan situation. "Five or six companies that hired Logan under different identities. That was Denton Pierce from the MJFDA."

Aric nodded. "Ah." He continued with the cable assemblies, opening up a new plastic bag of power cables. "Any luck tracking him down?"

Adam shook his head. "Certainly not as Logan Mathias." He sighed. "I know this isn't a Christian thought, but sometimes I just wish people like that would die, meet their Maker."

Aric stopped what he was doing and looked intently at his older brother. "You're right. It's not how we should think, but I'd be lying if I said I never thought that way. Thing is, we *all* deserve to die. We *all* deserve damnation. It's only through the gift of grace through Christ, and Christ alone, that we all don't end up that way."

Adam smiled. "Preach it, little brother." Leave it to Aric to work in the gospel message, even to him. Or maybe especially to him. Adam had to admit that his fledgling Christianity needed a boost now and then.

Aric laughed. "Sorry, guess I'm preaching to the choir now." He resumed his work. "A thought just came to mind. You know the Bible talks about spilling blood, like Abel's blood speaking to God from the earth. What about a virtual death, so to speak? I mean, the guy has done it to himself, killed himself off, at least six times that you've confirmed, if you count Logan Mathias as the sixth."

Adam saw where this was going? "Don't you think that's stretching things a bit?"

Aric shook his head. "I guess I see it more like eliminating a lie." He grinned. "Okay, maybe I'm stretching things some, but I see it as a perfectly fitting demise, or retribution, or whatever. What's the worst that could happen? He has to rebuild his virtual life? He loses his bank accounts? Oh yeah, like you lost yours."

Adam slid off the stool and motioned Aric to follow. He sat down at his workstation and began to work. Using UltraNet, he set up a profile. He'd already tried searching using the name Logan Mathias, so this time he entered the man's school credentials and work history, basic demographics, and the like. He entered enough information that his software should only come up with one name. After all, everyone's life was unique, built upon their experiences.

"Hey, don't forget his photo," said Aric. "That should cinch it."

Adam debated that option. "Unless he uses images with different facial hair, different colored contact lenses, or maybe even . . . no, you're right. Facial rec should still ID him, and if it doesn't, we can search again without it." With the press of a key, he launched his search with UltraNet. It shouldn't take long. Once a new identity was found and confirmed to be him, it wouldn't require much effort to virtually delete his entire life history. Let him try to find work, do banking, get references, and more without that.

He turned back to his brother and saw Aric, brow furrowed, looking at an adjacent monitor. He'd forgotten that he'd left that on display. He pressed a function key to turn off the monitor.

"Hey!" Aric turned toward with a serious look bordering on anger on his face. "What was that? Someone found you? That means someone has been looking for you. Who? What did you do?"

Adam put both palms up and out toward Aric in a defensive stance.

"Whoa. You already know what I did. I took down the globalists' attempt to rebuild AlterNet."

Adam still had a few secrets that he kept from his brother, but AlterNet—now evolved into his UltraNet—was something Aric had firsthand knowledge of. He, too, had been exposed to the dangers it posed when Wallace Chamberlain and his goon, Henry "Buck" Buckner, were hunting them both four years earlier.

Adam popped the monitor back on so that the message was visible.

"You know who Werner Koch is, right? The World Order Council?" Aric nodded. "Well, he was behind the attempted resurrection of AlterNet. They were also responsible for that engineered enterovirus that was released last year. At that time, I discovered info that led me to believe he was hunting for me. Why? I'm not sure. At first, I thought he wanted to find me to help rebuild AlterNet. Then, I grew suspicious that it was for a more nefarious end."

"And they found you?"

Adam shrugged. "Evidently this female Russian hacker did. Read it all." He gave his brother a minute to digest what the text said. "I set up an elaborate web of potential suspects, all linked together in their effort to eliminate the WOC's plans. I made it look like they were the ones who took down AlterNet, and I linked it back to the head of the FSB in Russia. Someone, her, I suspect, managed to follow every trail. That alone took some skill. How she ultimately found me, I haven't figured out yet."

"And this CISA thing?"

"Yeah, well, I did that in a fit of anger, and I realize I handled that wrong. That was one of the things Denton called me about. He knows all about it, too."

He explained what he had discovered and what he had done to retaliate. Aric kept shaking his head.

"But if she could find you, can't they? And what if the WOC folks discover that she knows and torture her for the info?"

"She's dead. I think."

"What?"

"I did some sleuthing of my own, and I'm pretty sure that CyberTsarina's real name is, or was, Yolina Zhdanov who worked for a company called Pozitiv Teknolodzhiz, a major technology firm in Russia. I found a news article that said that Yolina Zhdanov was killed in a suspicious house fire outside Moscow. Her co-workers were mourning her death."

"When?"

"About the same time that I received that message. Actually, from the timing of the call to the fire department, I think she was already caught in that fire and just wanted the satisfaction of letting me know that she found me. But that's just speculation on my part."

Aric had not stopped shaking his head. "But if she found you, aren't you worried that the others will, too?"

Adam wanted to answer in the negative, but he couldn't, if he was honest with himself. Inevitable: unable to be avoided, evaded, or escaped; certain; fated: an inevitable conclusion. The word and its definition kept running through his head. Had he simply delayed the inevitable?

FORTY-FIVE

It was now the last week of March, spring recess for students at UMSL, and Aric and Jess drove through the rain that Monday to trade temperatures rising to the 70s by the end of the week in St. Louis to temps stagnant in the 40s in Kenosha. Both locations were forecast to see sunny days midweek with increasing clouds toward Easter. Jess' parents had an engagement party all set up for that Thursday evening and the couple would stay for Easter Sunday's service at her father's church before driving back that afternoon. It was a trip they seemed destined to make many more times before graduation.

The entire trip was consumed by talk about their upcoming nuptials—the arrangements that had already been made and the decisions still to be made. The hardest part was the invitation list. Like most couples, they had limitations determined by the size of the reception venue. The church could hold an easy 300 people, but the banquet facility could hold only 200. And their budget was more like 100.

Listing family members and old family friends was easy. The list of younger friends was more difficult. Aric wanted to invite his buddies from the college football team there. They had, after all, helped protect him from the LGBTQ+ activists in their old dorm. Jess wasn't sold on that group. They agreed upon friends from their Christian groups at the college and church. Jess wanted to invite old schoolmates dating back to elementary school, people whom Aric had never met, and he wasn't committed to them any more than she was to his jock friends. The list was a work in progress.

But now, Thursday evening had arrived. The day had been sunny and mid-40s, and with daylight savings time, the light would extend into the early evening. They couldn't ask for better weather. Well, they could, but it *was* Wisconsin in late March. It had snowed a week earlier and was forecasted for the following week, too.

They stood in the front room of the Larson's home and greeted guests as they arrived. The pattern of arrival seemed to be the same. The guys would greet and congratulate them. The gals would greet them and insist on seeing the ring. Why was that?

"Jessssss! Let me see, let me see!" Jess's good friend, Ericka, rushed up to greet her with a hug before grabbing her left hand to see the ring. "Wow! It's beautiful." She poked Aric in the upper arm. "Good job there, Aric with an A."

He grinned. "Thanks, Ericka with a K."

As Jess and Ericka talked, Jess saw Mitch and two others from the football team arrive. Rather than disturb Jess, he walked over to the front door to greet them. Mitch entered the home with Brian and Zach right on his heels. They greeted each other with man hugs and moved away from the front door.

"So, she finally convinced you, eh?"

Aric smiled. Since that first class he and Jess shared, he hadn't needed any convincing.

"Yeah, finally." He laughed.

"So, how'd you do it?" asked Zach. "I need some ideas."

Aric raised his brow. "You gonna ask Emilia? Way to go."

The guy nodded. "Haven't decided on timing yet. That's

why I need ideas. I keep reading about all these extravagant proposals, but that's just not me." He paused. "But I still want to do something memorable."

Aric described his scenario at the botanical gardens in St. Louis. "Zach, trust me, just getting down on one knee and asking will always be memorable for both of you." He looked at Mitch. "So, where's Dan? I thought he'd show up with you all."

All three men's brows furrowed, and their faces filled with sadness. "You didn't hear?"

"Hear what?"

"He died," said Brian.

"What?"

"Yeah, went to bed one night and never woke up. His roomie found him dead in bed the next morning. Happened right before finals last semester," said Mitch.

"How?"

"Word we got from coach is that he had a heart attack or something." Zach shook his head. "Can you imagine that? Twenty-one years old, a college athlete in great shape, and he died of a heart attack?"

Mitch shook his head, too. "Most of the team think it was that COVID jab they forced us all to take. We keep reading about all the myocarditis and heart issues that have developed because of it, and you read about all these young athletes and celebrities dying young the same way. A third of the team made appointments with cardiologists to get checked out. It's kinda scary. I personally don't want to dwell on it."

As friends for over two years, Aric had wanted to share the gospel freely with these guys, but the timing never seemed right. He had prayed for an opening to reach out to them. And now he had it. "Guys, you know where I stand. I know that I know that I know that if I died suddenly, I would find myself in the arms of Jesus and have eternal life. How about you?" He went on to present the gospel to them and invite them to church for Easter.

After they all moved on to get drinks and food, Aric found Jess and told her about what had happened.

"I hope they show up Sunday," said Jess. Aric nodded.

They enjoyed the evening and seeing old friends. Lynch and Amy arrived late.

"Sorry, babysitter issues," said Amy as they entered the house and greeted the couple.

As Aric shook hands with Lynch, he asked, "Any chance we could get together and talk about world events tomorrow?"

Lynch frowned. "I don't think so. I have faculty meetings pretty much all day, and we already have evening plans. Sorry. What about Saturday?"

Aric shook his head. "Nope. We're committed all day Saturday. Rats."

Amy tugged Lynch's sleeve. "We could stay a little later tonight. The kids will be in bed, and Carly said she didn't mind staying later if we wanted some time out together."

Lynch nodded. "Okay."

After calling their sitter, Lynch and Amy moved on to greet Jess's parents, while Aric and Jess rejoined a group of their college friends. The party continued for another hour or so, and the invited guests began to dissipate. Soon it was just the couple of honor, her family, and the Cullys. They all grabbed drinks and moved to take seats in the Larson's family room.

"So, Aric, what's on your mind?" asked Lynch.

Aric took a sip of his hot tea before replying. "Gee, I guess world events in general. People keep talking about the war between Russia and Ukraine leading to world war three. Israel continues fighting Hamas in Gaza, finding and destroying miles of tunnels, and preparing to move into southern Gaza. Up until now, the Sidon administration seemed supportive of Israel's efforts, but just this week, the UN approved a resolution calling for a complete ceasefire and withdrawal from Gaza. In previous resolutions, the U.S. insisted on wording calling for the release of all hostages, and Russia and China would veto the resolution. This latest one had no such clause, so Russia and China voted for it. I would have expected the U.S. to veto it, but no, the Sidon administration abstained, allowing it to pass. That seems to me to be another step toward Armageddon. What do you think?"

Lynch nodded. "The word Armageddon is being thrown about a lot these days, but most people have it all wrong, just like they do about a person they call the Antichrist. The word comes from Har Magedon. Har means mountain, but translators chose to use hill, which isn't correct. Either way, there is no hill or mountain in the Jezreel Valley. The fortress ruins of Megiddo are an archaeological tell. It doesn't qualify as either. Magedon gets a bit technical. In Hebrew, it's M-G-D. Vowels are assumed. The G is where it gets technical. If you use gimel for the G sound, the translation could lead to Megiddo. But if you use 'ayin, as in Gomorrah, it translates to the mount of assembly, which is in Jerusalem. Personally, I think Armageddon is the same as the War of Gog and Magog in Ezekiel, and that's a war for Jerusalem. So, yes, we're definitely heading down that path."

The conversation drifted into numerous world issues—

illegal immigration and the very real threat of terrorist activity on U.S. soil, the war in Ukraine as a means of using U.S. taxpayer dollars to enrich the military-industrial complex, the menace of China, and finally, the very real threat of a cultural implosion across the globe.

Lynch went on. "The demographics of the U.S., western Europe, China, and Russia all point to cultural collapse. Our populations are aging, and the birth rates aren't high enough to replenish the population, so the economies will fail because they're all built on money that doesn't really exist and on growth that isn't there. The Book of Revelation foretold this in chapters 17 and 18. We're about to see it happen."

Aric rubbed his temples. He thought back to their last visit with Lynch.

"Do you still think we're just months away from the Lord's return? Last time we talked, you mentioned this fall as a possibility."

Lynch nodded. "Lots of people believe we're not to know the hour or the day of the Lord's return. But that's really a hint that points to Yom Teruah, the Jewish holiday known as the only one for which the hour and day was not known. It was determined by spotting the new moon and could only be announced by the high priest. In reality, Jesus told us we're not to know the hour, but we can discern the day."

Pastor Larson shook his head. "I disagree."

Lynch smiled. "Most Christians in this country would, but reread Matthew 24, verses 36 to 44 where Jesus talks about it. At the end of that section, He says only that He would return at an hour we do not know. Mentions nothing about a date or day."

Jess's dad pulled out his phone, apparently to pull up his

Bible app. A moment later, he raised his brow and waggled his head, "You're right. That's what it says. So, are you saying you have a date, that you know when He's returning?"

Lynch offered a nonchalant shrug. "I can't say with 100% assurance, and I have no 'thus saith the Lord', but yes, I do."

Author's Note

Revelation 13:16-17
Also it causes all, both small and great, both rich and poor, both free and slave, to be marked on the right hand or the forehead, so that no one can buy or sell unless he has the mark, that is, the name of the beast or the number of its name.

Over the centuries, many have speculated over the nature of "the mark of the beast." Many theologians think it's a spiritual mark, much like the seal on the forehead given to believers in Christ in Revelation 7. I suspect that there is that spiritual aspect to it, but an invisible, spiritual mark isn't likely to affect one's buying and selling. After all, how would any merchant know, if it's an invisible mark?

As such I've expected that this mark would have a physical component to it. For many years, students of the End Times speculated that this mark would consist of a tattoo or such on the back of the right hand or on the forehead. Then came electronics and an embedded chip of some kind that could be scanned by a reader became fashionable. Bill Gates funded the development of a digital tattoo, and this became a contender for "the mark" (especially coming from Mr. Gates).

Following the COVID pandemic, with the release of the so-called vaccine for that virus, I saw the possibility of a vaccine passport becoming or evolving into the mark of the beast. The EU's Green Pass was publicly stated to be a means of limiting travel between countries during a pandemic, mainly for those without the "requisite" vaccines. After all, if these could be used to limit travel, it wouldn't take much to "tweak" them into allowing or disallowing someone to buy and sell.

In 2023, as I started writing this story, I learned about new automations in retail stores that were being touted as convenience features while holding the threat of limiting shopping to "approved" groups as well. One of the newest Aldi grocery stores in the Netherlands requires the chain's app to even enter the store. You have to scan the app to get in, use the app to scan each item, and ultimately use the app to make your purchase. Here in the U.S., Sam's Club has been pushing its own version of this with its Scan'n Go feature in its app. There is now technology using RFID tags on items to let the store's computer know that it's been placed in your cart, negating the need to scan it. It doesn't take a great stretch of one's imagination to see how someone's app could be turned off to deny access or a purchase if that person was no longer deemed acceptable to society. Plus, it wouldn't take much programming to tie such apps and passports together.

And then in early 2024, I read about the new digital IDs being promoted here in the U.S. There are currently two versions of what's being called a mobile driver's license or mDL. Apple has been promoting one, into which its Apple wallet is also installed. One version utilizes facial recognition, while the other requires both a retinal scan and right palm print. This allows either biometric marker to be used for identification. In the story I mention that all mDLs become standardized on the latter because deep fakes could fool a facial scanner. That is speculation on my part, but it's true that facial rec can be fooled by a deep fake image, so it's a reasonable speculation.

You can expect to see more marketing soon about mDLs.

In fact, your state's DMV may already be offering one when you need to renew your driver's license. They will be pushed for convenience, for stopping identity theft, for safe travel and passing through TSA checkpoints in airports, and more. And I'm again speculating that once they achieve a certain level of acceptance, merchants will clamor to come on board. My comments about Amazon One in the story are true.

Would you take the mark? If you're considering it, please consider the following, which I don't include in this particular book:

Revelation 14:11

*And the smoke of their torment goes up forever
and ever, and they have no rest, day or night, these
worshipers of the beast and its image, and whoever
receives the mark of its name.*

Revelation 16:2

*So the first angel went and poured out his bowl on
the earth, and harmful and painful sores came
upon the people who bore the mark of the beast
and worshiped its image.*

Revelation 19:20

*And the beast was captured, and with it the false
prophet who in its presence had done the signs by
which he deceived those who had received the
mark of the beast and those who worshiped its
image. These two were thrown alive into the lake
of fire that burns with sulfur.*

Now perhaps you understand the dilemma faced by Aric in

being required to get a mDL. Am I saying that mDLs are unequivocally the mark? No, I can't claim that, but I will say that we need to be aware of this potential. Yes, think carefully about accepting the mark.

While I don't utilize the concept of the number of the beast in this story, you'll note at the beginning of this note (Rev 13:16-17) that it is mentioned along with the mark. Just what is this number, the infamous 666? [Note: Some first century texts had the number as 616.] As with the concept of the mark, there's lots of speculation on this one, and my take on it is very, very different than conventional teachings.

Lots of people want to tie the idea of a number to a specific person (Antichrist) by using the numeric values of the letters in his or her name. That's called gematria. Irenaeus, in the second century AD, confirmed that John said the number was 666 and proposed gematria for determining it. The name he proposed was the Greek word for 'titan.' Other believers did that to label Nero as the Antichrist, but which of his four official names should they have used? Likewise today, if you want to use gematria to identify some candidate for Antichrist, what name do you use? Middle name, no middle name, middle initial, and so on. No, gematria is far too broad. And, as I state in the story, the beast from the sea in Rev 13 is not a person but a global government.

Some think the number 666 seems to point to humanism as the spirit of antichrist. Six is the number of man, and man is composed of body, mind, and spirit. So, using six for each the number could be presented as 666.

As stated above, my take is very different. The Greek word used for 'number' in that verse is used for a census count everywhere else in the Bible. As such, what could 666 be with respect to a census? Maybe, a percentage, 66.6% or two-thirds. Perhaps two-thirds of the population at the time will take the mark.

Do I have other scripture to back up that claim? Yes. When King Ahab's son, Ahaziah, sent captains of fifty to get Elijah, three companies were sent, and the soldiers of two of them died by fire from the Lord. Only a third survived. Take a look at Zechariah 12-13. In verse 13:8, we read:

> *In the whole land, declares the LORD, two thirds shall be cut off and perish, and one third shall be left alive.*

We also see this idea in Ezekiel 5:2, 12:

> *2 A third part you shall burn in the fire in the midst of the city, when the days of the siege are completed. And a third part you shall take and strike with the sword all around the city. And a third part you shall scatter to the wind, and I will unsheathe the sword after them. ... 12 A third part of you shall die of pestilence and be consumed with famine in your midst; a third part shall fall by the sword all around you; and a third part I will scatter to all the winds and will unsheathe the sword after them.*

One-third gets scattered and emptied out but are still alive. Two-thirds perish. So, maybe my interpretation isn't farfetched at all. Oh, and there's also 2 Samuel 8:2, where David defeated Moab and laid out the people in three lines, two of which he killed and one he left alive.

In the story, I present one other prophetic "concept" that

falls well outside the accepted teachings about the End Times and Revelation: that we are not to know when Christ will return. Some will look to Acts 1:7 where, prior to His ascension, Jesus says, *"It is not for you to know times or seasons that the Father has fixed by his own authority."* If you look at the Greek, 'times and seasons' means the epochs in history. We are not to know the various epochs of history that the Father had determined, not the timing of Christ's return. Indeed, Jesus, in the parable of the fig tree, told us we are to be aware of the seasons, particularly when summer (His return) is near.

In Matthew 13:11, he says: *"To you it has been given to know the secrets of the kingdom of heaven, but to them it has not been given."* And in 1 Thessalonians 5:4, we're instructed that we *"are not in darkness, brothers, for that day to surprise you like a thief."*

So, if this is true, how do we reconcile Jesus' teaching in Matthew 24:36-44 where He begins by saying *"But concerning that day and hour no one knows, not even the angels of heaven, nor the Son, but the Father only . . ."?* As I mention in the story, this is a clue. Yom Teruah (the Feast of Trumpets) called Rosh Hashanah today, is the only Jewish holiday to fall on the first of the month, with the sighting of the new moon. The Sanhedrin would send out watchmen to look for the new moon, and when two or more reported seeing it, they would tell the high priest. Only the high priest could announce the beginning of the holiday, just as only the Father can tell Christ when it's time for Him to come back. Because of the Jewish day beginning at sunset, the new moon could be spotted on either of two days and at any hour because of weather conditions. Thus, the holiday was known as the one where no one knew the day and hour of its start.

Oh, and the high priest would announce the holiday with the blowing of the shofar, the trumpet, giving the holiday its name. And Who is returning with the blowing of trumpets? You guessed it.

Also stated in the story, Matthew 24:44 says, *"Therefore you also must be ready, for the Son of Man is coming at an hour you do not expect."* Date or day is not mentioned. So, can we know the day? I believe so. In fact, I've calculated it out. Revelation 13 says the beast will have 42 months to reign. I believe that means just what it says, 42 months. After all, when God revealed the seven years of feast and of famine to Joseph, precisely seven years of each occurred. When he told Abraham that his descendants would be enslaved in Egypt for 400 years, they were . . . for 400 years. God is a god of order. So, to me, 42 months means 42 months.

If we accept the idea that the Deep State came into its full reign in the spring of 2021 when Biden took full reigns of the U.S. government, that it was given 42 months to reign, and that Christ is returning on Yom Teruah in 2024 (six months from now as I write this), what happened 42 months before Yom Teruah 2024?

Yom Teruah falls on October 3-4 this year. That is, it starts at 6 pm on 2 October and ends at 6pm on 4 October. [BTW, Yom Teruah is celebrated over two days because of the tradition of not knowing which day it would start.] Was there an event of Biblical importance that happened 42 months earlier? Yes. PRECISELY 42 months before 4 October 2024 was 4 April 2021—the last day of Passover Week AND Easter. I checked this timing all the way out to 2040 and only one other period comes close, being just three days off.

Easter is celebrated by a manmade tradition on the first Sunday following the first full moon of spring. In reality, it rarely falls during Passover Week. As an example, this year (2024) Easter is a full three weeks before Passover. And yet, in 2021 Easter occurred on the last day of Passover Week and both were *precisely* 42 months before Yom Teruah this year.

Now, does this mean we drop everything and wait for Him? Not at all. I have no assurance that I'm right. You won't see me walking the streets in a white robe carrying a sign stating that the end is near, although the timing is really, really interesting and compelling. No, we are to continue buying and selling, marrying and being given in marriage, planting and building, and eating and drinking. That said, though, if He is actually that close to returning, we should step up our game and become more fervent witnesses. Do you have family members and friends who aren't following Christ? Maybe now is the time to try reaching them, whether for the first time or umpteenth time. Think and pray about it.

Until the next book . . . *The Fall.*

Acknowledgments

As always, I again want to acknowledge and thank my dear wife, Paula, for her help, encouragement, and putting up with my spending time to write. With the retirement of my main proofreader, I started using *Grammarly* for additional error checking. If you find any errors, it missed them. So, please let me know.

And my sincerest compliments to Adrijus Guscia, of Rockingbook Covers, for his incredible covers.

About the Author

Braxton can't lay claim to wanting to be a writer all his life, although his mother and seventh grade English teacher were convinced he had what it would take. A bachelor's degree in Bio-Medical Engineering led to medical school and a residency in Emergency Medicine. He served for a decade in the U.S. Army Medical Corps with tours such as the Chief, Emergency Medical Services at Fort Campbell, KY, and as a research Flight Surgeon at Fort Rucker, AL. Who had time to write?

By the 1990s, as a civilian, his professional and family life had settled down, somewhat, and his mother once again took up her mantra, "Write a book. You're a good writer." In 1997, a Valentine's Day writing contest convinced him that maybe he could write fiction. He spent the next fifteen years learning the craft of writing.

Now, twenty-plus years after that first hesitant start, he has sixteen novels published, as well as non-fiction books and a children's book, and can't find enough time to write. As a Christian, he writes "true-life" Christian fiction (suspense and thrillers) that many call "cutting edge," as he's not afraid to take on such issues as human trafficking, racism, and more. His characters are real-life as well, with all the flaws and blemishes real people have. As such, his books are never likely to gain acceptance by the Christian Bookseller Association. But then, he never intended to tell stories just to the choir.

Books by Braxton DeGarmo:

Still Here Series:

The End Begins – 1
The Shaking – 2
The Beasts – 3
The Trumpets – 4
The Mark - 5

Non-Fiction Study Guides:

Still Here! Surviving the End Times
Still Here! The Apocalypse is Now
Still Here! Countdown Revelation

MedAir Series:

Looks that Deceive – 1
Rescued and Remembered – 2
The Silenced Shooter – 3
Wrongfully Removed – 4
A Zealot's Destiny – 5
Kidnapped Nation - 6
The Khmer Connection - 7
Resurrected Trouble - 8

Seamus O'Connor Thrillers:

The Militant Genome
Ten Seconds 'Til

Other Books:

Indebted

Children's Books:

The Toucan Who Can Can-can

www.ingramcontent.com/pod-product-compliance
Lightning Source LLC
Chambersburg PA
CBHW071238190726
48292CB00007B/2348